GENERALLY SPEAKING

For almost three years, novelist and short-story writer Lawrence Block's monthly column, "Generally Speaking," was one of the most popular features in *Linn's Stamp News*. A general collector of pre-1940 issues, Block had the entire world of stamps as his subject, and he turned in 33 columns before he decided it was time to stop.

But Keller, the author's fictional character, never lost his enthusiasm for philately. A wistful and introspective killer for hire, Keller rekindled a boyhood passion for stamps at the end of *Hit Man,* the first of a series of books about him. Like Block, Keller collects the whole world through philately's first century. (How's that for coincidence?) And the nature of his profession gives Keller more discretionary income than Block—and a lot more money to spend on stamps.

Published here for the first time is the full run of columns from *Linn's,* along with six selections from the Keller saga chosen for their philatelic perspective.

More by Lawrence Block

NON-FICTION

STEP BY STEP • GENERALLY SPEAKING • THE CRIME OF OUR LIVES • HUNTING BUFFALO WITH BENT NAILS

NOVELS

A DIET OF TREACLE • AFTER THE FIRST DEATH • ARIEL • BORDERLINE • CAMPUS TRAMP • CINDERELLA SIMS • COWARD'S KISS • DEADLY HONEYMOON • FOUR LIVES AT THE CROSSROADS • GETTING OFF • THE GIRL WITH THE DEEP BLUE EYES • THE GIRL WITH THE LONG GREEN HEART • GRIFTER'S GAME • KILLING CASTRO • LUCKY AT CARDS • NOT COMIN' HOME TO YOU • RANDOM WALK • RONALD RABBIT IS A DIRTY OLD MAN • SINNER MAN • SMALL TOWN • THE SPECIALISTS • STRANGE EMBRACE • SUCH MEN ARE DANGEROUS • THE TRIUMPH OF EVIL • YOU COULD CALL IT MURDER

THE MATTHEW SCUDDER NOVELS

THE SINS OF THE FATHERS • TIME TO MURDER AND CREATE • IN THE MIDST OF DEATH • A STAB IN THE DARK • EIGHT MILLION WAYS TO DIE • WHEN THE SACRED GINMILL CLOSES • OUT ON THE CUTTING EDGE • A TICKET TO THE BONEYARD • A DANCE AT THE SLAUGHTERHOUSE • A WALK AMONG THE TOMBSTONES • THE DEVIL KNOWS YOU'RE DEAD • A LONG LINE OF DEAD MEN • EVEN THE WICKED • EVERYBODY DIES • HOPE TO DIE • ALL THE FLOWERS ARE DYING • A DROP OF THE HARD STUFF • THE NIGHT AND THE MUSIC • A TIME TO SCATTER STONES

THE BERNIE RHODENBARR MYSTERIES

BURGLARS CAN'T BE CHOOSERS • THE BURGLAR IN THE CLOSET • THE BURGLAR WHO LIKED TO QUOTE KIPLING • THE BURGLAR WHO STUDIED SPINOZA • THE BURGLAR WHO PAINTED LIKE MONDRIAN • THE BURGLAR WHO TRADED TED WILLIAMS • THE BURGLAR WHO THOUGHT HE WAS BOGART • THE BURGLAR IN THE LIBRARY • THE BURGLAR IN THE RYE • THE BURGLAR ON THE PROWL • THE BURGLAR WHO COUNTED THE SPOONS • THE BURGLAR IN SHORT ORDER

Generally Speaking

All 33 columns, plus a few philatelic
words from Keller

LAWRENCE BLOCK

A LAWRENCE BLOCK PRODUCTION

FOREWORD

It was in the late summer of 2009—ten years and a few months ago as I write these lines—that I wrote a brief essay about my own return to philately. By then I'd been collecting again for more than a dozen years, and I'd had occasion to write about stamps ever since Keller, my fictional assassin-for-hire, had himself returned to the hobby in the final chapter of *Hit Man*.

He'd been looking for something to keep him busy in his planned retirement, but if you're a collector yourself you can probably guess what became of his retirement fund. Keller went on working—through *Hit List, Hit Parade, Hit & Run*, and *Hit Me*—and his philatelic adventures have played an increasing role in his life, and in the books.

I think it was Michael Laurence, then editor of *Linn's Stamp News*, who first took official notice of Keller. Other writers and other publications followed, with mentions and reviews. Randy Neal serialized several Keller stories in *American Stamp Dealer & Collector*. Charlie Peterson, sadly gone now, helped spread the word about Keller in the philatelic community, invited me to address the Tiffany Dinner at the American Philatelic Society convention in Hartford and, with Robert Odenweller, sponsored me for membership in the Collectors Club.

By the time *Hit & Run* was published, Keller had enough of a philatelic following to sustain a special philatelic edition of the book, signed, numbered and limited, with a custom made postage stamp tied to the title page with a special cancellation.

So that was all background to the aforementioned essay, "A Dream of Lost Stamps." I sent it off to Michael Baadke, and before either of us quite knew what had happened, I had agreed to write and he to publish a monthly column consisting of the ruminations of a general collector. I called it *Generally Speaking,* and it would go on to appear in monthly installments for almost three years.

This was not my first experience with a regular magazine column. For four-teen years, from 1976 to 1990, I wrote a monthly instructional column on fiction writing for *Writer's Digest.* That column yielded four books (*Telling Lies for Fun & Profit, Spider Spin Me a Web, The Liar's Bible,* and *The Liar's Companion*) and led indirectly to two others (*Writing the Novel from Plot to Print* and *Write for Your Life*), but that was by no means all it did for me. One way or another, it informed both my reading and my writing. I've often thought it made me a better writer.

After I'd been writing *Generally Speaking* for a few months, I realized how much I'd missed having a monthly slot to fill. But it wasn't until I was well into the column's second year that I brought over the kids—Arnold and Rachel and Edna and the gang—who'd served me so well in the *Writer's Digest* days. If you haven't met them yet, I can only hope you'll enjoy making their acquaintance.

By the time *Generally Speaking* was two years old, I'd discovered eBook self-publishing. The eBook of *Generally Speaking: A Philatelic Patchwork* made its appearance, and I figured there would eventually be a sequel, or at least an expanded edition, because I was confident I'd be writing the column for years.

But that wasn't to be the case.

I'm not sure what happened, but something shifted—and not in the audi-ence or the magazine but in my own self. I was late with my 33rd column, so much so that it was delayed a full month. And, while it was a perfectly decent column, and one I liked no less than its fellows, shortly after I turned it in I realized I was done.

I don't know why. I don't know where the urge to write about my hobby had come from in the first place, and now it was gone, and I couldn't explain that, either.

I mused a bit in the eBook introduction:

"Has writing Generally Speaking made me a better philatelist? The question itself may be unwarranted, in that stamp collecting is essentially a pastime, and thus not a pursuit at which one succeeds or fails. But it seems clear to me that I've gotten more from the hobby by virtue of having to come up with a couple of thousand words every month. For some of the columns, I've had to sift my own experience and examine my own feelings and perceptions on a particular subject. For others, I've had to inform myself on various topics in order to convey that information to my readers.

"I've been rewarded, too, by the response I've had throughout the past two and a half years. It's a rare column that doesn't bring email from readers, many of them sharing their own thoughts and experience.

"Occasionally readers will tell me that my column led them to my books—to Keller, most often, but sometimes to my other fiction as well. And Keller fans often express the hopeful thought that the books might draw new entrants to the hobby, or at least render it a bit less unfathomable to them. ("Thanks to Keller, my wife finally thinks what I'm doing isn't completely hare-brained," one fellow wrote.)"

Whenever a door closes, it's been observed, another one opens. Well, okay. But there's another way to look at it.

Whenever a door opens, you know it's going to swing shut again sooner or later.

So it was with the column. And, so it also proved to be, for this dedicated philatelist, with philately itself.

It took a while. After I stopped writing the column, I went on studying and collecting stamps as ardently as ever. As always, there were fallow stretches of inactivity, but each would be followed by a stretch of renewed enthusiasm. I'd send off orders, attend a conference or an auction or a club meeting, mount stamps in my albums, and get the special pleasures and satisfactions that the hobby had always held for me.

But, along with *Linn's* and my Scott catalogue, I could read a few other things as well—the calendar, for example. And the handwriting on the wall. I'd had a longer-than-usual stretch of not buying any stamps, of not keeping up with the literature, of overall philatelic inactivity. A glance at my shelf of albums engendered more guilt than pride, and a reluctance to pick one up and open it.

Sooner or later, I knew, my collection and I would part company. When I took leave of the world, I wouldn't be taking my stamps with me. They'd then be an added burden, something for my heirs to dispose of—and for less than I could realize by taking that chore off their hands.

And so, just as there had been a day when it was time to abandon my column, so there came a day when I was ready to let go of my collection. I consigned it to an auction, and some months later I received a check.

(Did I come out ahead? No, of course not. I hadn't owned my stamps long enough for their appreciation in value to cover the difference between a buying and a selling price, nor had my purchases been made with an eye toward investment. The remarkable thing, really, is that I'd spent money on an engaging and entertaining pastime—and actually realized a substantial sum. A friend of mine had to give up golf when he couldn't swing a club without pain. He'd devoted years to the game, and what do you figure *he* got back?)

More recently, another close friend who has spent a lifetime collecting books made a similar decision for essentially similar reasons. Now he had always been a more passionate collector than I, and his collection had always been his highest priority. (The house he'd built included a library that was truly state-of-the-art; it inspired and is described in a short story of mine, "The Burglar Who Smelled Smoke.")

I dined with him not long after his shelves had been stripped bare, and while he was comforted by the financial gain he stood to realize, he confessed to being desolate over the removal of the books. It made him ill to look at the bare shelves.

I've had the occasional pang looking at the shelves where my albums used to repose, but the sense of loss has never been intense, nor has it lingered long.

What I've felt mostly is relief at having dealt with a future problem in an intelligent and foresighted fashion.

My column in *Linn's* was always well illustrated with color photos of the stamps. Sometimes I scanned specimens from my own collection; sometimes *Linn's* furnished the illustrations.

It would be nice to reproduce all of those illustrations here, but cost and space are limiting factors. We've picked out appropriate illustrations for the start of each chapter, and I hope you'll find them interesting and attractive, but the main thing you get here is words. And you get them pretty much as they appeared in the magazine, because I haven't attempted to edit the columns, or to hide the fact that they are indeed individual monthly installments written one by one over a period of thirty-three months.

To compensate for the lack of photographic illustration, I've chosen to include some passages from my various writings about Keller, the philatelically-inclined hit man who got me into all this, and whose adventures I've been able to chronicle in six books so far, five novels—*Hit List, Hit Parade, Hit & Run*, and *Hit Me*—and a novella, *Keller's Fedora*. While I may have disposed of my own collection, Keller's done nothing of the sort—although there have been times when that was an iffy proposition . . .

When I was writing this column, I had the great good fortune to work with a superb editor, Michael Baadke. As I noted in this book's initial edition:

> *"Those mere words to which I'm limited are insufficient to convey what a thoughtful and sensitive editor he has proven to be; any editor who would allow a writer to hang the title 'How Much is That Dachshund in the Fenster?' on a column about the 1923 inflation in Germany is worth his weight in Penny Blacks.*

"It is my great pleasure to dedicate this book to Mike. I hope he won't mind sharing this distinction, such as it is, with my wife, Lynne, whose unflinching acceptance of the time and money I devote to little scraps of paper is quite remarkable."

While Mike is no longer my editor, as I've long since stopped giving him anything to edit, it's gratifying to me that he remains my friend. Our paths cross infrequently, but we do stay in touch, and catch up for coffee when we can.

And now let's get on with it, shall we? First with an introduction to Keller and his reintroduction to philately, and then we'll get to the columns . . .

GENERALLY SPEAKING

Contents

Keller Finds a Hobby
—From *Hit Man*

"I collected stamps when I was a boy," Keller told the stamp dealer. "I wonder whatever became of my collection."

"Might as well wonder where the years went," the man said. "You'd be about as likely to see them again."

"You're right about that. Still, I have to wonder what it would be worth, after all these years."

"Well, I can tell you that," the man said.

"You can?"

He nodded. "Be essentially worthless," he said. "Say five or ten dollars, album included."

Keller took a good look at the man. He was around seventy, with a full head of hair and unclouded blue eyes. He wore a white shirt with the sleeves rolled up, and a couple of pens shared his shirt pocket with some philatelic implements Keller recognized from decades ago—a pair of stamp tongs, a magnifier, a perforation gauge.

He said, "How do I know? Well, let's say I've seen a lot of boyhood stamp collections, and they don't vary much. You weren't a rich kid by any chance, were you?"

"Hardly."

"Didn't get a thousand dollars a month allowance and spend half of that on stamps? I've known a few like that. Spoiled little bastards, but they put together some nice collections. How did you get your stamps?"

"A friend of my mother's brought me stamps from the overseas mail that came to his office," Keller said, remembering the man, picturing him suddenly for what must have been the first time in twenty-five years. "And I bought some stamps, and I got some by trading my duplicates with other kids."

"What's the most you ever paid for a stamp?"

"I don't know."

"A dollar?"

"For one stamp? Probably less than that."

"Probably a lot less," the man agreed. "Most of the stamps you bought probably didn't run you more than a few cents apiece. That's all they were worth then, and that's all they'd be worth now."

"Even after all these years? I guess stamps aren't such a good investment, are they?"

"Not the ones you can buy for pennies apiece. See, it doesn't matter how old a stamp is. A common stamp is always common and a cheap stamp is always cheap. Rare stamps, on the other hand, stay rare, and valuable stamps become more valuable. A stamp that cost a dollar twenty or thirty years ago might be worth two or three times as much today. A five-dollar stamp might go for twenty or thirty or even fifty dollars. And a thousand-dollar stamp back then could change hands for ten or twenty thousand today, or even more."

"That's very interesting," Keller said.

"Is it? Because I'm an old fart who loves to talk, and I might be telling you more than you want to know."

"Not at all," Keller said, planting his elbows on the counter. "I'm definitely interested."

"Now if you want to collect," Wallens said, "there are a lot of ways to go about it. There are about as many ways to collect stamps as there are stamp collectors."

Douglas Wallens was the dealer's name, and his store was one of the last street-level stamp shops in New York, occupying the ground floor of a narrow three-story brick building on Twenty-eighth Street just east of Fifth Avenue. He could remember, Wallens said, when there were stamp stores on just about every block of midtown Manhattan, and when Nassau Street, way downtown, was *all* stamp dealers.

"The only reason I'm still here is I own the building," he said. "Otherwise I couldn't afford the rent. I do okay, don't get me wrong, but nowadays it's all mail-order. As for the walk-in trade, well, you can see for yourself. There's none to speak of."

But philately remained a wonderful pastime, the king of hobbies and the hobby of kings. Kids still mounted stamps in their beginner albums—though fewer of them, in this age of computers. And grown men, young and old, well-off and not so well-off, still devoted a substantial portion of their free time and discretionary income to the pursuit.

And there were innumerable ways to collect.

"Topical's very popular," Wallens said. "Animals on stamps, birds on stamps, flowers on stamps. Insects—there's series after series of butterflies, for example. Instead of running around with a net, you collect your butterflies on stamps." He thumbed a box of Pliofilm-fronted packets, pulling out examples. "Very attractive stamps, some of these. Railroads on stamps, cars on stamps, paintings on stamps—you can start your own little gallery, keep it in an album. Coins on stamps, even *stamps* on stamps. See? Modern stamps with pictures of classic nineteenth-century stamps on them. Nice-looking, aren't they?"

"And you just pick a category?"

"Or a topic, which is what they generally call it. And there's checklists available for the popular topics, and clubs you can join. You can design your own album, too, and you can even invent your own topic, like stamps relating to your own line of work."

Assassins on stamps, Keller thought. Murderers on stamps.

"Dogs," he said.

Wallens nodded. "Very popular topic," he said. "Dogs on stamps. All the different breeds, as you can imagine . . . . Here we go, twenty-four different dogs on stamps for eight dollars plus tax. You don't want to buy this."

"I don't?"

"This is for a kid's Christmas stocking. A serious collector wouldn't want it. Some of the stamps are the low values from complete sets, and sooner or later you'd have to buy the whole set anyway. And a lot of these packet stamps are garbage, from a philatelic point of view. Every country's issuing ridiculous stamps nowadays, printing up tons of colorful wallpaper to sell to collectors. But you've got certain countries, they probably don't mail a hundred letters a month from the damn place, and they're issuing hundreds of different stamps every year. The stamps are printed and sold here in the U.S., and they've never even seen the light of day in Dubai or Saint Vincent or Equatorial Guinea or whatever half-assed country authorized the issue in return for a cut of the profits . . . ."

By the time Keller got out of there his head was buzzing. Wallens had talked more or less nonstop for two full hours, and Keller had found himself hanging on every word. It was impossible to remember it all, but the funny thing was that he'd *wanted* to remember it all. It was interesting.

No, it was more than that. It was fascinating.

He hadn't parted with a penny, either, but he'd gone home with an armful of reading matter—three recent issues of a weekly stamp newspaper, two back numbers of a monthly magazine, along with a couple of catalogs for stamp auctions held in recent months.

In his apartment, Keller made a pot of coffee, poured himself a cup, and sat down with one of the weeklies. A front-page article discussed the proper method for mounting the new self-adhesive stamps. On the "Letters to the Editor" page, several collectors vented their anger at postal clerks who ruined collectible stamps by canceling them with pen and ink instead of a proper postmark.

When he took a sip of his coffee, it was cold. He looked at his watch and found out why. He'd been reading without pause for three straight hours.

"It's funny," he told Dot. "I don't remember spending that much time with my stamps when I was a kid. It seems to me I was outside a lot, and anyway, I had the kind of attention span a kid has."

"About the same as a fruit fly's."

"But I must have spent more time than I thought, and paid more attention. I keep seeing stamps I recognize. I'll look at a black-and-white photo of a stamp and right away I know what the real color is. Because I remember it."

"Good for you, Keller."

"I learned a lot from stamps, you know. I can name the presidents of the United States in order."

"In order to what?"

"There was this series," he said. "George Washington was our first president, and he was on the one-cent stamp. It was green. John Adams was on the pink two-cent stamp, and Thomas Jefferson was on the three-cent violet, and so on."

"Who was nineteenth, Keller?"

"Rutherford B. Hayes," he said without hesitation. "And I think the stamp was reddish-brown, but I can't swear to it."

"Well, you probably won't have to," Dot told him. "I'll be damned, Keller. It sounds for all the world as though you've got yourself a hobby. You're a whatchamacallit, a philatelist."

"It looks that way."

"I think that's great," she said. "How many stamps have you got in your collection so far?"

"None," he said.

"How's that?"

"You have to buy them," he said, "and before you do that you have to decide exactly what it is you want to buy. And I haven't done that yet."

"Oh," she said. "Well, all the same, it certainly sounds like you're off to a good start."

"I was thinking about collecting a topic," he told Wallens.

"You mentioned dogs, if I remember correctly."

"I thought about dogs," he said, "because I've always liked dogs. I had a dog named Soldier around the same time I had my stamp collection. And I thought about some other topics as well. But somehow topical collecting strikes me as a little, oh, what's the word I want?"

Wallens let him think about it.

"Frivolous," he said at length, pleased with the word and wondering if he'd ever had occasion to use it before. Not only did you learn the presidents in order, you wound up expanding your working vocabulary.

"I've known some topical collectors who were dedicated, serious philatelists," Wallens said. "Quite sophisticated, too. But all the same I have to say I agree with you. When you collect topically, you're not collecting stamps. You're collecting what they portray."

"That's it," Keller said.

"And there's nothing wrong with that, but it's not what you're interested in."

"No, it's not."

"So you probably want to collect a country, or a group of countries. Is there one in particular you're drawn to?"

"I'm open to suggestions," Keller said.

"Suggestions. Well, Western Europe's always good. France and colonies, Germany and German states. Benelux—that's Belgium, Netherlands, and Luxembourg."

"I know."

"British Empire's good—or at least it was when there was such a thing. Now all the former colonies are independent, and some of them are among the worst offenders when it comes to issuing meaningless stamps by the carload. Our own country's getting bad itself, printing stamps to honor dead rock stars, for God's sake."

"Reading the magazines," Keller said, "it made me want to collect everything, but most of the newer stamps . . ."

"Wallpaper."

"I mean, stamps with Walt Disney characters?"

"Say no more," said Wallens, rolling his eyes. He drummed the counter. "You know," he said, "I think I know where you're coming from, and I could tell you what I would do in your position."

"Please do."

"I'd collect worldwide," Wallens said, warming to the topic. "But with a cutoff."

"A cutoff?"

"They issued more stamps worldwide in the past three years than they did in the first hundred. Well, collect the first hundred years. Stamps of the world, 1840 to 1940. Those are your classic issues. They're real stamps, every one of them. They aren't pretty in a flashy way, they're engraved instead of photo-printed, and they're most of them a single color. But they're real stamps and not wallpaper."

"The first hundred years," Keller said.

"You know," Wallens said, "I'd be inclined to stretch that a dozen years. 1840 to 1952, and that way you're including the George the Sixth issues and stopping short of Elizabeth, which was about the time the British Empire quit amounting to anything. And you're also including all the wartime and postwar issues, all very interesting philatelically and a lot of fun to collect. A hundred years sounds like a nice round number, but 1952s really a better spot to draw the line."

Something clicked for Keller. "That's very appealing," he said.

Wallens suggested he start by buying a collection. He'd save money that way and get off to a flying start. Two whole shelves in the dealer's back room held collections, general and specialized. Wallens showed him a three-volume collection, stamps of the world, 1840 to 1949. No great rarities, Wallens said as they paged through the albums, but plenty of good stamps, and the condition was decent throughout. The catalog value of the entire lot was just under $50,000, and Wallens had it priced at $5450.

"But I could trim that," he said. "Five thousand even. It's a pretty good deal, but on the other hand it's a major commitment for a man who never paid more than ten or twenty cents for a stamp, or thirty-two cents if he was getting ready to mail a letter. You'll want to take some time and think about it."

"It's just what I want," Keller said.

"It's nice, and priced very fair, but I'm not going to pretend it's unique. There are a lot of collections like this on the market, and it wouldn't be a bad idea for you to shop around."

Why? "I'll take it," Keller said.

A Dream of Lost Stamps

I sat up, stared at my wife. "Why," I demanded, "did you sell my hat?"

She stared right back at me.

"Oh, it must have been a dream," I said. "You know that fedora of mine, with the hole in the crown that looks like a cigarette burn? I dreamed you sold it for ten dollars."

"Why would I sell your hat?"

"That's what I wanted to know. But it was a dream, so—"

"And why would anybody buy it? It's an old worn-out hat and there's a hole in it."

"I know."

"Ten dollars," she said. "If anybody wants to pay ten dollars for that hat, I'm all for selling it. But I'd ask you first. I mean, it's your hat."

We were in Listowel, a town in North Kerry, in the West of Ireland, and I didn't know then and don't know now why I should have dreamed about my hat, and the selling thereof. Maybe it was something in the water. If so, it was still there a day later, because I awoke the next morning fresh out of another harrowing dream, and I shot Lynne a look that would have curdled milk.

"My stamp collection," I said.

"Your stamp collection?"

"Why did you—oh, hang on, it must have been another dream."

"And just what did I do this time?"

"You sold my stamp collection."

"I did no such thing," she said. "Wait a minute. What kind of dream is this, anyway? *What* stamp collection? You don't *have* a stamp collection."

The day before, when I'd discovered that she hadn't sold my old hat after all, I had felt an inexplicable sense of relief. And now, realizing she hadn't sold my stamps, I felt nothing so much as a bottomless sense of loss. Because she was right, she hadn't sold my stamp collection. How could she? Twenty years earlier, before we'd even met, I'd sold it myself.

I must have been seven or eight years old, and I was born in 1938, so you can do the math. I was at my grandparents' house for a family dinner, and one of my mother's two brothers showed me a book of stamps. Both Hi and Jerry had collected as boys, and one of them had his album there, and I looked at it and could see right away that collecting stamps would be a Good Thing to Do.

Then somebody gave me a Modern Stamp Album and a packet of hinges, and my Aunt Nettie began supplying me with stamps. She was my mother's aunt, and she worked as secretary to the president of Trico, a local firm that supplied windshield wipers to the world. Trico did a lot of business overseas, and Nettie opened the mail and clipped off the corners of the envelopes with the stamps. And gave them to me.

I dutifully soaked them off their paper backing, dried them, found room for them in my stamp album, and hinged them in place. A lot of them, as I recall, were from South and Central America.

When my collection outgrew that first album, I upgraded to a two-volume Scott's International. I still got stamps from Aunt Nettie, and I bought some as well from approval dealers. "Have fun," one advertised. "Add thousands of stamps to your collection with my bargain-priced penny approvals."

I think I had just started high school when I decided to specialize. I received the birthday present I requested, the Scott Specialty Album for Great Britain, British Europe, and British Oceania. This must have been in 1952–3, because it ended with the last of the George VI issues—and that struck me as a perfectly fine place to stop. I didn't want to keep up with new issues. I wanted to concentrate on the stamps for which my album had spaces.

But by my senior year in high school, I'd lost interest. I certainly didn't want to sell my collection, I figured I'd get back to it someday, but for the time being I was content to leave it on the shelf.

When I resumed collecting, I was out of college and married, with a kid on the way. And now it was coins, not stamps. I started out going through rolls of coins from the bank, and in very little time was serious about the pastime, joining coin clubs, attending auctions, and devoting a good deal of time and much of my discretionary income to the hobby.

Next thing I knew I was writing for a couple of numismatic publications, and one of them offered me a job. We up and moved to Racine, Wisconsin, where I edited the *Whitman Numismatic Journal* and handled various other chores in the coin supply division.

And that sent me back to stamps.

After eight hours at a desk mucking about with numismatics, I very much wanted a change when I got home. And of course my stamp album had made the trip to Racine, and so I took it up and returned wholeheartedly to philately. I had a couple of dealers sending me approvals, and I took the train to Chicago once or twice and spent some time and money at stamp shops in the Loop. I continued to collect stamps for that British Europe album, and I added another collection by picking up the Specialty Album for Benelux.

I stayed at Whitman until early 1966, then moved back to the New York area. I continued to collect, but other activities got first crack at my time and money. I'd go months without looking at my stamps.

In 1973 my marriage broke up, and I moved to a studio apartment in New

York. And sometime that year or the next, because I sorely needed the money, I took both of those stamp albums to a dealer in midtown Manhattan. And that was that.

Sometimes, over the years, I'd remember my days spent with hinges and tongs and a perf gauge. But I didn't spend much time thinking about my stamps, because it always made me sad. Still, I don't think I felt the full impact of the loss until that morning in Listowel, when I woke up from that dream.

I'd formed a few haphazard collections over the years, but hadn't pursued anything with any seriousness. And the dream made me realize how much I missed it all.

The answer, of course, was to resume collecting stamps. But it took me a while to figure it out.

2

Nothing About Everything

In scholarship as in philately, there are specialists and there are generalists. And there's a longstanding explanation of the difference between the two. The specialist, it is said, keeps learning more and more about less and less, until he knows everything about nothing. The generalist, on the other hand, keeps learning less and less about more and more, until he knows nothing about everything.

When I decided in my mid-fifties to return to a hobby I'd abandoned twenty years earlier, I didn't know what sort of a collector I'd be. As a boy I'd started out collecting everything, then narrowed my focus to British Empire—specifically, to the Scott Specialty Album for Great Britain, British Europe, and British Oceania. In my mid-twenties I'd begun collecting Benelux as well, and in my mid-thirties, when my first marriage ended, I sold everything.

Now I was starting over. Fine. I'd be a stamp collector again. But what would I collect?

Well, I'm a writer, and had accumulated a nice collection of portraits of writers from the old *Vanity Fair*. Why not collect writers on stamps? A little research revealed this to be an abundant topic, with most stamp-issuing countries given to honoring their literary stars philatelically. There was a sub-group of the American Topical Association, JAPOS, devoted to the topic—the acronym is Journalists, Authors, and Poets On Stamps. I joined, and went through catalogs, and began acquiring stamps.

And never really got caught up in it. For one thing, the stamps themselves did not strike me as inherently interesting. They were mostly portrait stamps, and they mostly depicted writers I'd never heard of, and found I had precious little interest in learning more about. And I didn't want to design album pages, and couldn't get much satisfaction out of housing my new acquisitions in a stockbook.

Beyond that, I came to realize that I lacked the mindset of a topical collector. I can certainly appreciate topical collecting and have no end of respect for its enthusiasts. Indeed, topical displays are often the ones I find most interesting at shows. But it was becoming clear to me that I was programmed to collect stamps on the basis of where they were from, not what they pictured.

So I began collecting the stamps of Ireland. I had long been fond of the country, knew a fair amount of its history, and liked the restraint the Irish had shown in their stamp-issuing policy over the years. (Two of my *Vanity Fair* prints turned up on a pair of stamps issued in 1980 to honor Oscar Wilde and George Bernard Shaw.) I sought out mint never-hinged stamps, housed them in a pair of Davo hingeless albums, and reached a point where there was nothing left for me to buy. I could still keep up with new issues, and buy annual album supplements to house them, but that felt like renewing a subscription to a magazine I never read.

Or I could specialize, seeking out minor varieties and errors, adding blocks and other multiples, picking up covers, working my way into postal history. I did pick up some forerunner issues, and quite a few booklets. But I found I didn't care about die breaks, or any of the minutiae you couldn't see without a magnifying glass. And I couldn't work up much interest in covers or postal history. In fact, now that my collection was essentially complete, I found myself not much inclined to open the albums. I was glad I had them, and it pleased me to see them on the shelf, but there they stood, untouched.

Which meant I ought to start another collection. But of what? British

Empire? A good possibility, as I'd always liked their stamps. Benelux? Again, I knew the stamps, and liked them well enough.

But I liked most countries' stamps, really, and to select one area for specialization was to neglect the rest of the world.

But I couldn't set out to collect the whole world, could I?

Well, why not?

It was one thing to collect worldwide. It was another thing to collect everything—and I knew better than to attempt that. I'd already discovered with my Irish collection that I wasn't geared for keeping up with new issues, and was more interested in earlier stamps. 1940 struck me as a good cut-off date. It wasn't until after that date—after World War Two, really—that countries went nuts on a grand scale, issuing stamps in enormous profusion. And the earlier engraved stamps appealed more to me aesthetically than the more flamboyant stamps facilitated by modern printing advances.

So I'd collect the stamps of philately's first century. That would keep me busy enough.

And I knew not to include the United States in my philatelic world. I'd collected U.S. issues avidly as a child, and it seems to me that most of my knowledge of my country's history was an unwitting by-product of my collecting. Like Keller, the stamp-collecting hit man I've written a few books about, I can still name the presidents in order. (So he told his associate, Dot. "In order to what?" was her perfectly reasonable response.)

But I'd be spreading my resources too thin if I tried to collect the U.S. and the rest of the world.

Once I'd made my decision, I wasn't sure what to do next. And then I saw a listing for a worldwide collection, 1840 to 1900, and the $1000 price seemed reasonable. The next thing I knew, I was the owner of an old Scott brown album containing a collection that had been put together eighty or more years before it came into my hands.

The dealer who'd sold it to me had done some cherry-picking first. I remember that there were no stamps on the pages for French Offices in China, but hinge marks to show they'd once been present. Iceland, too, was empty, and who knows what individual rarities may once have been present. It looked at first as though I had a truly valuable run of several Central American countries, until I discovered that the stamps were all Seebeck reprints. Most of the European issues were used, and condition throughout was what dealers call *mixed*.

No matter. There was plenty of value there, and, more to the point, it got me started.

First thing I did, once I'd familiarized myself with what I had, was start buying stamps to add to it. I found some dealers who sent out weekly lists, and a couple who sent out approvals, and I even found one fellow who ran a cubbyhole shop weekends in a nearby antique mall. It didn't take me long, though, before I became dissatisfied with that old album, and realized that what I wanted to house my new collection was the Brown Album reprint I saw advertised in *Linn's*. I bought a set of pages and binders and set about remounting my collection.

And that turned out to be the best thing I could have done. It took months, and by the time I was through I was truly acquainted with the stamps in my collection. Before long I had bought more pages through 1940 and binders to accommodate them.

There was a point, after I'd finally gotten around to assembling all the albums with all the new pages, that what I had was a handful of pages with stamps on them floating like islands in a virtual sea of blank pages. But the blank pages didn't bother me, and it was satisfying every time one of them got a stamp mounted on it. There are fewer blank pages in those albums now, but there are still some to be found, and they still don't bother me. And I still find it satisfying every time I get to mount a stamp or two on one of them.

3

THE MIRACLE OF EMPTY SPACES

After I bought that first old Scott album (worldwide, 1840–1900), my wife asked a perfectly reasonable question. What would I do, she wanted to know, when I'd filled every one of its spaces?

"Should I live another three hundred years," I told her, "and should I become wealthy beyond the dreams of avarice—two eventualities which strike me as equally possible—I would still be unable to fill this book."

"Well, that's a load off my mind," she said. "I was worried you'd be hanging around the house with nothing to do."

Different collectors, I've come to realize, regard empty spaces differently. An empty space provides graphic evidence that one's holding of a particular group of stamps is not complete, that one's work remains unfinished.

And certain spaces guarantee that the work will be forever unfinished. For example, my own album has room for Sweden 1a, the unique three-skilling error of color. Even if the stamp's current owner should decide to sell, the likelihood of my being able to buy it is, uh, remote. And the Swedish stamp is hardly unique in its uniquity; my albums have room for any number of stamps of which only a single copy exists, stamps unknown outside permanent institutional collections, stamps that, should I exceed Croesus in wealth and Methuselah in length of days, will still never be mine.

Indeed, even if I could wrap myself in a cloak of invisibility and pilfer all those rarities from all those royal collections, I'd still have empty spaces to look at. Because my Brown albums are reproductions of early albums, and some of the stamps included are ones that never existed in the first place.

Some collectors prefer to design and produce their own pages, an endeavor that has become a good deal simpler in the era of desktop publishing. There are many satisfactions in so doing—one can arrange the stamps to please one's eye, or one's sense of order—but not the least consideration is that the collector can limit the spaces to ones he can reasonably expect to fill. (Or *wants* to fill—if you find certain minor varieties and shades to your taste, make space for them; if not, include them out.)

If the permanently unfillable space can be daunting, it at least teaches the valuable lesson of acceptance. But what about the space that ought to be easy to fill, but somehow remains forever empty? Now *that's* infuriating.

When I was a boy with the Scott Specialty Album for Great Britain, British Europe, and British Oceania, I had no end of empty spaces, and most of them were ones I never expected to fill. But among my holdings were three of the four stamps of the 1935 Silver Jubilee issue for Fiji. Somehow I'd managed to acquire all but the lowest value, the 1-1/2 penny carmine and blue. Nowadays it catalogs $1.10, but this was long ago, and it was valued at whatever Scott's minimum may have been back then, or close to it. I'm sure I could have filled that space for a dime—if I could have found the damn thing offered for sale.

I had no end of opportunities to buy the whole set, and inexpensively enough, but why buy three stamps I already owned in order to get the one really cheap one that I lacked? I figured it would turn up offered as a single if I just waited long enough, and I waited for years, and when I finally sold that collection in my mid-thirties, that particular space remained empty.

Twenty or more years later, when I resumed collecting, I still remembered that stamp. I even remembered the catalog number, Scott #110. Amazing isn't it, the kind of clutter that lodges in the corner of one's mind?

I haven't bought any partial Silver Jubilee sets lately, and I have the Fiji set intact. But I didn't have to look it up just now in order to include the catalog number here. That empty space stayed with me better than most of the filled ones.

In the main, I learned the lesson of Fiji #110—don't buy partial sets. But this principle is one I sometimes honor in the breach. One dealer in particular often lists partial sets at extremely attractive prices, and now and then I bite. And it seems to me the frustration of the blank space, so much greater when what's missing is one of a set, is more than offset on the happy occasion when I'm able to fill it in.

Philately is by no means my only obsession, and I have a number of other pursuits with their own blank spaces. My wife and I are ardent travelers, for example, and some years ago visited out hundredth country and thus qualified for membership in the Travelers Century Club. There were, when last I looked, 321 countries on the club's list, and our own total now stands somewhere between 135 and 140, so we have a long way to go. We'll add several on a Cape Town-to-Gibraltar cruise of West Africa in the spring, but we're in no great rush to complete our set, and there are a couple of spots on the globe we're as likely to reach as I am to get hold of Sweden 1a. And that's okay.

I'm a racewalker and runner, too, and my chief interest in that area is marathons. While I haven't formally joined the 50 States club, I do have the goal of completing a marathon in every state, and my count as of this writing stands at 18. I don't know how many years of marathoning I've got left in me, but I'd be surprised if there are enough to get me all fifty states. And that's okay, too.

A little over twenty years ago, Lynne and I set out on a curious pursuit. I'd grown up in Buffalo, New York, and we decide to drive around and see how many other Buffalos we could visit. We knew of twenty when we got the idea, and extensive library research stretched the list to forty. Within a few years we'd visited 82 of them, and know of about a dozen we haven't gotten to yet. (Buffalos, we discovered, are like subatomic particles; the mere act of looking for them causes new ones to spring into existence.) We haven't been to a new Buffalo in several years, and I can't say whether we'll ever resume the Buffalo hunt. But we're okay with that.

Come to think of it, I find it somehow reassuring that there are still pristine Buffalos out there, and unvisited countries, and states where I've not yet run my 26.2 miles. The satisfaction of the 321st country or the 50th marathon might be considerable, but would it offset the hollow feeling that would almost certainly accompany it? A triumph, perhaps, but one with a tragedy fast on its heels, because there would be no more countries, no more states, no more wide places in the road.

Alexander, we are told, wept when he realized there were no more lands left to conquer.

One begins a journey with an eye on one's destination. Somewhere along the way, one learns (if one's lucky) that it's the journey itself that's important.

One buys a stamp album with the intention of filling it—but it is in moving toward this goal that satisfaction lies, not in attaining it.

Consider Mayotte. It's one of the Comoro Islands in the Indian Ocean, lying between Madagascar and Mozambique (and fitting neatly between them alphabetically, come to think of it). A French colony, it issued 32 stamps between 1892 and 1912, and one needn't take out a second mortgage to own them all. I filled them in over the years as the opportunity arose, and just a couple of months ago I bought #19, the 1 franc bronze green on straw. I cut a mount for it and fastened it in place, and I now had the country of Mayotte complete.

A triumph, but not without its bittersweet aftertaste. Because now I'd have no reason to scan Mayotte listings, and not much reason to look at those pages in my album. Mayotte and I are, alas, done with one another. (Unless, of course, Lynne and I travel there sometime, and I get to check it off another list.)

But wait a moment.

Mayotte 22–32 are eleven stamps from the first set, surcharged "05" or "10". Double surcharges exist for three of them, and I could try to add them, if I wanted. And all eleven exist with the surcharged numerals more widely spaced, and are listed in Scott as minor varieties. And, yes, the double surcharges exist on the wide-space varieties, too. So that means there are seventeen more stamps from Mayotte I could seek out.

And then there are blocks and other multiples, not to mention covers. The whole world of postal history could ensure against the possibility of ever bringing a collection of Mayotte to completion. I don't think I'll go that route, I don't even know that I'm interested in chasing down the wide-space stamps, let alone the double surcharges—but it's comforting to know they're there if I want to pursue them.

You never fill all the spaces, not really. And I find that enormously comforting. In philately, Alexander would have had nothing to worry about. There are always fresh worlds to conquer.

4

Mint or Used?

The columns I've written about my return to stamp collecting and my evolution as a general collector have drawn some interesting (and very welcome) responses from readers. Many of you have reminisced about your own collecting histories, and have noted how they were similar in some respects to mine and different in others. A few have asked questions, and one question turned up in several of your emails. I've said that I collect worldwide, which is to say all countries but my own, and that I limit myself to philately's first century, stopping at 1940. But, you wonder, are the stamps I collect mint or used?

It's a perfectly reasonable question, and one I could answer with a single word. But that would leave me 1499 words short of a column, which is manifestly worse than being three bricks short of a load.

And a longer answer might lead us someplace interesting.

When I started collecting, used stamps were my only option. My Aunt Nettie clipped them from her firm's overseas correspondence, and I soaked them and dried them and mounted them with hinges in my Modern Stamp Album. I obtained U.S. stamps from the family's mail, dutifully soaking and mounting any I didn't already have. (The good news was that postage meters were less widely used in the late 1940s, so most of the mail bore stamps. The bad news was that the stamp in question was almost invariably Scott 807, the 3¢ deep violet from the Presidential series, picturing Thomas Jefferson. It's a perfectly nice stamp, but it didn't take me long to grow tired of the sight of it.)

Before long I moved on to a two-volume version of the Scott International Album. I was getting an allowance, and I earned extra money mowing and raking the neighbors' lawns, and shoveling their walks and driveways. Some of this wealth went into my stamp collection. There were a couple of dealers who sent me low-priced approvals, and I'd pick out a dollar's worth, say, and return the rest along with my payment.

I found I preferred to buy unused stamps. I liked the way they looked, fresh and new, the gum intact, with no cancellations obscuring their design. Some I'm sure had been hinged before they came to me, while others had not, but I never noticed the difference; I hinged them all, and mounted them in my books.

Meanwhile, my father was briefly enthusiastic about U.S. stamps as an investment. Like many men in those years (and, alas, many since) he figured you couldn't possibly go wrong buying unused stamps from the Post Office. Even if they didn't shoot up in value, they'd always be worth what you paid for them, wouldn't they? And you could take them back to the Post Office and get your money back. Right?

Ah well. I don't think he lost any serious money at this pursuit, although I seem to remember that the family's outgoing mail bore copies of the 3¢ Everglades stamp a good ten years after it was issued in 1948. But while he was loading up on sheets and plate blocks, he'd pick up singles of whatever they had that I lacked. I got most of the Prexy series that way, although I don't believe the 17¢ Andrew Johnson ever did turn up.

By the time I was in high school I was specializing. I had the Scott Specialty Album for Great Britain, British Europe, & British Oceania, and I honestly don't remember what became of my earlier albums, the Modern that started it all or the International that followed. I bought stamps mostly unused, from dealers, and hinged them.

I had lost interest by the time I went away to college, but the stamps were there when I was ready to return to them in my early twenties. I ordered stamps from ads in *Linn's*, and received selections on approval, and started a second collection as well, in the specialty album for Belgium, Netherlands, & Luxembourg.

By this time I was quite certain I preferred mint stamps, but would weigh my preference against the question of cost. There was often a huge discrepancy, with used copies of classic Nineteenth Century European issues going for a few cents, while their mint counterparts might bring hundreds or thousands of dollars. I might find a mint copy more attractive than a used one, but was that reason enough to blow my whole stamp budget on it when I could fill the same space for ten or twenty cents? And there were some stamps, inexpensive enough in used condition, that I couldn't even dream of buying mint. Wasn't a used specimen preferable to leaving it blank?

Let's flash forward. I'm an aging fellow rediscovering the joys of philately, first collecting Ireland, then experimenting with topical collecting, and eventually picking up an old 1840-to-1900 worldwide album. Its contents were a mix of mint and used, with most of the European issues used and a fair proportion of British and French colonials mint. (There were a lot of unused Central American issues, too, but almost all of them turned out to be Seebeck reprints.)

At the beginning, as I familiarized myself with the collection and began adding to it, I took it for granted that I'd continue to buy either mint or used stamps, depending what was on offer and what sort of price discrepancy existed. There were, to be sure, some stamps—from Italy, for various German states—where the genuinely used stamp was worth far more than the mint one. In those cases I'd buy the mint stamp, of course, and when the numbers were reversed I'd fill the space with the used stamp.

And if they were about the same price, as was not infrequently the case, I'd go for the mint stamp.

Because, I realized, that was still what I preferred. I just plain liked the way the unused stamps looked on the page, and when one stamp in a row was canceled, it looked to me as though it didn't belong. Even if it was worth as much used, even if it was worth *more*, it sat there on the page looking like a poor relation at a banquet.

So, if I preferred mint stamps, why buy used ones?

My first decision, then, was to stop buying used stamps. I'd leave a space blank until I could afford a mint copy.

But the used stamps I already owned could remain where they were, filling their spaces. Oh, if I could replace one of them with a mint copy for a few cents, then I'd do when I got the chance. But I had used early stamps from Germany and France that would be expensive to replace, so I'd keep those, wouldn't I?

At first I did. But some of them were pretty ratty, little more than space fillers, and I replaced them when I could. And then I bought unused replacements for some perfectly acceptable used specimens, because I liked unused stamps better, and it was my collection, wasn't it? So couldn't I decide what to buy and what not to buy?

Somewhere along the way I began using my Scott Classic Catalog as a checklist, circling the catalog number of a stamp to indicate that I owned it. I color-coded my list, using pencil if my copy was used, red ink if it was mint.

(An aside—I think I'd buy the catalog annually if it weren't so much of a chore to transfer the information from the old volume to the new one. Switching back and forth from a pencil to a red Flair pen made the whole business impossibly onerous, so I soon stopped keeping track of the used stamps and circled only the mint ones. At which point my decision to buy a stamp was uninfluenced by my already owning a used copy, because I wouldn't know offhand whether I did or not.)

Please don't think that I am here to argue the natural superiority of mint stamps. I don't even believe it myself, so why would I want to persuade you of it? I'm familiar with the argument that a used stamp, one which has seen postal duty and actually served its purpose of carrying the mail, is of far more historical interest than one that never did more than go from a post office into a file drawer, and then into a stamp album.

Nor would I presume to argue that a canceled stamp cannot be every bit as attractive as a used one. I understand the appeal of a socked-on-the-nose CDS cancellation, and some of the interesting geometric and figural handstamp cancels employed in the 19th century. When a canceled stamp particularly appeals to me, I'll happily retain it—as I've done with several early Russian stamps, with their start cancels, and a few particularly nice socked-on-the-nose issues from various countries. But I'll keep each as an adjunct to the mint example.

The reader will note that I've used the terms *mint* and *unused* interchangeably, and might well wonder what exactly it is that I collect. Some philatelists, to be sure, limit the use of *mint* to stamps that are Post Office fresh, their original gum never touched by a hinge. Anything else is to be called *used*.

Others divide the category of mint stamps into *hinged* and *never hinged*, with a stamp designated as *hinged* presumed to have at least some of its original gum. Without the gum—but without any evidence of cancellation—it's *unused*. "NG," it'll say in a dealer's listing, indicating that it has No Gum, and bearing a strong subliminal hint that it is therefore No Good.

Ah, the wonderful world of gum. What a marvelous subject for discourse!

But it'll have to wait. I'm out of space, and so important a topic as gum deserves a column all its own.

5

Buying the Same Stamp Twice

Keller sat in his hotel room with his purchases on the desk in front of him, pleased with what he'd acquired and the bargain prices he'd paid, but a little bit anxious at having spent so much money.

He had dinner again that night with McEwell, and confided some of what he was feeling. "I know what you mean," McEwell said, "and I've been there myself. I remember the first time I paid over a thousand dollars for a single stamp."

"It's a milestone."

"Well, it was for me. And I said to the dealer, 'You know, that's a lot of money.' And he said, 'Well, it is, but you're only going to buy that stamp once.'"

"I never thought of it that way," Keller said.

—*HIT MAN*

Yeah, right. If only.

I haven't bought any thousand-dollar stamps more than once, or any hundred-dollar ones, either. But it's almost as aggravating, if less financially damaging, to buy at any price a stamp for which I have no use.

And it happens again and again. In my stamp room (well, my wife thinks it's the dining room) I have an extremely attractive artifact about the size and shape of a cigar box. It's made of porcupine quills, and I bought it in Hobart, Tasmania, a little over a dozen years ago, from a fellow who was about to close his antique shop and do all his business on-line. I have always suspected the box originated elsewhere, as I don't believe they have porcupines in Tasmania, and whether they do or not they don't have this box, as I bought it and took it home with me.

I only had to buy it once.

At the moment, it's filled with stamps I bought and have no use for. Soon I'll empty it and mail its contents to a dealer friend, and before the parcel reaches him I'll have begun the process of filling it up again. With stamps I neither want nor need.

Endless, the whole business.

How did these various philatelic treasures come to be nestled beneath the canopy of porcupine quills? Let me count the ways:

First of all, there's human error—specifically mine. Because I collect worldwide 1840–1940, the catalog I use is the Scott Classic, which covers that specific period. And, whenever I acquire a stamp, I circle its identifying number in my catalog. (With a felt pen, one that won't bleed through, and in red, because it's more visible that way. That's if it's unused. I own an ever-diminishing number of used stamps which I'm gradually replacing, and early on I used to circle their numbers in blue, until I decided that was a waste of time. Where philately is concerned, I'm quite particular about how I waste my time.)

Thus the catalog serves as my checklist, and is ideal for the purpose. When I'm going over a pricelist, printed or on-line, I'd have the book at hand anyway, so it's easy enough to tell at a glance what I have and don't have. It's a little heavy to take along to stamp shows, and it gets a little beat up from all that schlepping, but it's manageable—and the more of a beating it takes, the more inclined I am to replace it with a new copy every couple of years.

So where does the human error come in? Well, sometimes I buy a stamp and mount it in my album without troubling to log it in my catalog. And later I find it offered on somebody else's list, and see that it's one I don't have, and buy it again. And then when I go to mount the new copy in my album, there's one already there.

Or I do make the appropriate entry when I buy the stamp. And a year or two later, when I've bought a replacement for my Classic Catalog, I go through the remarkably tedious process of circling in the new book everything I'd circled in the old. If I were a perfect person, perhaps I could do this perfectly . . . but I'm not, and I can't. Some of the information doesn't get copied, and sometimes I buy the stamp all over again.

I hate it when this happens. But I don't lose sleep over it, because it rarely happens with costly material. I'm more apt to know if I do or don't have a pricey stamp, and if there's any doubt I go over and look for it in the appropriate album, and settle the question then and there.

How else do I add to my box of duplicates? Well, there's another sort of human error that sometimes applies, but in this case the error is not mine but a dealer's. Sometimes a stamp is not the variety it's supposed to be. Sometimes a stamp is used instead of mint, or damaged in a way that renders it unsuitable for my collection.

Dealers are human, and mistakes are inevitable, and all I have to do is send the stamp back and its cost will be refunded. But when the stamp cost me 20¢, do you think I ought to spend 44¢ to return it? Plus the cost of the envelope, plus the nuisance of addressing the envelope and mailing it . . . all in all, a stamp has to cost at least couple of dollars for me to bother. Easier by far to tuck the thing in the quill-covered box and move on.

That pretty much covers the duplicates I buy by accident. But then there are the ones I buy on purpose.

Here's an example. Consider French India, a French administrative unit of five settlements on India's east coast, with its capital in Pondicherry. Two of its long series of regular issues are Scott 25–49, issued in 1914 and 1922, and

Scott 54–79, issued from 1923 to 1928. The stamps are not expensive; the first set lists at $33.05 in my 2009 catalog, the second at $75.35. I have been filling in these sets when I get the chance, and at the moment I lack #39 and #49 in the early set and #58, #60, #65–6, #69, #73, #76, and #78 in the later set. These ten stamps will complete the two sets—and, in fact, will complete French India for me.

As I said, these are not high-ticket items. Two of them list for less than a dollar, and the most expensive is $15.00. If I were to pay full catalog for them, I'd fill all ten empty spaces for something like $36.80. So all I have to do is wait and acquire each stamp as it becomes available, right?

Well, yes, at least in theory. But what happens, more often than not, is that a stamp I need is grouped in a single lot with one or more other stamps that I don't need. I need French India #39, cataloging 90¢, and it might well be offered in tandem with #38 ($2.40) or #40 ($1.40). Or both of them.

Or the lot on offer might consist of #74 ($1.10), #75 ($3.50), and #76 ($7.00). Say the dealer priced the group of three at $7.50, approximately two-thirds of Scott value. Reasonable enough, but how good a deal is it for me, if I only need #76? Do I wait another five years in the hope that the stamp will come my way with no baggage attached? Or do I buy the three stamps and toss two of them in the box?

Decisions, decisions. Sometimes the answer's obvious, when the cost of the extra stamps renders the purchase disproportionately high. By the same token, passing up a stamp I want because buying it might require the expenditure of an extra 20¢ for a stamp I don't need, would only make sense if my name were Penny Wise. But the decision isn't always that clear-cut.

For example, the 1925 postage due issue of French New Hebrides, J1–5, catalog $50 per stamp. Over the years I had acquired nice copies of J3 and J5, and then the full set turned up in an auction with a starting bid that was several dollars lower than I would have cheerfully paid for the three stamps I lacked. I bid the minimum, and when it held up I had my set completed—along with two stamps cataloging a cool hundred bucks to add to my box of duplicates.

Sometimes, even when it's worth too little to interest a dealer, the unwanted stamp is still not a total loss to me. I always compare the duplicate to the specimen I already have, and sometimes the new arrival is a little bit the better of the two. Superior centering, brighter color, less heavily hinged. On such occasions it's the original stamp that joins the duplicates, supplanted in its mount by my new acquisition.

It sometimes seems to me, as I weigh the relative merits of buying a stamp I don't need against waiting for the one I do need to be offered unencumbered, that philately is far and away the area of my life where I spend the most time and effort making genuinely inconsequential decisions. And perhaps that has something to do with the extraordinary satisfaction it affords. When I settle into my stamp room (and it's not a dining room, no matter what fantasies Lynne's able to entertain) I am entirely engaged in an activity that is at root entirely unimportant.

6

THE STICKY SUBJECT OF GUM

When I found my way back to philately, it took me a little while to decide just what I would collect. As I've explained previously, I became a general worldwide collector of the first hundred years of stamps, 1840 to 1940. And, because I found unused stamps more visually pleasing than canceled ones, they were what I chose to collect.

But what about the back of the stamp? Did it matter if it had the original gum?

Obviously, it mattered to some people, as the price of a stamp typically increased substantially if it bore its full complement of original gum, unmarred by any evidence that it had ever been sullied by a hinge. And that price dropped according to the extent to which the gum was impaired: a lightly hinged specimen was worth less than a never hinged one, full original gum was more desirable than part original gum, and, at the bottom of the pile, one found specimens designated NG, which would seem at a glance to be No Good, but which of course indicated they had No Gum.

It seemed to me, as I scrutinized price lists and tried to determine what to buy, that uncanceled stamps lacking gum constituted a bargain. A stamp with no gum was not infrequently priced at half of its hinged counterpart. And sometimes, I was surprised to discover, that ungummed stamp was pegged substantially lower than a used copy.

Early on, that was hard for me to understand. Here were two stamps, both identically devoid of gum, and one marred by a cancellation. Yet the canceled stamp cost more! In the fullness of time, of course, I came to understand this; collectors who sought used stamps wanted them to be canceled, albeit lightly and attractively, while collectors of unused stamps wanted them as close as possible to their original state, which is to say with gum on their backs.

But from my point of view, the ungummed stamp was more desirable if uncanceled. And, all things considered, would look every bit as good in my album as if its back were as pristine as its front. The front of the stamp was all I'd be looking at once I'd mounted it, and all anyone else would ever see.

Indeed, the only person who will ever see the backs of my stamps is the dealer who will someday acquire my collection—and by then I expect to have little interest in the matter.

Given the nature of my collection, my albums will always have a large number of empty spaces. That's perfectly fine with me, and the fact that completion is not even a goal, that there will be stamps I lack for longer than I'll be around to seek them, strikes me as a plus. All the same, if I can fill some of those spaces at a lower price, why wouldn't I want to do so? And if the stamps I fill them with are visually just as nice for half the price, why should I shun them?

Consider Italy's first postage due issue, Scott #J1. The value in the 2009 catalog is $2000 mint, or $3000 never hinged. A used specimen catalogs $225. But an unused copy without gum, Scott tells us, is a mere $85.

That particular space in my album is filled, and the stamp that's filling it is an attractive one. If you were to examine its back, you wouldn't find any gum. That makes it a good deal less valuable, but it wouldn't look any better with gum on its back.

I'll tell you this—I'm happy to have it. If it were canceled, I'd always be looking to replace it with an unused specimen. If it was thinned, or had a corner missing, or was otherwise visibly impaired, I'd hope for a replacement. But my stamp's sole flaw is its lack of gum, and that doesn't bother me a bit.

I'll keep it.

Sticky, the whole question of gum.

I'm sure I'd take a different tack if I were collecting, say, the stamps of the past half-century. These more recent issues are rarely offered without gum, and the prices in Scott are for NH specimens.

But that's not the case with the stamps in my collecting range, and the farther back you go, the greater the proportion of NG stamps you'll encounter. In the early days of the hobby, the only attention collectors were apt to pay to gum was to remove it in order to preserve the stamp. The chemical composition of some early varieties of gum would eventually discolor or otherwise ruin the stamp, so collectors would soak off the gum before mounting the stamp.

(That seems so Nineteenth Century, doesn't it? Then again, everything new is old again, and there's been more than a little speculation on what will eventually become of today's self-adhesive stamps. Will the adhesive simply degrade until the stamps fall free of their backing? Will it harm the stamps? I've heard a good many educated guesses on the subject, but haven't paid too much attention—because, as a collector of earlier material, I'm blissfully unconcerned.)

Forever unhinged Nineteenth Century stamps are scarce because virtually every collector hinged his stamps; that's how one mounted them in one's album. If a stamp of that era survives in Never-Hinged condition, that's either because it was part of a sheet or block, or because it spent its days in the possession of an accumulator, who wanted to own it but didn't feel the need to affix it in an album.

I've heard collectors of postally used stamps explain that the cancellation legitimizes the stamp for them, showing that it served the purpose for which it was intended—i.e., carrying a letter through the mail. By the same token, one could argue that a hinge mark, or even a hinge remnant, legitimizes a mint stamp, showing that it occupied a place in the collection of a philatelist, instead of having been merely tucked away in a box of glassine envelopes or forgotten in a desk drawer.

Another very real advantage of No Gum stamps is that one is spared the worry that they might have been regummed. A regummed stamp is one which has lost its original gum somewhere along the way, only to have it replaced with new gum. When the equivalent is performed on, say, a Rembrandt oil painting, we call it restoration; when such restoration is performed on a postage stamp, we're more apt to regard it as a crime against nature, and a clear-cut example of philatelic fraud.

Since I'm not much inclined to pay a premium for gum in the first place, I don't think it would greatly upset me to learn that one of my stamps had been regummed. I wouldn't be surprised to learn that I have a few regummed stamps in my collection, and I'm sure I'm not alone.

One encounters people who will tell you that they can always spot a regummed stamp. There are, to be sure, ways to detect regumming, but I can't believe they work 100% of the time, any more than I believe the folks who assure you that they can always spot a toupee. I know of a fellow, a salesman of quality human hair goods, who used to steer conversations to the point where someone made that statement. "Oh, really?" he'd say—and remove his own rug, to their astonishment. And to his own profit, as you can be sure he sold a lot of wigs that way.

I don't want to give the impression that I'm contemptuous of gum, or that I give the back of my hand to the back of the stamp. If I wind up with more than one copy of the same stamp (and that happens all too often, as I confessed in last month's column), I have to decide which specimen to keep and which goes in the box of duplicates. Sometimes centering makes the choice for me, but when the two stamps are more or less equal in this respect, I'll turn them over. And I'll choose hinged over no gum, and never hinged over hinged.

I make this choice not merely on the basis of value, but also for personal aesthetic reasons. I can appreciate the appearance of a stamp with its gum present and unimpaired, and I can remember how much I warmed to the phrase *Post Office Fresh* the first time I encountered it. Who wouldn't rather have a stamp that was Post Office Fresh than one that was, oh, Cat Box Stale? But it's not something I insist upon, or for which I want to pay a substantial premium.

If you don't care all that much about gum, it's not hard to guess how you mount your stamps. You hinge them, right?

Well, no. I don't. Each stamp goes in its own black-backed plastic mount.

Hang on, LB. You're no fool, you don't let hinges lower the value of whatever NH copies come your way, but how about the others? How about the NG ones, those poor devils with not a trace of gum to protect? Surely they don't wind up in mounts.

Ah, but I'm afraid they do. So in fact do the handful of used stamps in my albums. This business of cutting mounts extends the time it takes me to add stamps to my albums, and I am not unmindful of the fact that I'm spending more to mount an extremely common stamp than the stamp itself is worth.

But here's the thing: it's my collection, even as your collection is yours. Just as I get to choose what stamps I collect, I can also decide how to house and display them. And I just plain prefer the appearance of a stamp in a black-backed mount. I like the way it looks. And it seems to me that any stamp worth holding a place in my album, even temporarily, is worth the cost in time and money to display it properly.

Gum—its presence or absence—seems to matter more or less to me, depending on the particular stamp. The greater the price differential between Hinged and NG, the more likely I am to go for the gumless stamp. In addition, my enthusiasm or lack thereof for a particular country plays a role. I may be a little more intent on adding more desirable specimens to a favored country, while ungummed and poorly centered stamps will serve well enough for those countries I care less about.

Wait a minute. Can a general worldwide collector care more about some countries than others? Is there a Most-Favored Nation clause in his contract with philately?

Ah. Wouldn't you know it? Now I've got a topic for next month's column...

Keller and His Stamps

—From *Hit List*

At home, he paged through one of his stamp albums. Many of his fellow hobbyists were topical or thematic philatelists, collecting stamps not of a particular country or time period but united by what they portrayed. Stamps showing trains, say, or butterflies, or penguins. A doctor might choose stamps with a medical connection, while a musician could seek out stamps showing musical instruments, or those with portraits of the great composers. Or you could collect rabbit stamps for no more abiding reason than that you just plain liked to look at rabbits.

Art on stamps was an increasingly popular topic. Early on, when postage stamps were commonly of a single color, reproducing a great painting on a scrap of paper was easier said than done. A monochromatic miniature of the Mona Lisa might be recognizable for what it was, but it lacked a certain something.

Those early stamps, skillfully engraved and beautifully printed, were to Keller's mind far more attractive than what they turned out these days, when virtually every stamp from every country was printed in full color, and any stamp-issuing entity could spew out gem-like reproductions of the world's art treasures. Collectors made such endeavors profitable, and, unlike animation art from Disney or Warner Brothers, the works of Rembrandt and Rubens were unprotected by trademark or copyright. Anyone could copy them, and many did.

Keller's 1952 cutoff date put most of the world's art stamps out of his reach. But some countries had issued such stamps back in the old one-color days, more out of pride in their artistic heritage than in a grab for the collector's dollar. The French were particularly eager to show off their culture, portraying writers and painters and composers at the slightest provocation, and Keller looked now at a set of French semi-postals that gave you a real sense of the artists' power.

And of course there was the Spanish set honoring Goya. One of the stamps showed his nude portrait of the Duchess of Alba. The painting had caused a stir when first displayed, and, years later, the stamp had proven every bit as stirring to a generation of young male philatelists. Keller remembered owning the stamp decades ago, and scrutinizing it through a pocket magnifier, wishing fervently that the stamp were larger and the glass stronger.

In the current issue of *Linn's*, as in almost every issue, there was a spirited exchange in the letters column on the best way to attract youngsters to the hobby. Evidently boys and girls were less strongly drawn to philately in a world full of computers and Nintendo and MTV. If kids stopped collecting stamps, where would the next generation of adult collectors come from?

Keller, having considered the question, had decided that he didn't care. All he wanted to do was add to his own collection, and he didn't really give a damn how many other men and women were working on theirs. Without new collectors joining the fold, stamps might eventually decline in value, but he didn't care about that, either. He wasn't going to sell his collection, and what difference did it make what became of it upon his death? If he couldn't take it with him, then somebody else could figure out what to do with it.

But others clearly did care about the hobby's future. The U.S. Post Office evidently saw a very profitable sideline threatened, and had responded by issuing stamps designed specifically to appeal to the young collector. When Keller was a boy, stamps showed great American writers and inventors and statesmen, people he mostly hadn't heard of, and in the course of collecting their images he had in fact learned a great deal about them, and about the history in which they'd played a part.

Nowadays, stamp collecting was a great way for young Americans to learn about Bugs Bunny and Daffy Duck.

Keller thought it over and decided they were doing it wrong. He'd collected avidly as a boy not because stamp collecting was designed for kids but because it was something undeniably grown-up that he could enjoy. If it had felt like kid stuff he wouldn't have had any part of it.

Would a stamp with Bugs Bunny's picture on it have prompted a young Keller to whip out his magnifying glass for a closer look?

Not a chance. If they wanted to get the kids interested, he thought, let them start putting naked ladies on them . . . .

By the time he got home the mail was in. Keller had never cared much about the mail, collecting it and dealing with it as it came, tossing the junk mail and paying the bills. Then he took up stamp collecting, and now every day's mail held treasures.

Dealers throughout the country, and a few overseas, sent him the stamps he'd ordered from their lists, or won in mail auctions. Others sent him selections on approval, to examine at leisure and keep what pleased him. And there were the monthly stamp magazines, and a weekly stamp newspaper, and no end of auction catalogs and price lists and special offers.

Today, along with the usual lists and catalogs, Keller received his monthly selection from a woman in Maine. "Dear John," he read. "Here's a nice lot of German Colonies, plus a few others for your inspection. Enclosed are 26 glassines totaling $194.43. Hope you find some to your liking. Sincerely, Beatrice."

Keller had been dealing with Beatrice Rundstadt for almost two years now. She enclosed a similar note with each shipment, and he always wrote back along the same lines: "Dear Beatrice, Thanks for a nice selection, much of which has found a home here on First Avenue. I'm enclosing my check for $83.57 and look forward to next month's assortment. Yours, John." It had taken well over a year of Dear Mr. Keller and Dear Ms. Rundstadt, but now they were John and Beatrice, which gave the correspondence a nice illusion of intimacy.

Just an illusion, though. He didn't know if Beatrice Rundstadt was married or single, old or young, tall or short, fat or thin, didn't know if she collected stamps herself (as many dealers did) or thought collecting stamps was a fool's errand (as many other dealers did). For her part, all she knew about him was what he collected.

And that was how he hoped it would remain. Oh, he couldn't avoid the occasional fantasy, in which Bea Rundstadt (or some other lady philatelist) turned out to be a soulmate with the face of an angel and the build of a Barbie doll. Fantasies were harmless, as long as you kept them in their place. His notes remained as steadfastly perfunctory as hers. She sent him stamps, he sent her checks. Why mess with something that worked?

You could generally hold a selection of approvals for up to a month, but Keller rarely kept them around for more than a day or two. This time all he needed was an hour to pick out the stamps he wanted. He could mount them later on; for now he wrote out a check and a three line note and went downstairs to the mail box . . .

7

THE ABIDING PATIENCE OF STAMPS

For the past couple of weeks I've been neglecting my stamps. There are several envelopes on my desk, and I did go so far as to examine them and log their contents by circling the corresponding numbers in my Scott catalog. (If I've remembered to do that, and if I've managed to circle the correct numbers, I'll be a little less likely to buy the same stamp a second time.) The next step would be to install these new acquisitions in what I like to think of as their permanent home. To mount them, that is to say, each in its allotted space in one of my albums.

Now that's generally the part of collecting that provides me with the greatest satisfaction. I take the album from the shelf, I open it on my desk, I consult my catalog and match the new stamp with its designated space. I find a mount of the right size, inset the stamp, trim it to fit with my guillotine-style mount cutter, and—well, you get the drift.

Then I sit and look at the page. Perhaps I've just mounted the initial stamp on a page that used to be blank. Perhaps I've filled the final space on that page. Or, as is more often the case, perhaps I've added a fifteenth stamp to a page, thus reducing its number of blank spaces from nineteen to eighteen. In any event, I'm looking at progress—and I take a moment to enjoy it.

Perhaps, while I'm at it, I look at the pages before and after the one I've just augmented. If it was a stamp from, oh, Bahrain, how do the other Bahrain pages look now? If I'm one stamp closer to completing Bahrain, how many of the ones I still need are likely to be inexpensive?

None of Bahrain's stamps, I note, are impossibly expensive. The priciest one I can see is #14, the 5 Rupee dark violet & ultra of 1933, pegged at $175 in my catalog. Bahrain doesn't boast many minor varieties, but there's #64a, a double surcharge in the 1948 Olympics issue, at $1750, and #78a, a surcharge variety, at $925. I don't care much about double surcharges, or minor varieties generally, so these are not stamps I'll feel a need to buy. But I'll take a moment to think about the one booklet listed, #15a, valued at $1500 and described as containing 16 copies of the 1 anna dark brown with watermark inverted, in four blocks of four. The booklet's cover, a note explains, is red and black on tan, with an advertisement on its front for Mysore Sandal Soup.

Now I'll probably never be offered a copy of that booklet, and could in any event almost certainly find a better use for the $1500, but my life seems richer for having spotted that note. Mysore Sandal Soup! A soup made from sandals? A soup in which sandals may be immersed, no doubt to their benefit?

Or could it be that the product was actually intended for the cleaning of leather, and that a miracle of modern typesetting has now transformed it from soap to soup? Oh, that's the mundane explanation, to be sure, but if it's all the same to you I'll sit here at my desk and enjoy the notion of sandal soup, Mysore's finest contribution to the cuisine of South India.

That's all very interesting—to me, at any rate. And I've spared you the fruits of ten minutes on Google and Wikipedia, where my faint curiosity about the general location of Mysore taught me more than I'll ever need to know about the history and geography of the place. But here's the thing—all of this Bahrain-Mysore-Sandal stuff came about because I had to pick an example to illustrate this column's argument. Those envelopes on my desk don't contain any stamps from Bahrain—although there are in fact twenty-one such stamps in my album, none of them of great value.

Meanwhile, the stamps in the envelopes remain unmounted. And dealer price lists accumulate unperused in another corner of my desk, along with a couple of unread issues of *Linn's*. I just haven't felt in the mood for stamps these past several weeks.

And that's one of the best things about the glorious hobby of stamp collecting. I can neglect it any time I want.

Now I can see how that might strike you as curious. After all, doesn't part of philately's attraction lie in the grip it holds on us? It is our eagerness to locate and acquire and add to our albums that testifies to our commitment to the hobby. If we weren't obsessed with stamps, we'd limit our engagement with them to the mailing of an occasional letter, and find other uses for our time and money.

We praise a book by stating that we couldn't put it down. So what sort of endorsement is it to say of our stamp albums that we can put them down whenever we wish, and indeed stay away from them for days or weeks on end?

I would contend that it's a great virtue. And I'd bolster the argument by pointing to some other activities that can't be so easily neglected.

Work, for one. A person with a job had better go to it, and a person with a business had better tend to it. As a self-employed writer, I'm able to set my own hours and schedule my time as I see fit, but I still have to get the work done. This column, for example, ought to be in my editor's hands—or at least his virtual mailbox—on a certain date. My books don't have due dates, but if I don't deliver them with some degree of regularity I won't have money to spend on stamps—or on some of life's less essential matters, like food and clothing and shelter.

But a hobby's not supposed to be work, and that indeed is one of its charms, that it provides a respite from work. Other leisure pursuits, however, are less forgiving than philately.

Anything living, for example, imposes its own responsibilities. You've got to walk the dog, refresh the cat box, feed the fish, water the philodendron. A few years ago some computer genius marketed a virtual aquarium, and added an element in the interests of realism; if you didn't do the necessary day-to-day maintenance, your virtual fish would drop virtually dead.

Athletic pursuits make their own demands. I'm a long-distance racewalker, and take the sport seriously enough to have written a memoir on the subject. I participate in marathons, and if I am to complete them I have to have trained sufficiently. Much of the time it's pure pleasure to get out and walk for an hour or two, but occasionally it's the last thing I want to do.

If I don't do it once it's no big deal. But if I skip enough sessions my condition will suffer, and I may not be able to finish my next race. Or I may skip that race altogether and take off enough time to get out of shape, and it is ever so much easier to get out of shape than to get into it again. And . . .

Well, you get the idea. And I get depressed just thinking about it.

Ah, the D word. Depressed.

I'm subject to occasional depression, and I'm sure there's a pill I could take for it, and I don't want to hear about it. Mine is not the paralyzing clinical depression that afflicts some people I've known, but it's enough to make me disinclined to do much of anything.

Sometimes philately is a help. On such occasions I'm entirely absorbed in my stamps, and they take me out of my mood. They don't cure it, the respite is only temporary, but while I sit there with tongs in one hand and a magnifier in the other, I'm a little less mindful of the fact that the world—from Aden to Zululand—is a horrible place.

When the depression's bad enough, of course, my stamp collection is just one more aspect of my life I can't bear to face. My albums, from Aden to Zululand, only deepen my mood. To glance at the shelf that holds them is to remind myself that here is another area in which I'm falling short. On the one hand, I have stamps on my desk and I'm not mounting them. On the other, I should never have taken up this hobby in the first place, and am a fool to have sunk so much time and money into it.

And so on.

The first time I went through this, perhaps a year or two after I returned to stamps a decade and a half ago, I thought I'd made a great mistake. What was I doing, trying to recapture an enthusiasm of my youth? Clearly I'd been pouring time and money into what was turning out to be yet another passing fancy.

And then *that* passed, as it has any number of times since.

Now I'm able to recognize, as the disembodied voice says in *Battlestar Galactica*, that all this has happened before, and all will happen again. Depressions come and go, and a passion for philatelic pursuits that wanes one day will wax another.

When I'm ready for them, my stamps will be ready for me. They won't have withered like unwatered plants or soiled the carpet like unwalked dogs. They won't turn out to be virtual fish, floating belly-up in a virtual aquarium. They've been around, some of them, for a century and a half. Keep them dry and out of drafts, as it were, and they'll be around forever.

And even now, as I fine-tune this column, I can feel the end approaching of my temporary estrangement from philately. Just yesterday another dealer's list turned up in my mailbox, and last night I found myself going over it. I circled some stamps I can use, and once I've sent off this column I may follow it with an email order for these stamps. (It would be a happy coincidence if they were from Bahrain, but they're not. They're from New Guinea.)

So maybe I'll order them, and maybe I won't. Maybe I'll just head for the kitchen. I've got a recipe for Sandal Soup I've been wanting to try out.

8

PLAYING FAVORITES

As a general worldwide collector of philately's first century, I collect stamps from every stamp-issuing country in the world. Every space in my set of albums is a vacuum to be filled when the opportunity presents itself and my own resources appear equal to the task. I'm equally enthusiastic about filling any of these spaces, and as avid a collector of the stamps of one country as another.

Uh, maybe not.

Remember *Animal Farm*? In his brilliant satire of Soviet communism, George Orwell's animal revolutionaries march to the slogan, "All animals are equal." But before long the pigs, who wind up running the show, amend the phrase a wee bit. "All animals are equal," the new motto proclaims, "but some are more equal than others."

In my collection, some countries are more equal than others.

Now if one is going to play favorites, a stamp collection is a benign medium in which to do so. If I turn out to be a more ardent buyer of stamps from the various French colonies, say, than of the Spanish colonial issues, I don't see that I'm hurting anyone. It's not like favoring one child over another, and I can't think that my favoritism will doom poor neglected Cape Juby to hours on end of psychotherapy, or that Gabon will strut about with a high-flown sense of entitlement. As with all the decisions I make regarding my collection, its impact outside the walls of my stamp room is less than minimal.

But why do I favor one country—or, more precisely, one country's stamps? Why choose one over another?

Well, there are a few reasons. In one case, it was my fondness for a particular country and my familiarity with its history that led to my interest in its stamps.

The country was Ireland. As a child I responded to Irish songs, and as a young man I began studying the country's history. My first trip to the place in 1964 felt curiously like a homecoming, and made me open to the notion of past lives. I spent a good deal of time there, at one point entertained the notion of moving there, and, when I decided about fifteen years ago to embrace philately again, I set out collecting the stamps of Ireland. It was not until I'd pretty much filled my Ireland album that I bought a pre-1900 worldwide collection and became a general collector.

(Now I could have stayed with Ireland forever. I'd begun acquiring booklets and forerunner issues and minor varieties, and I could have added covers and multiples and postal history and blossomed as a specialist. But a little taste of life as a specialist helped me realize that my true calling was that of the generalist, and a couple of years of dutifully keeping up with new issues made it clear that I wanted a cutoff date, and that 1940 seemed a sound choice.)

I have all my Irish stamps, and I cherish them, although I haven't added anything to that collection in quite a few years, and thus hardly ever open those albums. But Ireland was a natural choice to collect, and my other most-favored nations seem less obvious.

Take Gambia, for instance. I've never been there—although I think that may have changed by the time this column appears, as Lynne and I are booked on a cruise from Cape Town to Gibraltar and it seems to me that Gambia (or the Gambia, as you prefer) is one of the many exotic places where we'll make landfall. Gambia's independent now, of course, but during the years I collect it was a British crown colony, and one of several such entities in Africa. Why should I be a more eager seeker of Gambian stamps than of, oh, Nigeria?

Here I was responding not to the fact of Gambia but to the aesthetic properties of its stamps, and specifically of its earliest issue. The embossed stamps, with the white silhouette of the young queen's profile, appealed to me. There were a couple of examples in the starter collection I'd bought, and others turned up on dealer lists, and I began filling them in.

And, once those early issues had triggered my interest in Gambia, that interest enlarged to embrace all of Gambia's stamps. The issues that followed, most of them of the standard British keyplate design, were no different from corresponding series from Nigeria—or Sierra Leone or, well, any land upon which the sun was not setting. But, because I liked those embossed issues, I liked Gambia overall, and filled its spaces whenever I could.

Then there's Belgium. In my early twenties I collected coins more ardently than stamps, and the offerings at one auction included an elderly priest's life-long collection of Belgian commemorative medallions. The price was low, and I bought it, and a lovely assortment it was, with many low-relief masterpieces by the art nouveau sculptor Godefroid DeVreese, and no end of stern effigies of Leopold I and Leopold II. I never could figure out what to do with them, but enjoyed owning them, and within a couple of years I'd begun collecting the stamps of Belgium—and, in the natural course of things, of the Netherlands and Luxembourg as well.

I sold that Benelux collection in the early seventies, but my familiarity with Belgian stamps made it a favorite country when I surfaced years later as a worldwide collector. I heaved a sigh—heaved it clear across the room, let me tell you—when I bought the Cardinal Mercier semipostal set a second time, at a far higher price than I'd paid for it in the mid-sixties. But the stamps, as I mounted them, were as welcome as long-lost friends.

France and her colonies became a special passion early on, although I'd had no experience with them until I bought that pre-1900 starter collection. Of the colonial issues, there was a decent representation of the Peace & Commerce issues, many of them mint, and I was able to find a good number of the ones I lacked at modest prices. They were easy to collect, too, in that there were no watermarks and no perforation varieties to contend with. Early issues of France were pricy, but I picked up some bargains at auctions. As my collection extended its range all the way to 1940, I found enough appealing stamps at low prices to get me going, and enough more elusive stamps to make the pursuit sufficiently challenging.

I found I was partial to Sarawak, and remembered I'd felt similarly drawn to the place fifty years ago. Did I just like the looks of the stamps? Was it the dynastic line of white rajahs that hooked me? I don't honestly know, but I acquired the stamps whenever I had the chance.

And I learned a further truth to the adage that nothing succeeds like success. The more extensive my holding of a country's stamps grew, the fonder I became of that country, and the more eager I became to get more.

Consider Armenia. There were, of course, no Armenian stamps in that starter album, as the country's first issues emerged in the wake of the Russian Revolution. I picked up a few when they showed up in dealer lists, but I didn't get more than a handful that way, and consequently paid little attention to those pages in my album, and rarely had occasion to consult the Armenia listings in my Scott Classic Catalog.

Then I bid on a collection of Armenia in an auction. I don't do that sort of thing often, because I dislike buying duplicates, and I only want unused stamps, so most collections and bulk lots don't really work for me. But these stamps were almost all mint, and I had too few Armenian stamps myself for duplication to amount to much. So I took a chance, and devoted several days to the absorbing task of figuring out just what I had and just where to put it in my album.

In a matter of days, I went from a scattering of Armenian stamps to a good working collection—and the result was that I became far more interested in the country's stamps. Consequently I now wanted to get more of them. When those pages had consisted mostly of empty spaces, I'd been reasonably content to let them remain empty; now that there were far fewer of those empty spaces,

I found I wanted to fill them. While earlier I'd only bought Armenian stamps if they were the more low-priced common varieties, I now found myself willing to buy some of the more expensive items.

I found the various plebiscite regions of considerable interest before I owned any of their stamps. In the course of remaking the map of Europe after the World War—we wouldn't come to call it World War I until its sequel was upon us—plebiscite elections were held in various disputed regions, to determine the wishes of the inhabitants and settle the matter accordingly. An extraordinary Wilsonian notion, that; the citizenry was to decide for itself of which nation it wished to be a part. The world outside of philately has largely forgotten this chapter in its history, and few of the names ring even a muted bell for the average citizen, whose grasp on history is anyway not terribly brawny. But just as we stamp collectors are able to name the U.S. presidents in order, so can we nod with recognition at Upper Silesia, Eastern Silesia, Memel, and Allenstein. (I'm sometimes a little vague on the precise whereabouts of either of the Silesias, but at least I'm aware that Silesia is a geographical entity, and not an emotional disorder.)

So in a sense I suppose the plebiscite regions were favorites of mine well before I began to acquire their stamps. And for some reason I had a special fondness for Allenstein.

I've no idea why. I may well have had an ancestor who tarried there, but that's true of most of Central Europe, from Strasbourg to Minsk. Maybe I just liked the name. When I was a schoolboy I knew a kid named Allen Stein. Or was his first name Albert? Yes, of course, and his last name wasn't Stein at all. Albert Durlach, that was his name, and I can but wonder what became of him—

But I digress.

The stamps of Allenstein consist of two series of overprinted German issues, the first overprint announcing the coming plebiscite, the second citing the applicable articles of the Treaty of Versailles. There are 28 stamps in all, and they're by no means expensive, with a total Scott value of around $50. They turned up on a dealer's list in two lots, and I bought them both, and went from having no stamps from Allenstein to owning the complete country. This gave me a sense of accomplishment, and I was happy to have them, but Allenstein was a dead country and I found myself at a dead end. Scott lists a handful of minor varieties—shades, for the most part, and doubled overprints—but I didn't know that I wanted that sort of specialization.

And then an auction catalog showed up in my mailbox with mint copies of four unlisted stamps from the first series, cited in Scott but unnumbered because, while overprinted, they were never issued. That appealed to me enormously, and I attended the sale and bought the stamps. Scott also mentioned a similar unissued stamp from the second series, and a couple of months later it turned up on eBay and, shortly thereafter, found its way to my album.

So it goes. Allenstein's a favorite country of mine, and so are the other plebiscite regions.

If I'm going to play favorites, it's inescapable that there will be other unfavored countries. And the nice thing about that is it gives me something to write about next month. Given the way one thing tends to lead to another, it may be a while before I run out of topics. Now if I can only figure out whatever happened to Albert Durlach . . .

LESS-FAVORED NATIONS

Last month I likened my enthusiasms as a general worldwide collector to the characters in George Orwell's *Animal Farm.* "All animals are equal," the pigs proclaimed, "but some are more equal than others." And I, who collect all countries equally, had to allow that I find some of them more equal than others.

I had, you'll recall, different reasons for different preferences. A lifelong fondness for Ireland and a fair knowledge of its history made Irish stamps appealing. I liked Belgium because I'd collected its stamps forty years ago, liked Gambia because the early embossed issues appealed to me aesthetically, liked Armenia because a bulk purchase had given me a good foothold on the country. And so on—and I somehow found enough things to say about enough countries' stamps to fill my allotted space, and it wasn't until the column's end that I began to address the implication of playing favorites.

I.e., if some countries are more equal, then other countries are inevitably less equal. So, if I'm busy looking for Irish and Belgian and Armenian stamps, what countries am I just as busily overlooking? And what, pray tell, are my reasons for overlooking them?

This brought a quick response from *Linn's* editor Michael Baadke, understandably concerned that a discussion of my less-favored nations might contain some uncomplimentary observations about some countries and their stamps—and, by extension, those philatelists who collect them with a passion. I was quick to assure him that I'd be doing nothing of the sort.

And how could I? Aside from the fact that the last thing I want to do is insult whole countries and their philatelic advocates, I don't know that I harbor any negative feelings toward any stamps or stamp collectors. My albums are designed to hold every postage stamp issued between 1840 and 1940, and, while there are innumerable spaces I never expect to fill, there's not a single one I wouldn't *like* to fill.

Will Rogers, whose likeness can be found on U.S. #975, famously observed that he never met a man he didn't like. (Maybe he didn't get out much.) I have, alas, met more than a few men for whom I cared little, but I don't think I've ever come upon a stamp that filled me with contempt. There are stamps that fall outside the scope of my collection, but as for the others, well, my albums have spaces for them, and I'd rather have them than not.

Still, some are more equal than others. So what are some of these less-favored nations, and how did they make the list?

Well, consider Nicaragua. It is, to be sure, a charming and interesting nation, and a valued supplier of bananas and baseball players. I spent a week there some years ago with my eldest granddaughter, riding in a dugout canoe while a guide pointed out and identified various tropical birds, the names of which I promptly forgot. I liked the place, and wouldn't mind returning.

And the stamps are interesting, too, and one played an interesting role in American history. When rival factions advocated both Nicaragua and Panama as the site for a canal to link the two oceans, the pro-Panama folks lobbied by sending around Nicaraguan stamps, showing the official seal of the country. The mountain depicted was volcanic, and the Nicaraguans put the darn thing right there on their stamps, and did Congress really want to situate a canal next to a volcano?

Who wouldn't want to collect stamps with such a sweet historical connection?

I might have collected them enthusiastically myself, but for the fact that my 1840–1900 starter collection already had the country virtually complete, and mint with original gum in the bargain. I was delighted to see them, and wondered at the bargain I'd landed, until I learned enough about them to realize that what I had were Seebecks. One N.F. Seebeck had a contract with the government of Nicaragua to supply the country with stamps, and retained the right to reprint them for the collector market. He apparently did so in great profusion, and one result a century later was that my own personal interest in the stamps of Nicaragua (and other Seebeck countries, like El Salvador and Ecuador) dwindled.

Now I could seek out genuine replacements for those Seebecks. But for now I seem to be content to let them remain as they are, with unfilled spaces in some of the sets, and to pay as little attention to them as possible.

After 1900, Mr. Seebeck's efforts cease to pose a problem. And I do fill in my holdings of Nicaragua when the opportunity arises. But I'd go after the stamps a good deal more avidly if I hadn't started out with all those Seebecks.

My own ignorance and laziness keeps much of the world off my list of favorite countries. I'm familiar with the Latin alphabet, and have the good fortune to encounter it on the stamps of all the Western Hemisphere nations, as well as most of the countries of Europe, and their possessions and colonies throughout the world. I learned the Hebrew alphabet preparing for my bar mitzvah, and I still recognize the letters even if I have no idea what the words mean. And I know the Greek alphabet—I was required to learn it, all the way from A to Ω, when I pledged my high school fraternity. And I have a passing acquaintance with the Cyrillic alphabet, and can at least sound out the inscriptions on the Russian and Eastern European stamps that employ it.

And what does that leave? Alas, a good deal of the planet. Japan, China, Korea, Thailand, the Arab world—the stamps, however attractive and interesting they may be, are largely incomprehensible to me. I feel like the dog in that commercial a few years ago for fake bacon, maddened by his inability to make out what it says on the package. "I can't read!" he cries out—and I know just how he feels.

I can still enjoy the stamps, but I enjoy them more when I can tell them apart, and get some sense of what they're trying to tell me. Many bear secondary inscriptions in a familiar alphabet; Lebanon and Syria, for example, show as much French as Arabic on their pre-1940 issues, and that has made me more inclined to collect them than, oh, Saudi Arabia or Afghanistan.

But there's always an exception, isn't there? Until the issues of the late 1920s, virtually all I could make out on Turkey's stamps was the face value. Many of the early issues just showed a lamp—Aladdin's, I suppose—with a numeral underneath, or in a corner, or somewhere. And yet somehow Turkey was to become a favorite country.

How did this happen? I'd be hard put to explain it. One way or another, I picked up enough Turkish stamps to tilt the balance in the country's favor. Familiarity soon helped me tell the similar issues apart, and as the pages started to fill in I found myself warming to their appearance. I think it probably helped that there were enough low-priced stamps available to allow me to get a grip on the country without a major financial commitment. By the time the more expensive stamps came along, I was fond enough of Turkey to pay the price.

There may be a lesson there. I mentioned in my last column how Armenia had become a favorite country almost overnight; I bought an auction lot of stamps, and by the time I'd sorted it all out and mounted the stamps, I not only had a decent representation of the country, but in the process I'd been forced to learn a bit about Armenian stamps. I suppose I did much the same thing with Turkey, but more gradually, one stamp at a time.

"There are no strangers," say people with a little too much aspartame in their bloodstreams. "A stranger is only a friend you haven't met yet." (A fellow I know has a version I like better: *A friend is just an enemy who has not yet betrayed you.*)

Perhaps my less-favored countries are simply those with whose stamps I have not yet become sufficiently acquainted. Suppose I relegated all those Seebecks to separate pages, and studied the stamps enough to tell the originals from the reprints, and begin to acquire the original issues I've been missing. Wouldn't that make me feel more favorably disposed toward Nicaragua?

And, toward that end, wouldn't I be more inclined to do this if my post-1900 Nicaragua pages had more stamps on them? Wouldn't improvement on the later pages spur me to do something about the earlier ones?

I wouldn't be surprised.

Even within a small group of similar countries, I find myself playing favorites. I mentioned how the aesthetic appeal of the early embossed issues of Gambia led me to favor that country over its neighbors in British Africa. Similarly, some special aspect can nudge a country into relative disfavor.

Portuguese India is a case in point. I enjoy collecting Portugal and its colonies, but I'm less enthusiastic about Portugal's former toehold on the subcontinent. Now I've been to Goa, a port-of-call on a cruise Lynne and I took a few years ago, and found it an extremely interesting city, but I haven't done much with the stamps they issued, especially the very early issues.

What's the matter with them? Well, for openers, I don't find them all that physically attractive. And there are a great many of them, and one looks rather like the next. They are unwatermarked, which eliminates one whole ocean of confusion, but they are available on thin transparent brittle paper or thick soft wove paper, on white laid paper or thin bluish toned paper, and with no end of perforation varieties.

Now all of this would make Portuguese India fertile ground for the specialist, while a generalist can find it discouraging. Still, familiarity might well banish contempt, as it did with me for Armenia and Turkey—two countries which generally seem to prefer not to be in the same room, let alone the same sentence. But this hasn't happened for me with Portuguese India, and it may be a while before it does, and for a very simple reason.

The stamps are expensive.

Not out-of-this-world expensive, except for a handful of them. But there are very few low-priced stamps in the first 150-plus listings, and a fair proportion in the hundreds of dollars, and more than a few in the thousands.

The later issues of Portuguese India aren't all that different in price or complexity from those of the other Portuguese colonies, and some are particularly appealing, like those marvelous provisional issues (#260C–289, #336–354) which are perforated through the middle. I add them to my collection when I can, but I'm sure I'd be more eager to do so if my passion weren't held in check by my problems with the earlier issues.

Now if I were to strike it rich, and if a nice holding of unused early issues of Portuguese India were to come my way . . .

Well, that could change everything, couldn't it?

10

MY LITTLEST STAMP ALBUM

DAKHLA, WESTERN SAHARA—I'm writing this month's column in my cabin on the *Corinthian II*, a 114-passenger cruise ship registered in Malta. Four weeks ago we set sail from Cape Town, and a week from today we'll disembark at Seville, where we'll board a plane to Madrid to connect with a flight home to JFK.

So far I've added four stamps to my collection.

Now my main stamp collection, which I tend to talk about in these columns, is a general worldwide one, limited to philately's first century, from 1840 to 1940. (Like the Scott Classic catalog, I make an exception for the British Empire, and include stamps issued through the end of George VI's reign.)

I haven't added to this collection during the past month. How could I? Good King George hasn't had a pulse since 1952, and all his old African colonies have long since been granted independence. Africa may move at a slower pace than I'm used to back home, but that doesn't mean the post offices over here are likely to have stamps issued back in 1940, or even in 1952.

But I have another collection, a much more limited one, but every bit as challenging, and almost as impossible to complete. It is housed in an album four inches wide and six inches high and perhaps a half-inch thick, and at the moment it contains 99 stamps—and yes, I just paged through it and counted them, something I'm unlikely ever to attempt with my main collection. None of them are at all valuable, yet when one factors in the cost of acquiring them, they're the costliest stamps I own. And all 99 of these stamps are canceled, but not a one of them qualifies as postally used.

This collection, as you may have surmised, combines two passions, travel and philately. Whenever Lynne and I visit a new country, or revisit one not yet represented in this album, we make it our business to visit a post office, buy a stamp, attach it to a page, and persuade the clerk to cancel it. (More often than not, the clerk's command of English is about as firm as our own command of, say, Latvian, or Serbo-Croatian. Miming the act of cancellation with a closed fist generally makes the point; when a postal clerk proves a little slow off the mark, we can always flip to another page and point to a canceled stamp. Sooner or later, the message gets through. [As Figure ?? in the original column shows, it got through in a big way to an obliging fellow in the Chilean Antarctic.)

It was in September of 1997 that we began this collection. I'd resumed collecting stamps three or four years earlier, and was greatly enjoying my return to philately. And Lynne and I, who had begun traveling in earnest ten years earlier, set off to explore Europe by train. We bought rail passes and flew from New York to Prague with the intention of visiting as many countries as we could, hoping to make some progress toward our goal of qualifying for membership in the Travelers Century Club.

We spent a few days in Prague and took a train to Cracow. (We went via Warsaw, though not by design; we missed our stop, got off in Warsaw, and spent a night in the train station there, in the company of a lot of folks rarely met outside the pages of a really depressing French novel.) Cracow was lovely; that was the year the Polish travel bureau came out with a poster with the slogan *Cracow: Like Paris Without the French,* and we lingered there a few days before heading on to Budapest. And it was there that one of us said, "You know, if we had a little book . . ." and the other finished the sentence: "We could buy a stamp every place we stop."

And so we did—in Budapest, in Vienna, in Bratislava and Ljubljana and Zagreb, in Venice and San Marino and Vatican City, in Monaco and Nice and Barcelona. (The postal clerk at the Vatican was happy to sell me a stamp, but flatly refused to cancel it. If I put it on a letter and mailed it, then he'd cancel it. Otherwise no. I have no idea why he held so adamantly to this position, nor can I guess why a Roman postal clerk wouldn't cancel my Vatican City stamp, either. The only thing even more incomprehensible is how much all of this annoyed me at the time.)

Other trips followed, and other stamps found their way into our little album. To enter a new country was no guarantee that we'd be able to get a stamp. We often traveled with tour groups adhering to a tight schedule, and couldn't always fit in a visit to a post office.

And when we did get to a post office, there wasn't always someone on hand to wait on us. In Sri Lanka (Ceylon, of course, in my main collection) our cruise ship arrived on a Sunday morning, and we spent a full day in the island nation, highlighted by a visit to an elephant orphanage and a train ride back to the port. It was a great visit, but it didn't add a stamp to our book. There may have been a main post office open that day in Columbo, but the provincial one we found was shuttered, and we sailed away without a stamp.

Still, the album constitutes an attractive log of our adventures, if an incomplete one. On a group trip through Belarus, Ukraine, Moldova and Romania, we and some fellow Travelers Century Clubbers persuaded the tour leader to cross into Transnistria, the breakaway Moldovan province whose separate status has been guaranteed by a couple of thousand Russian troops. They had their own stamps, and at their post office I changed a single U.S. dollar into Transnistrian rubles, bought some stamps, and still had a few million left in Transnistrian 100,000-ruble notes. A powerful currency, the Transnistrian ruble.

The following day, the young woman at the Kishinev post office's philatelic window was so goodhearted and obliging that I wound up buying a slew of Moldovan stamps; it shares a page in my album the stamp from Transnistria.

In 1989 we vacationed on Tobago, and bought a stamp; a few years later a cruise ship stopped there, and I had just enough time to get to the post office. Both stamps are from the same series, and depict birds; they too share a page.

The cruise we're on as I write these lines has been deeply satisfying in many respects, but from a philatelic standpoint I'd have to call it a near washout. We boarded our ship in Cape Town in mid-March and made our way north along Africa's Atlantic coast, stopping in turn in Namibia, Angola, Gabon, Sao Tomé and Principe, Benin, Togo, Ghana, Liberia, Sierra Leone, Senegal, and Western Sahara. Tomorrow we'll be in Morocco, and two days later we visit Gibraltar. A day after that we sail up a river in Spain, dock in Seville, and fly home.

That's fifteen countries, and we've thus far netted a mere four stamps. We might get one or two more, but I wouldn't bet on it.

I could have gone to the post office in Cape Town, but had added a stamp there five years ago when my granddaughter Sara and I spent two weeks saving the penguins on Robben Island. (Don't ask.) In Namibia, a gift shop in the ghost town of Kolmanskop sold postcards, and I spotted some stamps on the counter, and a canceling device as well, so it seemed we were off to good start. We were shut out in Angola, but in Gabon a bit of ill fortune for the whole group turned lucky for us; a mix-up with visas led to our entire group's being bussed from the dock to the Libreville airport, where we went through an elaborate and nearly eternal process of photos and fingerprints. But there was a post office right there in the airport, and a money changer adjacent who was willing to convert a U.S. dollar into CFA francs, and we walked out of there with a nicely canceled Gabonese stamp.

In the former Portuguese colony of Sao Tomé and Principe, we spent a day on each island but couldn't get to a post office. Same story in Benin. We'd been to Togo in 1987, well before I resumed collecting stamps, and I asked our tour guide if he could possibly stop at a post office, showing him the book and explaining our goal. That wasn't possible, our schedule was too tight, but on his own he sent an assistant to the post office in Lomé and returned with a pair of Togolese stamps tied to an envelope with a nice cancel. If I'd known what he had in mind, I'd have let him take the book along, but I'm happy enough with the canceled stamp pasted "on piece" into our book.

But we struck out again in Ghana. In Monrovia we met with the Harvard-educated son of a former president of Liberia, and in Freetown the U.S. chargé d'affaires talked with us, but we never got anywhere near a post office. In Senegal we had some free time on Goree Island, and managed to get a stamp and a cancellation from a sullen postal clerk. And that's been it so far. Our first stop in Western Sahara was pleasant enough, but philatelically unrewarding, and we've another coming up tomorrow in Laáyoune. We'll see how it turns out.

RABAT, MOROCCO—No luck in Laáyoune, where the post offices close early on Friday, not that we'd have had much chance to get there anyway. Saturday was a day at sea, and Sunday, when we docked at Sayi and boarded buses for a tour of Marrakech, all government offices were closed. They were probably open the following day in Casablanca and Rabat, but we never had enough time to ourselves to find out.

Yet it seems petty to complain. We've been seeing wonderful sights and having a superb time, and if we don't get to paste little pieces of paper in our little book, well, is that so terrible?

GIBRALTAR—Success! While most of our shipmates took a cable car to the top of the Rock, made faces at the Barbary apes, and had a look at a cave of undoubted historical significance, Lynne and I treated ourselves to a few glorious hours of wandering Gibraltar's streets. We found the post office with no trouble, picked out a stamp depicting a hoopoe, complete with selvage that told us all about it, and for 44 pence added it to our album. The clerk handed me the canceller, and I got to do the job myself.

Back on the ship, the resident bird expert admired the stamp, and confided that the hoopoe in flight looks like the world's largest butterfly. I have to say he looks pretty good just perched in our album.

And what a splendid philatelic ending to our cruise!

We get a lot of satisfaction out of our littlest stamp album. But I was struck in the course of this cruise by the many ways in which my philatelic experience enhanced our travel. And, by the same token, I realized how this trip will broaden and deepen my feeling for stamps from this part of the planet.

You won't be surprised to know that I'll have a few thoughts to share on that subject. But I'm afraid it'll have to wait for another column . . .

11

PHILATELY AND THE "H" WORD

Monday nights my wife and I have taken to watching a reality show on the A&E network. It's called *Hoarders*, and it was clearly inspired by A&E's long-running hit, *Intervention*. That show deals with alcoholism and drug addiction, and each episode examines two addicts, demonstrates the effects of their addiction on them and their families, and traces their stories through intervention and treatment. Some of them stay clean and sober, at least until the program airs; others have trouble, and suffer relapses.

Hoarders is like that, but its subjects don't have a problem with drink or drugs. You could say that their problem is less with what they do than what they don't do—and what they don't do is throw anything away.

Now if you haven't seen the program, you might find it hard to believe that this is the stuff of which exciting television is made. Where's the drama in watching some fellow sit around not wheeling the trash cans to the curb in time for Tuesday's pickup? What's the big deal if some lady still has the newspaper from the day before yesterday?

Well, the pathology runs a little deeper in those poor souls whose cases wind up on TV. One woman's house looked as though the county had been using it for years as a landfill, and midway through the second day of professional cleaning, a workman got to the bottom of a pile in her living room and found a dead cat.

"I always wondered what happened to that cat," the woman said. One sensed she was grateful for the closure. Then a few minutes later she got still more closure when a second cat turned up, every bit as dead as the first.

"All very interesting," you say. (Or maybe you don't.) "But what's that got to do with stamp collecting? Unless you're suggesting a new area for topical collectors, Dead Cats on Stamps, in which case—"

Never mind.

Hoarding and collecting are two different things, although there's a certain degree of overlap, in that many of the documented cases include collections among their holdings. One man collected beer cans, and claimed to have some 50,000 varieties. (He also had perhaps three times as many duplicates, many of them dented and rusty and of use to no one.) He'd built a room onto his garage to house his cans, and it was filled floor to ceiling with crates of the things; they were also piled haphazardly in every room in his house.

Another fellow, a designer by profession, had been gifted with an artist's eye. He couldn't pass a thrift shop or a Dumpster without spotting something he found beautiful, and if he saw it he simply had to take it home. If he had five others just like it, well, wouldn't it be nice to have a sixth? If it was broken, he told himself it could be fixed—although he never seemed to have fixed anything at all.

Both of these fellows were more discriminating in their pursuits than the lady with the dead cat collection. But their hoarding got them in trouble; the beer can guy was in danger of having his property condemned, and the designer had already been threatened with eviction.

I have to admit I didn't have a whole lot of sympathy for the dead cat lady; I just wished the chaps in the white coats would haul her out of there, fumigate her, and tuck her away in a rubber room. But I could identify with the two gentlemen, because we have something in common. I too am a collector—and I have to be ever so careful not to step over the line into hoarding.

When I returned to philately in middle age, I was pleased to find how it lent itself to life in a New York apartment. I started out with a single album, Worldwide 1840–1900. With time I extended my range to 1940, but even so my albums don't take more than six or seven running feet of shelf space, with another foot or so for mounting materials and philatelic paraphernalia.

But early on I found my hobby spreading out, and it wasn't the stamps that were eating up space. I was finding other things to accumulate.

I subscribed to this estimable publication, and to a few others as well. I read them all avidly, and it seemed sensible to hang on to them. At the time, some of you will recall, *Linn's* was not the slick and slender magazine it is today, but a far bulkier tabloid newspaper. It didn't take too many months before my various philatelic back copies filled a couple of cartons, and I could see where this was headed.

But suppose I wanted to refer to one of them at some later date? I thought about that, and realized that several months had gone by, and that I had not once had the impulse to refer to any of the back issues. It was all I could do to keep up with the current ones.

Out they went, to be processed into something else through the miracle of recycling. Tax forms, I suppose. Parking tickets. Chinese restaurant take-out menus. But whatever socially useful role they eventually play, they won't be taking up cubic footage in my apartment.

There are, I've learned, three principal arguments to rationalize keeping something around the house. At one time or another, I've had all of them rattling around in my mind. Here they are:

I might have a use for this someday.
This is (or will be) worth some money.
Somebody somewhere would like to have this.

It was the first notion that led me to keep those back issues—and it wasn't until I'd learned otherwise that I felt free to get rid of them. In much the same fashion, I've found myself hanging on to other items I've since learned to live without.

Dealers package the stamps they sell in a variety of ways. The great majority use glassine envelopes, generally noting the country and catalog number on the envelope, and often the catalog value and retail price as well. My purchases stay in their glassine envelopes until I transfer them to an album, and then the glassine, having been used only once, and capable of years of further service, goes in the trash.

Early on, I was not so quick to discard them. Suppose I needed something to put a stamp in? A duplicate, say, or a used stamp I'd been able to replace with a mint one. Why buy a box of glassines for such a contingency, when I was getting free ones with every purchase?

And so I began tucking them into a shoebox. I didn't save every one that came into my hands, but I set aside enough to realize I'd surely run out of shoe-boxes long before I ran out of glassine envelopes. I noticed, too, that some of the glassines that came my way were pristine, never having been written upon. Those were the ones to keep—so I discarded the others, and saved the blank ones.

Until those too began to mount up, even as it was becoming increasingly clear that I wasn't going to have any use for them. When I bought a mint stamp and had a used one to dispose of, all I did was slip it into the envelope the mint one had come in; that saved me the trouble of writing anything. I did essential-ly the same thing when I bought a set of which I already owned a stamp or two; the duplicates went into the envelope that had contained the set.

It made sense to keep back ten or a dozen glassine envelopes. But a shoebox full? No, I don't think so.

Some dealers choose sturdier packaging for their pricier specimens, slipping them into a semi-rigid plastic sheath. So of course I started setting those aside, sure I'd want them eventually—and when I didn't, I tossed all but a few, to keep as company for the ten or a dozen glassines.

My stamp purchases brought me more than a glut of glassine envelopes. For starters, they drowned me in stamps—not only the worldwide issues I'd ordered, but no end of U.S. stamps that dealers had used to mail their goods to me. These were generally commemoratives, and sometimes half a century or more had passed since their issue dates, and the dealers who made use of them were killing two birds with one stamp—they were supplying their customers with postally used copies of collectible stamps, and they were trimming ten percent or so from their own shipping costs by using postage bought at a discount.

A win for all concerned, wouldn't you say? My wife, who mostly thinks of stamps as little pieces of paper that have reduced our discretionary income while depriving her of a dining room, could only admire the pretty envelopes that kept coming into our home. And I had my nostalgia button pressed every time I recognized a stamp I'd collected as a boy.

Wonderful. But what was I supposed to do with the things?

Throw them out?

For heaven's sake, how could I do that? The hoarder's three arguments stopped me cold. *I might have a use for them someday*, I told myself, might in fact decide to start a collection of used U.S., and here was a good start on it, coming into my mailbox every couple of days, at no cost whatsoever.

Furthermore, they were worth some money. Well, not a whole lot of money, to be sure, but every now and then someone advertised a willingness to pay so many cents per hundred for off-paper U.S. commems. Now the likelihood that I was going to put in the requisite hours to soak the little darlings off their envelopes was, I must admit, anorexically slender, and the yield on such an enterprise would be somewhere in the neighborhood of seventeen cents an hour, but did that mean I could consign the stamps to the trashcan? Look at this envelope, will you? That's a plate block of the 1948 Everglades stamp. Do you expect me to throw it away?

And, finally and irrefutably, *somebody somewhere would want to have them*. Some eager youngster, the protagonist of so many of the stories we tell ourselves, that boy or girl who would much rather collect stamps than watch TV or play video games or pursue any of the other exciting activities that didn't exist when we ourselves were children. Of course what those kiddies really want is the opportunity to stick stamps in an album, and what will get them started like the gift of a slew of their own country's stamps?

The last argument has the great value of sparing me any guilt over failing to soak the stamps from their envelopes. I can safely leave them as they are, leaving to the philatelists of the future the fun of soaking and sorting.

And so I slip each commem-clad cover into a large envelope designated for that purpose, and when it's full I transfer its contents to a suitable container, along with the picked-over remnants of whatever large lots I may have acquired, and any other stamps I don't want to keep and can't readily sell. I bundle it up and send it to one or another stamp charity, and what they do with it is something that doesn't greatly concern me. The stuff's out of my apartment, and I've managed to divest myself of it in a manner that leaves me wonderfully guilt-free—and that's enough to justify the nuisance of hauling it to the post office and the expense of sending it on its way.

I'm on the mailing lists of a couple of stamp auction houses, and while I'm not in a position to do much bidding, I've evidently bought enough over the years to keep receiving their catalogs. And they are beautiful volumes indeed, well printed and abundantly illustrated, and I always look through them and admire what's on offer. Some are general, and always have something of interest; others are highly specialized, and interesting to peruse even when they don't touch on my own collecting interests. Indeed, it's the catalog of Russian Zemstvo Locals, or Bessarabian Postal History, that is most apt to strike me as Something Worth Keeping.

And so I tended to keep them, because they were just too nice to throw out. After a while I decided they were very nice indeed, but that didn't mean I had to own them forever. I generally have one or two catalogs on hand, to thumb through during idle moments, and when a new one comes into the house, an old one goes out.

Which is something like the way I cycle my Scott Classic Catalogs. I use the book not only for reference but as an inventory of my collection, and every other year when I buy the new catalog I face the Herculean task of transferring all my data to it. I keep the old catalog, but the one before that gets sent on its way. (Since I use the book as a checklist, carting it to shows and auctions, its condition at the end of two years is somewhere between Poor and Space Filler. When its turn comes round, out it goes.)

And so it goes. I don't want to suggest for a moment that I've found the right way to keep hoarding at bay, and that if you do it differently you're doing it wrong. My own feeling is that there is no wrong way to collect stamps, any more than there are right and wrong areas of philately in which to concentrate one's efforts. The accumulator, with his acquisitions stuffed into boxes in no apparent order, is every bit as acceptable a philatelist as the collector trying slowly and painstakingly to fill, with flawlessly centered, post office-fresh examples, all the spaces in a single hingeless album. We're all in this together, and I figure whatever system we devise for ourselves is just fine.

It's my own nature and circumstances that have determined the way I cope; if I lived in a sprawling Victorian mansion with an attic, or in a significantly smaller apartment, I might take a looser or stricter stance.

But I draw the line at dead cats.

12

THE SYNERGY OF TRAVEL AND PHILATELY

In the spring my wife and I spent five weeks on the *Corinthian II,* cruising the West African coast from Cape Town to Gibraltar. On our return I wrote a column about the pocket-size stamp album that has accompanied us on our travels for the past fifteen years. I explained that, whenever we get to a country new to us, we try to visit a post office, buy a stamp, stick it on a page, and get the clerk to cancel it. It makes a nice ongoing souvenir, and ties together two compelling pastimes, travel and philately.

Since then I've had occasion to think about the ways my stamp collecting and globetrotting have buttressed each other. And it seems to me that my little album, for all the pleasure it provides, is really the least of it. My stamps have furnished me with knowledge and perspective, historical and geographic, which light up dark corners of the globe for me; at the same time, getting out and actually having a foot on the ground sharpens my philatelic interest and enthusiasm.

But let me give you a few examples, starting with Namibia. It was our first stop out of Cape Town, and we docked first at Luderitz, where we visited a ghost town, and then at Walvis Bay, where we rode out on the dunes, sported with the harbor seals, and feasted on the best oysters I've ever tasted. (I could tell you why they were so good, but it'd be off-topic, unless the Namibians put them on a stamp.)

I don't collect Namibia as such, since the country came into independent existence (named for the Namib desert) long after my collection's cut-off date of 1940. But two of its earlier designations have space in my albums—German Southwest Africa and, after World War I, as mandated by the League of Nations, the British-run territory of South West Africa. So I knew a little of its history, while most of my fellow passengers didn't know much more about the place than that it is the only country around that rhymes with tibia.

The ghost town we visited was a German mining settlement, long abandoned, and it brought the region's background as a German colony into sharp relief. And we learned that Walvis Bay, the source of those spectacular oysters, had not been a part of the German colony, that the British crown had retained Walvis Bay and administered it through the Cape colony.

That left me wondering about the postal history. Might one find Walvis Bay covers bearing Cape of Good Hope stamps—and, a little later, stamps of the Union of South Africa? I don't collect postal history, my general world-wide collection spreads my resources thin enough as it is, so I haven't made much effort to find out more. But I've enjoyed wondering about it.

And I'll enjoy it when I add to my holding of either of Namibia's earlier philatelic incarnations. I haven't had occasion to do so yet since our return, but when I do I'll remember the time we spent there. And, not to belabor the point, I'll remember those oysters.

A couple days out of Walvis Bay, we landed in Gabon. They don't get a lot of tourists there, nor does the former French colony spend a lot of time in the headlines, as the government has been atypically stable ever since independence.

I, of course, knew Gabon from its stamps. The first issues, from 1886 to

1889, were French Colonies issues handstamped GAB. The first stamps specifically printed for Gabon appeared in 1889, a pair of homemade-looking typeset stamps, comprising a 15-centime black on rose and a 25-centime black on green.

It's hard, isn't it, to say just what makes a stamp appealing? These two stamps, Scott 14–15, are hardly the sort of thing one would hang on the wall between the Cezanne and the Renoir, but I responded instantly to them just on the basis of the illustration in my Scott catalog. When the opportunity came my way, I picked up one of them in a Cherrystone auction; a year or two later, I was able to get the other. They didn't come cheap, but I've never regretted the purchase. I like looking at them, and I like owning them.

And they give me a connection with Gabon, a bond that is all the stronger now for my having been there. Our time in Gabon was not the stuff of which tourist brochures are made; our stay began with a bureaucratic boondoggle that sent us on a tedious bus ride from the dock to the airport, and consisted in large measure of more rides through Libreville's traffic-clogged streets. The American ambassador came to dinner on our ship one night, and four of her staff members joined us the next day at a beach resort.

I haven't bought any Gabonese stamps lately. The ones I need are hard to find and harder to afford. But when I look at the stamps I have, I look with the eyes of one who's been to the country, and that seems to make a difference.

My collection has never been very strong in Spanish Africa. While I've managed a fair representation of other Spanish colonial issues—Puerto Rico, Cuba—my holdings are spotty at best of Rio de Oro, Fernando Poo, Cape Juby, and the rest of Spain's African possessions. And my knowledge of these places was at least as spotty. I suppose I knew they were all in Africa, and probably West Africa, but that's about as far as I went.

Well, the *Corinthian II* didn't get to any of these places. But the trip gave me a better sense of them all the same.

Because they had a map of Africa posted on Deck Three, and I checked it frequently to see where we were and what was nearby. And what did I see off shore one day but an island identified as Annobón. I looked some more, and there was Elobey, and Corisco. *I know those places,* I thought. *I've got stamps from Elobey, Annobón & Corisco. Not many, but a few, anyway.*

It was, I must say, an uncommonly useful map. I found Fernando Poo as well, right off the coast of Equatorial Guinea—which was the stamp-issuing entity of Spanish Guinea before independence. I found Rio de Oro and Cape Juby in Western Sahara, which used to be Spanish Sahara and which is now a part of Morocco, although there's a separatist movement that thinks otherwise. My own National Geographic atlas shows some of these places but not others, because names have changed in recent years; Fernando Poo, for example, now bears the name Bioko. (It was discovered in 1472 by the Portuguese navigator Fernão do Pó, who named it *Formosa Flora,* or Beautiful Flower. Twenty-two years later it was renamed for its discoverer. Did you know any of this? Well, I didn't. But I do now, and so do you.)

Except for Western Sahara, where we did make a couple of landings, I didn't set foot on any of these places. But I came back with a sense of them I hadn't had before, and that may have had something to do with an order I sent off just a couple of days ago, in response to a list that turned up in the mail. I ordered stamps from all of these Spanish colonies, and did so with interest and enthusiasm that I can attribute to my experience on the ship, just looking at that map.

We went ashore on both Sao Tomé and Principe. I knew that former Portuguese colony from its stamps; what I didn't know was that Principe, the smaller island, was so named when the king of Portugal gave it to his daughter, the princess.

We spent a day in Benin. I knew it had been Dahomey before independence; now it's Benin, but I learned that the ancient African kingdom of that name was actually located a long ways away in Nigeria.

Then Togo, then Ghana. And from Ghana we sailed for Liberia.

I knew a little about Liberia—that it was founded in the 1820s as a home for freed American slaves repatriated to Africa. In the days before our arrival in Monrovia, the capital, I found a book in the ship's library, *The House at Sugar Beach, New York Times* reporter Helene Cooper's memoir of her girlhood as a member of the Liberian upper crust. I doubt I'd ever have looked twice at it if Liberia hadn't been on our itinerary, but that was enough to make me pick it up, and the story she told was riveting.

I hadn't known that Liberia was a two-class society, with the descendants of the returned slaves—known as the Congo People—essentially running the country for a century and a half, and lording it over the region's original inhabitants, the Country People. And, while I'd known the country had been a wartorn mess for some time, I hadn't realized that the place had been in turmoil from the 1980 coup that ousted the Congo people until several years after the turn of the century.

The book was good preparation for a visit to Liberia. But then so was philately.

Once again I looked at the map of Africa on Deck Three, and this time my eyes fastened on Liberia. And there was Monrovia, the nation's capital, named for U.S. president James Monroe—the fifth president, as every philatelist knows, whose likeness may be found on Scott 810, the 5¢ bright blue of the 1938 Presidential series, as well as Scott 325, the 3¢ violet of the Louisiana Purchase issue. But I saw some other Liberian cities on the map as well, and was puzzled by the fact that I recognized their names. Greenville, Robertsport, Buchanan, Harper—now why on earth should I be familiar with those cities?

From Liberian stamps, of course. I didn't have very many stamps from that nation, but my collection did include several sets of Liberian registration stamps, and each stamp bore the name of one of the five cities. I hadn't thought I was paying any attention, but evidently the information found its way to an unoccupied brain cell and took up residence.

So did some other philatelic bits and pieces. One of the public buildings we visited in Monrovia featured a hall of Liberian presidents, with portraits of the various men who'd held that office since the foundation of the republic. I'd have told you I didn't know anything much about Liberia's history in general or its presidents in particular, yet as I looked at their names and faces I found several of them curiously familiar. There was Hilary R. Johnson, shown on three stamps from the 1892 series; Arthur Barclay, portrayed on a stamp of 1906 and two of 1909; Daniel E. Howard, who appeared in the 1921 series; and Charles Dunbar Burgess King, whose bespectacled countenance can be found on two stamps in the 1923 series and one in 1928.

Later that day they held a reception for our party at a resort on the outskirts of the city, and after the welcoming dance—there's always a welcoming dance, wherever you go, and as far as I can tell it's always the same dance—we were addressed by Richard Tolbert, the nephew of William R. Tolbert, the Liberian president whose assassination touched off the 1980 military coup.

Richard, a Harvard graduate, lived in exile for twenty-five years in New Rochelle. In 2006 he returned to Liberia to chair the national investment commission, and his talk was an interesting one. It was designed to encourage us to invest in Liberia, and in a sense it worked, because when we got home from the cruise I found myself eager to add stamps to my Liberia collection. I can't see how this will constitute a contribution to the Liberian economy, or even to the personal financial picture of the several stamp dealers I've patronized, but I have to say I've been enjoying myself. My Liberia pages have still got more blank spaces than stamps, but they're beginning to fill in, and I've even added some more of the Registration stamps; now, when I see Buchanan and Greenville and Harper and Robertsport, they're not just words. They're dots on a map.

Philately and travel, it seems to me, complement each other nicely. Both open windows on the world, letting in light and knowledge. The stamp collector can pursue his philatelic ends without ever leaving his house; the traveler can roam the world unceasingly. Either pursuit can be undertaken at minimal expense; on the other hand, each—like a taste for cocaine—can easily consume whatever funds are available for it.

The educational aspects of both pastimes would seem to be infinite, but I have to say that an increase in knowledge is not what motivates me to add visas to my passport or stamps to my albums. What knowledge I gain is a purely a byproduct of an activity that is enjoyable in and of itself.

It may well be that all of humankind's leisure activities, all of our hobbies and pastimes, bring us new knowledge without our seeking it. "If the fool would persist in his folly he would become wise," wrote William Blake; he also observed that "the road of excess leads to the palace of wisdom." I'm not quite ready to start picking out drapes for the palace of wisdom, but I have every intention of persisting in my twin follies. Hey, you never know . . .

13

Condition, Condition, and Condition

When it comes to real estate, the conventional wisdom holds that three considerations reign supreme; they are, as you've probably heard, location, location, and location.

Back before retail stamp shops joined the whooping crane on the endangered species list, location had a role to play; it wasn't sheer coincidence that led all those dealers to Nassau Street. But even then it was condition, condition, and condition that mattered most in philately.

And, I suspect, in all collectibles. When a non-collector comes into a stamp or coin or comic book or baseball card, the first thing he wants to know is what it's worth, and the first mistake he makes is to overlook the question of condition; he assumes the figure in the price guide is the right price for his own specimen. Sooner or later it falls to someone to point out that the prices supplied are for essentially pristine examples, while the years have dealt harshly with his. That auction quote he's quick to cite is for a never-hinged, superbly centered stamp, with jumbo margins and great color; his own stamp was poorly centered the day it was born, has lost its gum and some of its paper in the bargain, and has been folded, pierced, and mutilated along the way.

I've been musing on the topic of condition ever since an earlier column of mine, on the subject of gum, brought an interesting response from a reader. I had allowed that, as a general worldwide 1840–1940 collector, gum didn't matter much to me, that while I was not witless enough to pay a Never Hinged price for a No Gum example, the latter would serve perfectly well to fill a space in my collection.

My reader wondered where else I drew the line. Did it bother me if stamps were thinned? If they sported a short perforation or two? If they were poorly centered? In short, just how much did I care about condition?

It's an interesting question, and one a general collector has to decide for himself, and a decision he needs to make over and over again. Before I started my worldwide collection, I collected Ireland—and from the onset bought nothing but mint never-hinged stamps. Out of ignorance, I at first paid rather less attention to centering than I might have, but I soon learned better and acted accordingly.

I saw right off that I couldn't collect the whole world that way. I discovered that I didn't mind if a stamp had been hinged, or if it still bore a hinge remnant. I found that I could be quite happy with a stamp that bore not a trace of its original gum.

On the other hand, while I didn't seem to care if the gum was gone, I found that I wanted all of the paper to be present. A stamp with a thin was not a whole stamp. Part of it was missing.

If the thin was substantial, you could detect it from the front; if it was less obvious, you had to turn it over or hold it to the light to spot the defect. In either case, I didn't really want it in my collection.

Same thing went for stamps with missing perfs and corners. If a stamp was torn, or badly creased, I didn't want it. Before long I learned not to order stamps tagged MD (for Minor Defect) when they turned up on dealers' lists. That saved having to return them.

That seems like a pretty clear standard, doesn't it? I wanted the stamp, the whole stamp, and (except for the occasional hinge remnant) nothing but the stamp. It made sense to me, and was a useful and workable policy when I was ordering from ads or lists.

But you have to understand that I wasn't acting in obedience to a high ethical principle, a moral imperative. What I was doing, really, was accommodating my own aesthetic sensibilities. I wanted my collection to consist entirely of stamps that it pleased me to look at. If I opened my album and my eyes hit upon a virtual pimple on the face of philately, well, that was a stamp I shouldn't have bought in the first place, and ought to replace when the opportunity presented itself. If, on the other hand, a particular stamp pleased me, it was a keeper—irrespective of some slight imperfection that might well merit an MD designation.

Thus the standard that serves me well when ordering online or by mail was subject to modification when I was able to see a particular stamp up close and personal. Among my Nineteenth Century French issues there are several with slight defects—here a barely perceptible thin, there an almost invisible crease. Some of these came from auctions at Stampazine, the firm run so well for so many years by the late Bert Taub. Such defects were dutifully noted in the catalogs, and I'd examine the lots that interested me to see if the flaw was enough to rule out the stamp. Sometimes it was, but sometimes it was not, and I was able to pick up at favorable prices a good number of classic stamps I'd otherwise have been unable to afford.

And the defects that kept the price down were not severe enough to make the stamps unacceptable to me. That, it seemed to me, was the criterion to be applied. The whole point of the collection was that it be pleasing to me; if I liked the stamp, if I didn't find myself making a face when I looked at it, then I was glad to own it, and delighted to have been able to buy it so inexpensively.

Subjective or not, this would all seem fairly clear-cut. Whether or not a stamp is acceptable for my collection would seem to hinge (so to speak) on my own aesthetic reaction to it. If I like the looks of it, it's in; if I don't, it's out—or it's in, but only until I can find a replacement.

Simple enough—but when I think about it, I have to admit that there's more to it than that. The more elusive a stamp is, and the higher its price, the more apt I am to make allowances for the odd flaw, the occasional minor defect.

I mentioned those French classics, the ones that proved acceptable on close examination. Now they really are nice enough, but the slight flaws they bear would rule them out if their catalog value was a few dollars apiece instead of a few hundred. Because they're pricey, and because those defects bring their prices down to where I can afford them, I become a good deal more forgiving of their faults. Like the professor grading the star quarterback's exam, I apply a gentler standard.

Sometimes it's not just the price as much as it's the elusiveness of the specimen. Before the French colonial authorities issued stamps for Madagascar in 1889, there was a stretch from 1884 to 1886 when the British issued stamps for their consular mail. Scott lists 56 major varieties, with the two cheapest valued at $90, and notes that the stamps were gummed only in one corner, and that most used examples have small faults.

Now I haven't gone out beating the bushes for these issues, but in the past fifteen years I've only run across one of them. It's unused, and the handstamped seal's not the best strike ever, and it's badly thinned where the gum used to be. The thin is all too evident when you hold the stamp to the light, but doesn't show when it's in a mount on its album page, where it looks okay to me. It's the only example I have of a British issue for Madagascar, and may retain that designation for quite some time. So, for all its faults, I have to say I'm glad to have it.

Or consider Annam and Tonkin. General issues for the French Colonies were overprinted in 1886 for use in these two Indo-Chinese protectorates, and Scott lists six varieties—the 1¢ on 2¢ brown, 1¢ on 4¢ claret, and 5¢ on 10¢ black, with the name given as A & T, and the same denominations with the name rendered as A - T. (My album has spaces for three more, originally listed by Scott as numbers 4, 5, and 6, with a horizontal bar at the bottom; I'm afraid they're unlikely ever to be filled.)

There's another stamp, noted but not given a listing by Scott, a 5¢ on 2¢ brown A & T, which is stated to have been prepared but not issued, and valued by Scott at $6750. (Yvert & Tellier lists it as #3, with a value of 8700 Euros.)

Now my album doesn't call for this stamp, but there's enough room on the page so that I didn't have trouble finding a spot for it when one of my regular approval dealers offered it to me.

The copy he had was severely damaged, in that the lower left corner was missing. That would have been enough to keep me from considering the stamp, but where would I ever find another example, and how could I afford it if I did? This one was priced reasonably, and I couldn't resist it. And, when I look at it, the missing corner doesn't bother me all that much; the stamp itself is special enough, and interesting enough, to make the flaw just part of its philatelic charm.

On the other hand, when I was looking through my French issues for a 19th Century stamp to illustrate this piece, I discovered that my copy of Scott 39, the 2¢ red brown on yellowish from the 1870 issue, is similarly lacking a corner, and badly thinned in the bargain. I can't believe I bought it so severely damaged, and suspect it came with the 19th Century starter collection that launched me as a general worldwide collector. It's not a cheap stamp, Scott pegs it at $275 mint, but I've made a note of the damage and will look to replace it when I get the chance.

We're all such quirky folks, aren't we? Grabbing up this stamp, rejecting that one, and always having a reason—whether or not it's terribly reasonable. And here's the best part of all: all of our reasons are right. Because this is, when all is said and done, something we pursue for our own pleasure and amusement. And if we think something belongs in our collection, then it does. And if we don't, then it doesn't.

Missing perfs, missing corners, missing gum, thins—all elements to weigh in the balance when making our decisions. I've barely mentioned centering, which sometimes bothers me and sometimes doesn't, and I'd be hard put to explain why it does when it does, or why it doesn't when it doesn't.

Nor have I mentioned the question of filling a space with a stamp that is not quite what is called for. Specimen overprints, official reprints, fakes and forgeries—how do I feel about them, and what role do they play in my collection?

Now that's a pretty interesting topic. But it'll have to wait for another month.

14

FILLING SPACES

In August I had the great pleasure of attending the American Philatelic Society's Stamp Show, held this year in Richmond, Virginia. I had a wonderful time, and spent the week after my return filling spaces in my albums with my new acquisitions. A stamp show, I've discovered, is a great place to find those low-priced singles that dealers can't always afford to list individually, and I gobbled them up with the avidity of an aardvark at an anthill. No end of spaces, long empty, are now full.

But I missed a chance to fill two more, two I'd always assumed would remain empty forever. If I'd dragged myself away from the bourse and gone to the auction—and if I hadn't by then spent all my money at the anthill—I could have enriched my collection with Mauritius #1 and #2, the famous Post Office issues.

How, you may wonder, could I have managed this feat? As a note in the Scott catalog makes clear, all unused copies of Mauritius #2, the 2p dark blue, are in museums. There are three copies of Mauritius #1, the 1p orange, in private hands, one of them unused. (Scott doesn't venture to guess how many used copies exist of #2, or where they are, but there can't be too many of them, as the used stamp's price is pegged at an even one million dollars.)

Here's Regency Superior's description of Lot 1200, offered at auction in Richmond:

"Complete set of 2 with matching large left margin, 1d in deep blue and 2d in deep orange, likely done in either 1912 for Royal Collection or 1930 for Burrus Collection. This is the only time we recall offering these reprints. No gum as issued, very fine."

The auction house estimated the price at $200. The hammer price was in fact $300, plus a bidder's premium of 17%.

The colors, you'll note, are reversed; these reprints weren't made with the intention of fooling anybody, but to spice up the collection of a prominent philatelist, either King George V or Maurice Burrus. (At the time of his death in 1959, Mr. Burrus owned five of the Post Office issues, all of them used. I can see why he'd have liked to add an unused copy of each, and the color be damned.)

Now as I said, I didn't get to the auction, but if I had I'd have had trouble passing this lot. My album has spaces for the stamps, and it's a good thing I don't find empty spaces maddening. In the early 1960s I owned a Volkswagen Beetle, the speedometer of which showed a wildly optimistic top speed of 120 miles per hour. That was a good 40 mph faster than I ever got that bug to go, and I'd have been a lot more likely to goose that earnest little car up to 120 than I will to fill those album spaces.

The reprints, I have to say, would be a perfectly acceptable substitute.

I wasn't thinking about the Mauritius issues when I picked the topic for this month's column. It came to me a couple of weeks before the APS show, when I was finishing up last month's column—which was about condition, and how I decide what's acceptable and what's not. Briefly, I said that I don't much mind the absence of gum, that I object strongly to thins, that my judgments tend to be subjective ("this one doesn't look too bad, but that one's a dog"), and that my standards ease visibly as the price rises. But, I mused, what about "the question of filling a space with a stamp that is not quite what is called for. Specimen overprints, official reprints, fakes and forgeries—how do I feel about them, and what role do they play in my collection?"

Well, let's start with specimen overprints. We can all recognize these readily enough—the word SPECIMEN is a dead giveaway—but why they were made, and what they're worth, is a tad less obvious. Here's a quick explanation from the website of dealer Jay Smith:

"Generally in philately, most specimen overprints were applied for security purposes either by countries submitting 'specimen' stamps to the Universal Postal Union or applied, in a few cases, by the UPU-member countries who received stamps that had not yet been overprinted. The UPU distributed the stamps of all members, to all members, so that postal administrations around the world could recognize what was (and potentially what was not) a valid postage stamp of another country. Generally speaking, specimen overprints applied by the issuing country usually exist in a quantity of only 100 to 400 examples and are usually quite scarce. Specimens applied by the receiving country—for example, the 'ULTRAMAR' (overseas) overprints applied by Portugal for onward distribution to the Portuguese Colonies—are usually rare."

The relative value of specimen overprints seems to be variable. As a general rule, such an overprint renders a common stamp more valuable and an expensive stamp less so. Consider, if you will, British East Africa. An 1896–1903 set, Scott #72–87, is valued at $528 mint and $378.50 used; the specimen set is listed at $325. On the other hand, mint examples of the three high values of the 1898 set, Scott #107–109, are priced at $425, $1000, and $2000 respectively—used copies are even more expensive—while the specimens are valued a good deal lower: $75, $150, and $300.

All things being equal, I'd have a slight preference for a regular stamp over a specimen. But I doubt that I'll ever pick up regular copies of those three high values, and I'd happily fill the spaces with specimens. I've done just that with the high value Kangaroo issues of Australia. My holding includes the two £2 stamps, Scott #102 and #129, which list at $4500 and $4000 respectively. I don't remember what I paid for the specimen overprints—Scott doesn't list them, though I'm sure Gibbons does—but I know it was a very small fraction of those prices. The spaces are filled, and I'm perfectly happy with the stamps filling them.

There's another type of overprint that shows up on mint stamps—of Mauritius, as a matter of fact. CANCELLED, it proclaims. In 1878 Mauritius changed its currency from the pound sterling to the rupee, and stamps issued that year were surcharged with values in the new currency. But earlier issues, still on hand in post offices, were overprinted CANCELLED and sold as remainders.

Scott lists thirteen such stamps. You might think they'd be regarded with the contempt visited upon modern canceled-to-order wallpaper, but that's not the case. They're all valued less than regular mint examples, but the difference isn't huge, and they remain considerably higher in price than postally used copies.

I have two, Scott #35 and #47. I suppose I'd prefer regular examples, but if I ever obtain them I'll still hang on to my CANCELLED copies. They look good on the page, and point up an interesting fragment of philatelic history.

During the nineteenth century, a number of countries reprinted some of their early issues using the original dies. France, for example, reissued Scott #1–11 in 1862, in lighter shades and on whiter paper than the originals, and these reprints are listed and priced in Scott, and highly regarded by collectors. (#7b, the Type Two 40 centime orange on yellowish of 1850, is priced at a hefty $25,000 unused; the reissue, #7e, is no redhaired stepchild, itself listed at $11,500.) The first six stamps of the 1863–70 Napoleon III series, Scott #29–36, were specially reissued as imperforates; known as the Rothschild issue, they were authorized exclusively for the banker's own use.

Now who wouldn't want one of those?

The French colony of Obock has had a couple of stamps officially reprinted, with discernible differences in the overprint. The reprint of Scott #3, worth $325 as an original, is valued at just $20; the very rare 5c postage due, J1, worth $7500, is listed as a reprint for $200. I managed to pick up a nice copy of J1 a few years ago, and it looks just fine on the page. The space for #3 is still empty, and someday perhaps I'll find something to mount therein; maybe in time I'll have both the original and the reprint, and won't they look nice side by side?

I can assure you they will—because I have a nice copy of Austria #2 and, mounted right next to it, a fine wide-margined example of the reprint.

My fictional hitman, Keller, buys a set of reprints of Sweden #1–5 in the opening chapter of *Hit & Run*; they cost him a few hundred dollars, as opposed to the originals, which list at $29,000. (But he pays cash, emptying his wallet in the process, and before he can get to an ATM, the whole world's after him for an assassination he didn't commit. A fat lot of good five Swedish stamps are gonna do him . . .)

I have those same five reprints, and figure I'm about as likely ever to own the originals as I am to pick up a copy of #1a, the presumably unique 3 skilling error of color. I'm happy with what I have—but less happy with some of the cheap reprints I own, produced long ago in great quantity for the packet trade. I've written before about the Seebeck reprints that filled pages in my started collection and put Nicaragua and other Central American countries on my list of less-favored nations. Similarly, I have a batch of Roman States private reprints, glossily mint and post office fresh, that fill spaces in my album without bringing me much pride of ownership. I'm not crazy about them, but neither am I much delighted at the prospect of paying substantial money to replace them with the real deal.

I have some fakes, too.

More, no doubt, than I'm aware of. François Fournier forged all the early French Colonial Peace & Commerce issues, among other items, and sold complete sets of them. Many of these stamps came in my starter collection, and I've added many since, and it wouldn't be all that difficult for me to hoist a good magnifier and go over every one of them. The forgeries aren't all that hard to spot.

Far as that goes, Scott points out that originals are perforated 14 x 13-1/2, while the forgeries measure 13-1/2 x 14. So I could whip out a perforation gauge, remove each stamp from its mount, and check its perfs.

Now how likely do you think it is that I'll ever get around to doing this?

Sometimes I buy fakes—knowingly, that is. The other day I picked up a low-priced lot of French Colonial fakes on eBay. I haven't had a chance to study them yet, but I suspect the bulk of them are Fournier fakes. I thought they'd be nice to own for reference, and doubt I'll mount any of them—although I do have a set of Fournier's counterfeits of French India 1–19, neatly mounted on the same page with my set of the originals. (Or what I dearly hope are the originals. I suppose I really ought to get out that magnifier and perf gauge!)

When a fake turns up on a dealer's list, and when the price is reasonable and the stamp itself strikes me as interesting, I'm likely to buy it—especially if it's from a country I'm enthusiastic about. On the other hand, I'm similarly apt to buy counterfeit stamps from some of my less-favored nations, just to fill the spaces at minimal cost. Iran's one such country, and Scott says over and over again that unauthorized reprints abound, often outnumbering genuine stamps by factors of ten or twenty to one, and that some of them are indistinguishable from originals. I don't honestly want to learn enough about Iranian stamps to tell the good ones from the bad, and I don't care all that much about filling the spaces. But if something comes along inexpensively enough, I'll pick it up—and simply assume it's a counterfeit.

Now I can't say I *approve* of counterfeit stamps. But it's hard for me to work up a lot of indignation at a forger who's been dead for the better part of a century. I wouldn't want to buy a fake sold as a genuine stamp, or an official reprint under the illusion that it's an original, but in certain cases and at the right price any of these oddities might find a welcome in my collection. They all make the philatelic universe even more interesting.

KELLER DOUBLES DOWN

—FROM *HIT PARADE*

It started with stamps.

He collected worldwide, from the first postage stamps, Great Britain's Penny Black and Two-Penny Blue of 1840, up to shortly after the end of World War Two.

When you collected the whole world, your albums held spaces for many more stamps than you would ever be able to acquire. Keller knew he would never completely fill any of his albums, and he found this not frustrating but comforting. No matter how long he lived or how much money he got, he would always have more stamps to look for. You tried to fill in the spaces, of course—that was the point—but it was the trying that brought you pleasure, not the accomplishment.

Consequently, he never absolutely had to have any particular stamp. He shopped carefully, and he chose the stamps he liked, and he didn't spend more than he could afford. He'd saved money over the years, he'd even reached a point where he'd been thinking about retiring, but when he got back into stamp collecting his hobby gradually ate up his retirement fund—which, all things considered, was fine with him. Why would he want to retire? If he retired, he'd have to stop buying stamps.

As it was, he was in a perfect position. He was never desperate for money, but he could always find a use for it. If Dot came up with a whole string of jobs for him, he wound up putting a big chunk of the proceeds into his stamp collection. If business slowed down, no problem—he'd make small purchases from the dealers who shipped him stamps on approval, send some small checks to others who mailed him their monthly lists, but hold off on anything substantial until business picked up.

It worked fine. Until the Bulger & Calthorpe auction catalog came along and complicated everything.

Bulger & Calthorpe were stamp auctioneers based in Omaha. They advertised regularly in *Linn's* and the other stamp publications, and traveled extensively to examine collectors' holdings. Three or four times a year they would rent a hotel suite in downtown Omaha and hold an auction, and for a few years now Keller had been receiving their well-illustrated catalogs. Their catalog featured an extensive collection of France and French colonies, and Keller leafed through it on the off-chance that he might find himself in Omaha around that time. He was thinking of something else when he hit the first page of color photographs, and whatever it was he forgot it forever.

Martinique #2. And, right next to it, Martinique #17.

He'd spent half an hour with the Bulger & Calthorpe catalog, reading the descriptions of the two Martinique lots, seeing what else was on offer, and returning more than once for a further look at Martinique #2 and Martinique #17. He interrupted himself to check the balance in his bank account, frowned, pulled out the album that ran from Leeward Islands to Netherlands, opened it to Martinique, and looked first at the couple hundred stamps he had and then at the two empty spaces, spaces designed to hold—what else?—Martinique #2 and Martinique #17.

He closed the album but didn't put it away, not yet, and he picked up the phone and called Dot.

"I was wondering," he said, "if anything came in."

"Like what, Keller?"

"Like work," he said.

"Was your phone off the hook?"

"No," he said. "Did you try to call me?"

"If I had," she said, "I'd have reached you, since your phone wasn't off the hook. And if a job came in I'd have called, the way I always do. But instead you called me."

"Right."

"Which leads me to wonder why."

"I could use the work," he said. "That's all."

"You worked when? A month ago?"

"Closer to two."

"You took a little trip, went like clockwork, smooth as silk. Client paid me and I paid you, and if that's not silken clockwork I don't know what is. Say, is there a new woman in the picture, Keller? Are you spending serious money on earrings again?"

"Nothing like that."

"Then why would you . . . Keller, it's stamps, isn't it?"

"I could use a few dollars," he said. "That's all."

"So you decided to be proactive and call me. Well, I'd be proactive myself, but who am I gonna call? We can't go looking for our kind of work, Keller. It has to come to us."

"I know that."

"We ran an ad once, remember? And remember how it worked out?" He remembered, and made a face. "So we'll wait," she said, "until something comes along. You want to help it a little on a metaphysical level, try thinking proactive thoughts."

Keller didn't know much about Martinique beyond the fact that it was a French possession in the West Indies, and he knew the postal authorities had stopped issuing special stamps for the place a while ago. It was now officially a department of France, and used regular French stamps. The French did that to avoid being called colonialists. By designating Martinique a part of France, the same as Normandy or Provence, they obscured the fact that the island was full of black people who worked in the fields, fields that were owned by white people who lived in Paris.

Keller had never been to Martinique—or to France, as far as that went—and had no special interest in the place. It was a funny thing about stamps; you didn't need to be interested in a country to be interested in the country's stamps. And he couldn't say what was so special about the stamps of Martinique, except that one way or another he had accumulated quite a few of them, and that made him seek out more, and now, remarkably, he had all but two.

The two he lacked were among the colony's first issues, created by surcharging stamps originally printed for general use in France's overseas empire. The first, #2 in the Scott catalog, was a twenty centime stamp surcharged "MARTINIQUE" and "5c" in black. The second, #17, was similar: "MARTINIQUE / 15c" on a four centime stamp.

According to the catalog, #17 was worth $7500 mint, $7000 used. #2 was listed at $11,000, mint or used. The listings were in italics, which was Scott's way of indicating that the value was difficult to determine precisely.

Keller bought most of his stamps at around half the Scott valuation. Stamps with defects went much cheaper, and stamps that were particularly fresh and well-centered could command a premium. With a true rarity, however, at a well-publicized auction, it was very hard to guess what price might be realized. Bulger & Calthorpe described #2—it was lot #2144 in their sales catalog—as "mint with part OG, F–VF, the nicest specimen we've seen of this genuine rarity." The description of #17—lot #2153—was almost as glowing. Both stamps were accompanied by Philatelic Foundation certificates attesting that they were indeed what they purported to be. The auctioneers estimated that #2 would bring $15,000, and pegged the other at $10,000.

But those were just estimates. They might wind up selling for quite a bit less, or a good deal more.

Keller wanted them.

What he needed, Keller decided, was fifty thousand dollars. That way he could go as high as twenty-five for #2 and fifteen for #17 and, after buyer's commission, still have a few dollars left for expenses and other stamps.

Was he out of his mind? How could a little piece of perforated paper less than an inch square be worth $25,000? How could two of them be worth a man's life?

He thought about it and decided it was just a question of degree. Unless you planned to use it to mail a letter, any expenditure for a stamp was basically irrational. If you could swallow a gnat, why gag at a camel? A hobby, he suspected, was irrational by definition. As long as you kept it in proportion, you were all right.

And he was managing that. He could, if he wanted, mortgage his apartment. Bankers would stand in line to lend him fifty grand, since the apartment was worth ten times that figure. They wouldn't ask him what he wanted the money for, either, and he'd be free to spend every dime of it on the two Martinique stamps.

He didn't consider it, not for a moment. It would be nuts, and he knew it. But what he did with a windfall was something else, and it didn't matter, anyway, because there wasn't going to be any windfall. You didn't need a weatherman, he thought, to note that the wind was not blowing. There was no wind, and there would be no windfall, and someone else could mount the Martinique overprints in his album. It was a shame, but—

The phone rang.

Dot said, "Keller, I just made a pitcher of iced tea. Why don't you come up here and help me drink it?"

"The horse's name is Kissimmee Dudley," Dot told him, "and he's running in the seventh race at Belmont Saturday. It's the feature race, and the word is that Dudley hasn't got a prayer."

"I don't know much about horses."

"They've got four legs," she said, "and if the one you bet on comes in ahead of the others, you make money. That's as much as I know about them, but I know something about Kissimmee Dudley. Our client thinks he's going to win."

"I thought you said he didn't have a prayer."

"That's the word. Our client doesn't see it that way."

"Oh?"

"Evidently Dudley's a better horse than anybody realizes," she said, "and they've been holding him back, waiting for the right race. That way they'll get long odds and be able to clean up. And, just so nothing goes wrong, the other jockeys are getting paid to make sure they don't finish ahead of Dudley."

"The race is fixed," Keller said.

"That's the plan."

"But?"

"But a plan is what things don't always go according to, Keller, which is probably a good thing, because otherwise the phone would never ring. You want some more iced tea?"

"No thanks."

"They'll have the race on Saturday, and Dudley'll run. And if he wins you get two thousand dollars."

"For what?"

"For standing by. For making yourself available."

"I think I get it," he said. "And if Kissimmee Dudley should happen to lose—where'd they come up with a name like that, do you happen to know?"

"Not a clue."

"If he loses," Keller said, "I suppose I have work to do."

She nodded.

"The jockey who beats him?"

"Is toast," she said, "and you're the toaster."

"A hundred bucks to win! Man, when you get a hunch you really back it, don't you?"

Keller didn't say anything. He had nineteen other tickets just like it in his pocket, but the little man didn't have to know about them. If the photo of the two horses crossing the finish line showed Dudley in front, his tickets would be worth $58,000.

If not, well, Alvie Jurado would be worth almost as much.

"I got to hand it to you," the little man said. "All that dough on the line, and you're calm as a cucumber."

Ten days later, Keller sat at his dining room table. He was holding a pair of stainless steel stamp tongs, and they in turn were holding a little piece of paper worth—

Well, it was hard to say just how much it was worth. The stamp was Martinique #2, and Keller had wound up bidding $18,500 for it. The lot had opened at $9000, and there was a bidder in the third row on the right who dropped out around the $12,000 mark, and then there was a phone bidder who hung on like grim death. When the auctioneer pounded the gavel and said, "Sold for eighteen five to JPK," Keller's heart was pounding harder than the gavel.

It was still racing eight lots later when the second stamp, Martinique #17, went on the block. It had a lower Scott value than #2, and was estimated lower in the Bulger & Calthorpe sales catalog, and the starting bid was lower, too, at an even $6000.

And then, remarkably, it had wound up sailing all the way to $21,250 before Keller prevailed over another phone bidder. (Or the same one, irritated at having lost #2 and unwilling to miss out on #17.) That was too much, it was three times the Scott value, but what could you do? He wanted the stamp, and he could afford it, and when would he get a chance at another one like it?

With buyer's commission, the two lots had cost him $43,725.

He admired the stamp through his magnifier. It looked beautiful to him, although he couldn't say why; aesthetically, it wasn't discernibly different from other Martinique overprints worth less than twenty dollars. Carefully, he cut a mount to size, slipped the stamp into it, and secured it in his album.

Not for the first time, he thought of the little man at the OTB parlor. Keller hadn't seen him since that afternoon, and doubted he'd ever cross paths with him again. He remembered the fellow's excitement, and how impressed he'd been by Keller's own coolness.

Cool? Naturally he'd been cool. Either way he won. If he didn't cash the winning tickets on Kissimmee Dudley, he'd do just about as well when he punched Alvie Jurado's ticket. It was interesting, waiting to see how the photo came out, but he couldn't say it was all that nerve-wracking.

Not when you compared it to sitting in a hotel suite in Omaha, waiting for hours while lot after lot was auctioned off, until finally the stamps you'd been waiting for came up for bids. And then sitting there with your pencil lifted to indicate you were bidding, sitting there while the price climbed higher and higher, not knowing where it would stop, not knowing if you had enough cash in the belt around your waist. How high would you have to go for the first lot? And would you have enough left for the other one? And what was the matter with that phone bidder? Would the man never quit?

Now that was excitement, he thought, as he cut a second mount for Martinique #17. That was true edge-of-the-chair tension, unlike anything those Jerry Orbach lookalikes in the OTB parlor would ever know.

He felt sorry for them.

What difference did it make, really, how the photo-finish turned out? What did he care who won the race? If Kissimmee Dudley held on to win by a nose or a nose hair, it was up to Keller to work out a tax-free way to cash twenty $100 tickets. If Steward's Folly made it home first, Alvie Jurado moved to the top of Keller's list of Things to Make and Do. Whichever chore Keller wound up with, he had to pull it off in a hurry; he had to have his money in hand—or, more accurately, in belt—when his flight took off for Omaha.

And now it was over, and he'd done what he had to, so did it matter what it was he'd done?

Hell, no. He had the stamps.

15

Stamps and Their
Infinite Variety

"Age cannot wither her," Shakespeare's Enobarbus says of Cleopatra, "nor custom stale her infinite variety."

There are, I submit, worse things a man could say about a woman, but it wasn't thoughts of women, however unwithered by age and unstaled by custom, that brought the line to mind. I was thinking about variety, and the infinite number of philatelic varieties, major and minor, which one can collect.

Or not collect.

And there, for the general collector, is a decision which has to be made time and time again. Does one make room in one's collection for perforation varieties? For sideways watermarks? For color shadings? For inverted overprints?

I'll tell you, it's enough to make one envy the specialist. If, say, you confine your collection to a single country, you just grab up everything on offer. The smaller the country and the less extensive its philatelic output, the more reason you have to seek out its stamps and covers in all their variety.

Indeed, you're virtually forced to do this—or it won't be long before you'll reach a point where the only stamps you lack are ones you can neither find nor afford, and what do you do then? Start a new collection? Take up golf?

Because I collect stamps of the whole world from 1840 to 1940, I'm never going to be forced to wander through the underbrush, trying to figure out where my tee shot went. I'll run out of time and money long before I run out of stamps to collect.

But deciding just what is or is not within the scope of my collection can be tricky.

Now I have to admit that my albums make part of that decision for me. My collection is housed in a dozen binders, containing the Scott Brown Album reproduction pages. These are four series of reprinted pages—1840 to 1900, 1901 to 1920, 1921 to 1930, and 1931 to 1940—and the simplest way for me to collect is to use the pages as a sort of Procrustean bed.

(You remember Procrustes, don't you? He was the chap with a guest bed designed to fit all comers. If you were too short for his bed, he had you stretched; if you were too tall, he cut you down to size. I suppose it worked for him, but he never did get the coveted Innkeeper of the Year award.)

With rare exceptions, my album doesn't bother with perforation varieties—so neither do I. It includes major watermark varieties, and makes room for some minor varieties and omits others, recognizes a few shades, has spaces for some errors of color.

Now I'd certainly prefer to think of myself as more than a mere filler of blank spaces, a spineless slave to my own album. And yet I can't deny that I've acquired any number of stamps that, but for the album's vagaries, I'd happily pass up.

For example, two master dies were used to print the George V keyplate issues of the British colonies. I can, if I consult the explanatory material in the introduction of my Scott Classic Catalogue, readily distinguish Die 1 and Die 2. (There's also a Die 1a and a Die 1b, but, really, who cares?) As I said, I can tell one from the other, but I'm incapable of retaining this information from one day to the next, so if I want to determine which variety I've got, I have to look it up anew. If a dealer has already made this determination, I generally take his word for it.

If I had my druthers, I wouldn't bother with the whole thing. There are perforation varieties, many of them considered major varieties and assigned whole Scott numbers, which my album ignores, and I happily ignore them myself. But for some reason—over-the-top Anglophilia would be my guess—the Brown Album decision-maker provided spaces for the George V die varieties. There are a lot of them, and most of them are not expensive, and those spaces look ever so much better with stamps in them.

So I buy them, and mount them in their appointed spaces, and am just as glad to have them. George V was an ardent stamp collector, of course, and wouldn't he want me to collect his own image in all its philatelic variety? I figure it's the least I can do.

The 1876–8 Peace & Commerce issues of France provide a similar batch of varieties, and they're major varieties as far as my Scott catalog is concerned. For Type I, the "N" of the INV subscript is beneath the "B" of REPUBLIQUE; for Type II, it's under the "U". Now that might seem like a subtle distinction, but it wins the different types whole numbers in Scott, and spots in my album. And, because both types were overprinted for French offices in Egypt, China, Morocco, Zanzibar, and the Turkish Empire, it adds up to a lot of spaces.

If I were less interested philatelically in France and her offices, I might be less motivated to grab up my magnifier and see where the N is. But I like the stamps, and so I endeavor to fill the spaces. (At least there's a rhyming mnemonic; *N under U, Type Two.*)

Now I don't feel compelled to seek out every stamp my album calls for, and it's just as well; I might have a hard time with British Guiana #13, for instance, or Mauritius #1 and #2, or Sweden #1a. And I wouldn't have it all that much easier with various stamps I can't identify by their Scott numbers because they don't seem to exist; my album thinks otherwise, but seems to be alone in that opinion. "No such stamp," I write in the unfillable space, and scowl at it.

But I think it may be more interesting to consider not what my album (or a dead English monarch) wants me to collect, but what I choose to acquire even in the absence of a designated space for it. It's the stamps I have to mount in the margins of my album pages that are in some respects the most interesting items in my collection.

Some are errors. There's Malta 20a, for example, the 2-1/2p dull blue; it's supposed to be surcharged "One Penny," but this variety has it "One Pnney." It's affordable, and visually remarkable, and I picked up my copy when it was offered in a block of four, with three non-erroneous companions.

Similarly, I have a block of four that includes an example of Hungary 393a, an otherwise unremarkable and inexpensive regular issue of 1924, a 600-kreuzer olive bistre stamp with the correct denomination in the upper left corner— and "800" in the upper right corner. It didn't come cheap, but it struck me as a wonderfully wacky variety, and especially interesting as part of a multiple.

Most errors don't move me all that much. Early Danish issues often have the frame inverted, and one can learn to tell the difference, but it's a subtle one, and the value is generally about the same either way—so what do I care? Inverted overprints are sometimes common and sometimes scarce, sometimes high-priced and sometimes not—and either way I feel no great urge to acquire them.

(But I have to admit I'm more impressed when it's not just some words and numbers that have been printed upside down but, say, an airplane; there's something irresistible about what we could call a Jenny overprint. Lebanon C13-16 exist with the overprinted plane flying upside down, noted but not formally listed in Scott and valued at $15 per stamp; I don't have these yet, but will snap them up if and when I get the chance.)

Some countries might almost be said to have specialized in inverted overprints, and inverted centers as well. Liberia and Somali Coast come quickly to mind, and I've a feeling some of those errors may well have been intentional, a matter of a printing house employee or government functionary amusing himself after hours. What's so tricky about running a few sheets through the press upside down?

Ironically, the more available and affordable such stamps are, the greater the likelihood that they owe more to mischief and chicanery than to sheer happenstance. Meanwhile, the genuine errors tend to be genuinely scarce—and correspondingly expensive.

As crowded as my album pages may get, I'm always able to create space for the stamps that strike my fancy, and they don't need to have whole Scott numbers, or even a listing, to win my heart. I'm a sucker for prepared-but-unissued stamps, like the six German stamps Scott notes as having been prepared for the Allenstein plebiscite territory. How could I not want to own these, just because they never found their way into the mailstream?

Of Spain's first airmail series, C1-5, dangerous counterfeits are said to be "plentiful." I don't own this set, genuine or counterfeit, but note that a sixth stamp, the 30¢ green, was authorized but never issued. It's not cheap, either, but if it were to come along and the price was right, I'd make room for it.

Speaking of widely counterfeited stamps, the post-World War One Hungarian occupation issues were so abundantly faked that even the most common issues may be assumed to be suspect until proven legitimate—and who's going to spend money on expertization of a 20¢ stamp?

That said, I have a special fondness for these stamps. The history is fascinating, with all those different occupying armies—the French, the Romanians, the Serbs. No sooner did they advance into Hungarian territory than they set about overprinting stamps so that they could write nice newsy letters to the folks back home. Doesn't that make you feel good all over? I want every variety Scott lists, and a few that it doesn't.

Consider the first Debrecen issue of the Romanian occupation. 2N42 is the 20 Filler dark brown, bearing a black oval overprint. I have it, and I also have the Scott-listed minor variety of 2N42b, with the overprint in red. Scott skips right over 2N42a, which suggests that a stamp that once existed with that designation has since been delisted. Well, I've got that one, too—the same stamp with a blue overprint. Is it legitimate? Gee, how would I know? Are any of them? All I can tell you for sure is I'm glad to own it.

Colombia 411–416, an attractive and inexpensive pictorial set, enhanced in my album by an accompanying set of imperforate specimen stamps in different colors. The 1919 14¢ on 35¢ overprints for the various French offices in China, with either a closed or an open "4". Welcome, I assure you, in my collection.

Consider Central Lithuania. But for a single rather pricey issue, Scott 13–22, all of the stamps of that short-lived postal entity are available either perforated or imperforate. Scott notes this, but doesn't list them separately, although the numbering system suggests this was not always the case; my album has spaces for both, and I've been happy to fill them. If my album were less accommodating, I'd find a way to make room for them. They're inexpensive, they're attractive, and they're interesting.

I'll say they're interesting. Central Lithuania, once a grand duchy of Lithuania, then under Russian rule from the end of the 18th Century. Occupied by Poland after the First World War, seized by the newly sovereign Lithuania, then recaptured by the Poles under General Zeligowski, during which time all of the country's stamps were issued.

Perforate? Imperforate?

I want them all.

16

THE PHILATELIC UPSIDE OF WAR

I had a dream the other night. It was a peaceful dream, and indeed it was specifically a dream of peace. A deep one, of the sort Abou Ben Adhem had.

Remember the Leigh Hunt poem?

> *Abou Ben Adhem (may his tribe increase!)*
> *Awoke one night from a deep dream of peace,*
> *And saw, within the moonlight in his room,*
> *Making it rich, and like a lily in bloom,*
> *An Angel writing in a book of gold . . .*

I won't tell you what passed between the angel and Mr. Ben Adhem, and instead encourage you to look it up and find out for yourself. But why should I keep you in suspense? It's my pleasure to assure you that things worked out just fine for Abou Ben Adhem.

Less so for me. I dreamed my deep dream of peace—an end to war, ushering in a Golden Age of lasting peace and prosperity in every corner of the globe. And I woke up, eyes wide, brow beaded with sweat, heart pounding.

"Great Scott," I cried, or words to that effect. "There'll be nothing interesting to collect!"

Conflict and turbulence, war and rebellion—these recurrent manifestations of man's inhumanity to man have a profound impact upon philately. The notion that war is the natural state of man seems almost irrefutable to those of us who collect the world's stamps. Occupation issues, provisional overprints, interrupted mail service, stamp-issuing entities appearing and disappearing, colonies transferred from one power to another before fighting their way to independence—how many of those would exist in a world of universal peace and harmony?

Toss in all the stamps issued to honor generals and military heroes, all those commemorating this battle and that glorious revolution. "It was a famous victory," Robert Southey wrote ironically of the Battle of Blenheim. Well, if it was any kind of a famous victory, you know someone somewhere has issued a stamp for it.

I was musing about all of this the other day, and thinking how much more evident it must be for the worldwide collector than for those among us who collect only U.S. issues. It's not as though our nation has managed to remain at peace since the first postage stamps appeared. The Mexican War had ended by the time Franklin and Washington lent their images to our letters, but philately was around for the Civil War, the Spanish-American War, the First and Second World Wars, Korea, Vietnam, and right up to the present.

But we've been blessed, in that most of the fighting has taken place offshore. Our borders haven't been redrawn, our cities have remained unoccupied. Oh, the war with Spain led to overprinted U.S. issues for Cuba, and for our new territories of Guam, Puerto Rico, and the Philippines, and we can't forget the whole run of Confederate philately. Still, those issues can't compare with the manner in which war has entirely remade the philatelic map of Europe.

Or so I told myself. Then I went to a meeting the first Wednesday of November and found out there might be more to it than I'd realized.

It's my good fortune to be a member of the Collectors Club. Twice a month we convene in an elegant brownstone on East 35th Street, where a member or a distinguished guest exhibits material from his collection and tells the rest of us about it.

On this particular evening, our guest speaker was Richard E. Drews, showing his prize-winning collection of the U.S. issues of 1861–6, Scott 63 to 111. The material was absolutely dazzling, but what caught me right away was when Rich explained why the whole series of stamps had come into existence in the first place.

When the Civil War began, it occurred to someone in Washington that the stock of United States postage stamps in the hands of postmasters in the Southern states constituted a considerable danger to the Union. Why, those stamps might be transported secretly across Union lines and sold at a discount to unscrupulous parties. Funds raised by this means could be used to further the rebel cause, and who was to say it wouldn't undermine the Union postal system in the process?

Nice try, Johnny Reb! But we'll just nip your nasty little scheme in the bud by recalling and destroying all of our existing stamp stock and rushing to replace the old stamps with new ones. That'll teach y'all!

Admittedly, I've got the benefit of a century and a half of hindsight going for me, but I have to say all of that strikes me as an act of harebrained postal lunacy that makes the intentional reissue of the 1962 Dag Hammarskjold invert look like a model of balanced judgment. Renegade postal clerks slipping across the border with their knapsacks full of stamps? Really? And, even if some equally brilliant Southerner had actually hatched such a scheme, could it possibly cost the North anywhere near as much as they spent to prevent it?

Never mind. The fact remains that a remarkable series of stamps was the result. And it became even more remarkable when postal paranoia kicked in, and a series of grills were impressed upon the poor stamps to prevent people from soaking them off and reusing them.

How much of a problem, in terms of dollars and cents, do you suppose the reuse of stamps constitutes? And how much do you figure the government spent on grills?

It's said of a type of larcenous individual that he'd rather steal a dollar than earn ten. It seems he has an opposite number, the government official who thinks it's sound policy to spend ten dollars to keep someone from stealing a buck.

And who benefits, in the long run? Why, we do. Just look at all the fascinating stamps out there for us to collect.

When I have a look at my own albums, it strikes me how thin they'd be but for war and rebellion. I collect worldwide to 1940, with a particular interest in the European nations and their colonies, and from a philatelic standpoint the First World War looms as the defining event of the hobby's first century. No sooner would an army march into enemy territory than a batch of clerks would rush in to overprint stamps for the occupation. And if the heat of the moment led them to dash off a batch of inverted overprints and double surcharges, well, is our pastime not the richer for it?

Hungary has a rich philatelic history, but it was during the war that it reached its heights. Eleven occupation issues produced innumerable stamps and varieties. "Counterfeits abound," my Scott catalog warns me, and I'll never know which of my own examples are bogus, because who'd spend $25 on a certificate for a stamp that's only worth 20¢ if genuine? True or false, the stamps make Hungary a joy to collect, though I don't suppose it was a very happy place to be while the war was going on.

And, of course, after the war came the republic, with the *Koztarsasag* overprints. And then, briefly, the Hungarian Soviet Republic, with five distinctive portrait stamps and a series of overprints. And then the restoration of the monarchy...

Or consider a single German colony, German East Africa. In my Scott Classic Catalog, it precedes two other German colonies, German New Guinea and German South West Africa. There are 23 stamps listed for German New Guinea, 34 for German South West Africa.

But there was a war going on in German East Africa. The German military commander was General Paul Emil von Lettow-Vorbeck, and his small army performed remarkably well; at the Battle of Tanga in November 1914 his soldiers were victorious over a British force eight times their size.

Von Lettow-Vorbeck was run off at last by sheer weight of numbers, especially after a Belgian force moved in from the Congo. He withdrew into Mozambique and Northern Rhodesia.

But will you look at the legacy he left behind?

The first stamps of German East Africa compare to those of the other colonies; there are the overprinted German issues, followed by the Kaiser's Yacht set, with and without overprint, running to 41 stamps in all.

And then there are the occupation issues. The Belgian forces began by overprinting a set of eight Belgian Congo stamps, once for Ruanda and once for Urundi. (Three more overprints, Karema, Kigoma, and Tabora, were not officially authorized, so we won't count them. Not that I wouldn't love to own them . . .)

Then the Belgians overprinted the same series with a four-line inscription in Flemish and French, slapped surcharges on five of them, and overprinted a Congo semipostal series with the initials A.O., for Afrique Oriental. After all, the mail must get through—and how could you manage that without overprinted semipostal stamps for occupied territory?

That was Belgium's contribution. That's 38 stamps, in case you lost count.

And now consider the British. They began by overprinting four stamps of Nyasaland Protectorate with the initials N.F., which stands for Nyasaland Force. (It was supposed to be N.F.F., for Nyasaland Field Force, but the telegraph operator goofed. Ain't philately grand?)

Only the troops were entitled to use the N.F. stamps; for civilian use, the British overprinted seventeen stamps from their colony of East Africa &

Uganda with the letters G.E.A., for (duh) German East Africa. Making 21 more in total.

And let's not forget Mafia Island, which you should note has nothing to do with Tony Soprano; the name comes either from the Arabic for archipelago or the Swahili for *a happy dwelling-place*. It's in the Indian Ocean, right off the coast of German East Africa, and the British captured it toward the end of 1914, and began overprinting stamps for civilian use on the island. In two years they managed to affix various overprints in various colors to various stamps from German East Africa, Zanzibar, and India. There are 98 of these, and none of them are inexpensive, and many of them cost the earth.

So what does that come to?

Well, I make it 198 stamps. That's not counting those 24 unauthorized Belgian overprints, or the many issues that Scott lists under Tanganyika. And we haven't even mentioned three stamps cited and valued by Scott, though not given listings. They're my favorites, because of the story that goes with them.

Here's how my catalog tells it:

In early 1916, German East African authorities ordered supplies of provisional stamps, printed by the press of the Evangelical Mission in Wuga. Three values in denominations most urgently needed were produced in March, but before they could be issued, new stocks of regular stamps were received from Germany.

Brace yourselves. Here comes the payoff:

To prevent their capture by the British, the provisionals were buried until 1922, when they were retrieved by the German government and sold at auction. Because of their long storage in the tropical climate, 90–95% of the stamps were destroyed and those surviving are usually brittle and somewhat faded. Value: 2-1/2h violet brown, $60; 7-1/2h carmine, $25; 1r pink, $1,450.

They buried them in the ground? Because otherwise the British might capture these pieces of paper and . . . and do what with them? Mail letters hither and yon?

And then they went and dug them up, and sold the moldering remnants at auction?

It sort of brings it full circle, doesn't it? In 1861, some genius in Washington rushed stamps into production to forestall some fancied Confederate operation to subvert the Federal mails. And half a century later some other genius in German East Africa picked up a shovel and started digging, all to keep the Brits from making off with some unissued provisional stamps.

The mind reels.

While I was writing this column, the month's copy of *The American Philatelist* arrived, with a feature article on Nicaragua by Louis E. Repeta. Here's how it opens:

> *The beauty of collecting Nicaragua stems in part from the inherent chaos that has pervaded the country for 150 years. This has led to political and fiscal chaos, rampant inflation, and problems in providing sufficient postage stamps with the required denominations for public use.*

Well, that's war for you. War and upheaval and chaos and disaster—hell to endure, heaven to collect. Let me close with one more quote, these lines voiced so memorably by Orson Welles in *The Third Man*:

> *In Italy for 30 years under the Borgias they had warfare, terror, murder, and bloodshed, but they produced Michelangelo, Leonardo da Vinci, and the Renaissance. In Switzerland they had brotherly love— they had 500 years of democracy and peace, and what did that produce? The cuckoo clock.*

Well, okay. On the other hand, there's plenty to get excited about in Swiss philately . . .

17

How Much is that Dachshund in the Fenster?

Last month I found some observations to make on war—less as a deplorable presence in the world than as a great enricher of philately. All those occupation issues, all those provisional overprints, all those countries changing their names, all those colonies shuttling back and forth. And, when the tumult and the shouting dies, all those commemoratives—to honor heroes and generals, to celebrate victories, and even to herald the unlikely outbreak of peace.

If one of the effects of war is to give us more stamps to collect, a result of collecting them is a greater appreciation of the history they reflect. In my own case, I thought I had a fair grasp of the first World War, and what went on between the assassination of the Archduke at Sarajevo and the armistice some four years later. Troops from Australia and New Zealand slaughtered at Gallipoli, and a whole generation of British youth climbing out of the trenches and into a barrage of German bullets, and clouds of mustard gas drifting back and forth over the trenches, killing troops on either side, and the Red Baron and his Allied counterparts in their little toy airplanes, wearing leather helmets and flight goggles and dueling in the sky, and—

And so on.

But until I had a good look at the stamps of German East Africa, I somehow missed knowing that the war was not limited to Europe. In addition to extensive fighting in German East Africa, there were clashes in Germany's three other African colonies, Togoland, Kamerun, and German Southwest Africa, and overprinted stamps provide evidence of the changed status of the overrun territories.

Since I submitted that column, I've found some paraphilatelic reminders of Germany's former colonies. Sometime in the following decade, private firms in Germany issued undenominated labels. One series, which I've had the good fortune to acquire, provides a stamp to mourn each of the ten lost colonies. The designs are identical, the bicolor stamps differing only in the colony's name and the second color of ink. Another series, with a stamp for each colony, shows stamps from the Kaiser's Yacht series, in color on a black background, with a surrounding legend that translates to "Never Forget Our Colonies."

Well, that's war for you. Philatelically speaking, it's the gift that keeps on giving.

This month I find myself ruminating upon another of the afflictions of mankind, inflation. Now let's be clear about this—the four horsemen of the apocalypse are Pestilence, War, Famine and Death, and inflation, however harrowing, is just not in their league. But neither is it a walk in the sunshine. And it gives dramatic philatelic evidence of itself.

I should point out that I am not talking about the ordinary inflation that appears to be a constant in any free economy. What that form of inflation does is enable each succeeding generation to bore its grandchildren senseless with interminable examples of how much cheaper everything used to be. I'm old enough myself to remember nickel candy bars and fifteen-cent beers, and can remember too when I was young enough to consume both with impunity.

I can get a vivid picture of the gradual march of inflation during my own lifetime just by looking at the various U.S. stamps that have had their turn carrying first-class letters. A 2¢ stamp, generally carmine rose in color, paid the rate for years, until it jumped 50% in the depths of the Depression. I was born six years later, in 1938, and the Post Office marked the occasion with the Presidential series. The 3¢ Jefferson showed up on most of the letters that came into our house, and the rate held for another twenty years.

And now it's 44¢.

Well, that's inflation. It happens, and we could debate whether it's good or bad, desirable or undesirable, but why bother?

Now if the cost of mailing a letter suddenly went from 44¢ to, say, $50,000,000—well, that would be a little different, wouldn't it?

Well, that's pretty much what happened in Germany in the early 1920s. Runaway inflation, hyperinflation—call it what you will, but what it amounted to was that the German government kept printing money, and the German mark kept dropping in value, and that forced the government to print more money, which further devalued the currency, and—

Just what happened, and just how and why it happened, is too complicated for the pages of a stamp publication; if you'd like to look further, a few minutes with Google and Wikipedia will prove enlightening. As philatelists, we can get a decent overview of the whole business by considering the stamps the Weimar government printed, when they weren't busy printing currency.

In 1920, the Germania series, Scott 118–132, ran from the 5 pfennig brown to the 4 mark black and rose. The following year saw the issuance of a regular series showing men at work—farmers, miners, iron workers—and Scott 137–155 range from the 5pf claret to the 20m indigo and green. Another set with a different watermark following in 1921–2, Scott 161–184, with a top denomination of 50 marks.

Scott 198–209, issued in 1922–3, has a 50m stamp as its lowest denomination, with a 100,000m vermilion stamp at the high end.

And they were just getting started. Their long set of 1923, Scott 241–278, consists of stamps surcharged with new inflated values. There's a 40 pfennig stamp raised to 5000 marks, a 400 mark stamp upped to 800,000 marks, and, finally, an already much inflated 5000 mark stamp surcharged with its new value of two million marks.

Next came a new design, with most of the stamp given over to its denomination—because the figures were high enough to take up some space. Scott 280 was the low-priced stamp, at 500,000 marks; the high value, Scott 299, came out at 50,000,000,000 marks. (That's fifty billion the way we count, though the Germans used the word *milliard* for our billion; their *billion* is our trillion.)

And what exactly could you do with these high-flying stamps? The only reason for their existence was to mail a letter or a parcel, and you had to do so in a hurry because they were likely to change the postal rates in the time it took you to lick the stamp and press it onto the envelope.

From the looks of things, not many of them ever made it onto envelopes. That high flyer, #299, is pegged by Scott at 20¢ mint, 90¢ never hinged. A postally used copy is $32.50, a cover $55. (The stamp's twin, Scott 309, serrate roulette instead of perforated, is more expensive at $1.60 mint and $5.25 never hinged, but commands a daunting $575 used and $775 on cover.)

It's not hard to see that this sort of hyperinflation couldn't go on forever. I don't know that anyone ever did literally load a wheelbarrow with money and trot down to the grocer to buy a loaf of bread, but that's been an enduring image over the decades. (And how could you go about buying the wheelbarrow in the first place? The money *that* would take would fill a railroad car . . .)

By the end of 1923, a new currency system was in place, and a set of postage stamps ranging from 3 to 100 pfennigs (Scott 323–8) had replaced its wildly inflated predecessors. Oddly enough, the design of the new stamps is virtually identical to the previous one; only the numbers have changed, and changed drastically.

The hyperinflated currency was widely collected outside of Germany, and in 1924 the *Los Angeles Times* speculated that there were more of the worthless German bills in the United States than in their country of origin. The same might well be true of the stamps. When I was a kid, buying packets and penny approvals and filling spaces in my Modern Stamp Album, nothing was easier to find and to afford than those German issues. Think of it, a stamp that cost fifty billion marks! And it was mine for a penny!

Back then, Scott listed them at 2¢ apiece. Now they're ten times that, but it doesn't mean they're worth any more than they were sixty years ago, just that creeping inflation has upped the catalogue's minimum to reflect the higher cost of doing business. But I liked collecting the stamps then, and when I resumed collecting I enjoyed them all over again.

There are enough more elusive examples to keep it interesting. Scott 264a, for example, was surcharged in black instead of green, while 267a is orange-red instead of green. Neither was ever put in use; thus they exist only unused, and Scott values them at $35 each. Scott 269b, 2 million mark surcharged on the 200 mark carmine rose (instead of rose red) catalogues $1250—unless it's watermarked sideways, in which case its price is only $1.40. And there are varieties with missing surcharges, and a scattering of imperfs, and one could fill one's philatelic hours just specializing in these extraordinary stamps.

While Germany set the mark (so to speak) for hyperinflation, other European stamp-issuing entities were tarred by the same brush. The Free City and State of Danzig, while under the protection of the League of Nations until its 1939 seizure by Germany, seems largely to have shared Germany's economy, and certainly fell victim to the same inflation. Stamp denominations in 1923 reached 500,000,000 marks. The currency reform at the year's end saw a new denomination replacing the mark; four stamps were surcharged with values in guldens, with the gulden equal to a hundred pfennigs.

Austria/Hungary was allied with Germany in the Triple Entente, and its two segments, separated after the war, both show philatelically that they did not go untouched by the 1923 inflation. Two Austrian sets, Scott 250–287 and 288–298, have as their highest denominations 4000 and 10,000 kroner respectively; previously, no Austrian stamps were valued higher than 10 kroner. The subsequent currency reform may be seen in the 1925 set, Scott 303–324, with hellers and kroner giving way to groschen and schillings.

Hungary had already gone through a siege of postwar turbulence, with the kingdom giving way to a republic, which was supplanted by a short-lived Soviet regime. The kingdom was restored late in 1919, and a lengthy regular issue of postage stamps, Scott 335–377, began in 1920 and continued over the next several years, with new stamps coming out in higher and higher de-nominations. The highest-priced stamp the first year was only 50 filler. In 1922 the series sported a 100 korona high value, with a 500k stamp in 1923, and a 2000k capping the set in 1924. In 1925 Hungary issued three commemorative stamps (Scott 400–2) to mark the centennial of the birth of novelist Maurus Jókal; the stamps are 1000k, 2000k, and 2500k, so inflation, while less a good deal extreme than in Germany, was still alive and well that year. Currency re-form came in 1926, when the korona was replaced by the pengo.

What was the effect of this phenomenon of hyperinflation? That's hard to say. It's often cited as a major factor in Hitler's rise to power, but the facts don't seem to support a direct relationship. The Hitler-Ludendorff Beer Hall Putsch did in fact occur in November of 1923; however, it's worth noting that by then currency reform was already underway, that the putsch was inspired less by lo-cal conditions than by Mussolini's successful march on Rome, and that Hitler's putsch was itself an abject failure. It wasn't until ten years later that Hitler was sworn in as chancellor and established the Third Reich.

Hyperinflation always falls most heavily upon the middle class. Savings be-come worthless overnight. The poor don't have any cash, so while they may be grossly inconvenienced, they don't lose anything. The rich may see their cash disappear, but in the end the still retain their real estate, their investments, their mines and factories.

Hungary's worst period of inflation followed not the first world war but the second, from late 1945 through the summer of 1946. The numbers are impossible to cope with, so let me put it this way—in Hungary's 1922–24 inflation, prices doubled every month. In July of 1946, prices doubled *every 13 hours*. On August 18 they replaced the pengo with the forint, and one new forint was equal to four hundred octillion pengo.

I'd love to show you some Hungarian stamps from that time, but my collection stops in 1940. And maybe it's just as well. I can only count so high.

War, rebellion, economic catastrophe—human history, like life itself, does seem to be one damn thing after another.

Isn't it a good thing that we've got stamp collecting to take our minds off all that stuff?

18

How to Spend $100

Let's say I've got $100 to spend on stamps this month. I've been looking over my worldwide collection, and lamenting the gaps in my Philippines holding. Remarkably enough, one of my favorite dealers sends me his list, and it's rich this month in Spanish Colonials. If I want to spend my $100 on stamps of the Philippines, I need look no further.

Because my dealer's list is an extensive one, and because my stock of Philippines is spotty at best, I can find a great profusion of stamps that would find spaces in my album. And, since this dealer's prices are approximately 50% of Scott catalog value, I can pick my way through his list and easily augment my collection by fifty or more stamps without going over budget.

Or I could select ten stamps with an average catalog value of $20.

Or—look what we have here! Scott C17, the one peso pale violet, over-printed to commemorate the flight of a pair of Spanish aviators from Madrid to Manila. I have several stamps from that set already, and it would be nice to acquire another. (Completing the set, however, will have to wait for a month with a larger budget; C7, for example, is listed at $3250, while C8 is an even $5000.)

It would be nice to have C17, and it's nicely priced on this list; Scott values it at $225, but I can buy it for precisely the $100 I'm planning to spend. (How's that for coincidence?)

So what do I buy? One stamp? Ten stamps? Fifty stamps? I can fill one space or ten spaces or fifty spaces, and whichever choice I make it's the same $100.

Tough call, isn't it? And it's one each of us has to make time and time again.

From an investor's point of view, the answer is simple. What I should do each month is spend my budget on the best stamp available to me. Scarcer, more desirable stamps tend to increase in value much more rapidly than common stamps, and indeed the commonest stamps don't go up at all.

The catalog, of course, shows an increase in price for common stamps that reflects the prevailing inflation. When I was a boy, right around the time of the Spanish-American War, Scott listed common stamps at 2¢. Now the minimum listing is 20¢, but that doesn't mean the stamps have increased in value by as much as a farthing. (If you pay 20¢ now, and would have paid 2¢ then, that's because your dealer's overhead has risen by a factor of ten. When it comes to selling, those 2¢ stamps were worthless then, and their 20¢ counterparts are worthless now. That doesn't mean they're not worth having—they're certainly not worthless to me, and I'm very glad to have them. But I'm well aware that their market value is nil.)

That being the case, there's a powerful argument for buying high-priced stamps and passing up the common ones altogether. If I'm buying primarily for investment, that's clearly the way to go.

What's that you say? I'd wind up with some very spotty album pages? Ah, but there's the beauty of the scheme—I wouldn't have spotty pages, because I wouldn't have an album in the first place. If I wanted to display my holdings with pride, I'd keep them in a stockbook; if I could get my ego out of the way, I'd leave them in the dealers' glassine envelopes, just the way they came to me, and arrange them in orderly fashion in stamp storage boxes.

Think what I'd save on albums! I wouldn't need plastic mounts, either, or much of anything but my storage boxes, and a ledger in which to keep an inventory of my collection.

As an apartment dweller, I've come to appreciate the compact nature of philately. I collect the whole world, and yet my albums take up just two shelves in a bookcase, with a little more space required for supplies. But boxes and a ledger wouldn't demand a third of that space, and would I even need the ledger? I could enter the data in a computer file, where it would be easy to update and even easier to ignore altogether.

And every time I glanced over at those boxes on the shelf, I'd get all choked up with the pride of ownership.

It doesn't sound much like collecting, does it? I had much the same thought when I read a very earnest piece in another publication, a dealer's thoughts on how a collector ought to prepare a collection for sale. Mounts particularly vexed him, because it added to the time required to examine and evaluate a collection. What suited him best, he explained, was for the collector to remove his stamps from their mounts, and indeed from the album itself, and to organize them in a stockbook.

Now I understood what he was getting at, but what he didn't seem to grasp was that our primary focus as collectors is not upon the eventual disposition of our collections. Arranging them on the page is part of the fun. Seeing at a glance what we have and what we don't have is one of the things that keeps the pastime alive for us.

Of course it's a comfort to think that at least some of the money I spend on stamps will return to me or my heirs when it's time for my little treasures to move on to other owners. Unlike golf or travel or no end of costly leisure-time pursuits, the collecting hobbies give something back to us at the end. If we factor in inflation, and all the expenses we run up along the way, I don't know that we come out ahead—but so what? That's not really the point, is it? I'm pleased to note that the stamp I paid ten dollars for ten years ago is now listed at several times that amount, but all that does, really, is help me rationalize spending more than I can afford on my hobby.

But I'm getting off the subject here. I'm not a philatelic investor, and my stamp collection is not going to make me a rich man, and that's fine. So let's get back to the $100 I've got to spend this month. What'll I buy with it? One stamp? Ten stamps? Fifty stamps?

While I may not think of my Philippine stamps as an investment, that doesn't mean I'm not mindful of what I pay for them. I want to fill those pages as economically as possible, and to do that I ought to buy the more expensive stamps first. They're the ones likely to appreciate in value, so it makes sense to get them now, and pick up their cheaper fellows later on.

Is that what you do, Dear Reader? Buy the expensive stamps first, and catch up on the low-priced ones a year or two down the line?

No?

You mean to tell me that you fly in the face of economic good sense, and spend your money on common stamps until there are no more of them for you to buy? And then you work your way up to medium-priced issues? And, when you've filled all the other spaces, then and only then do you go after those hundred-dollar stamps—which by then have risen a good ways past that hundred-dollar mark? Is that what you do?

Yeah, I thought so. Me too.

It seems counter-intuitive, doesn't it? Or let's save five syllables and call it dumb. But it's what I do, more often than not, and as far as I can tell I'm not alone here. Most collectors seem to operate this way, easing into a country or a collection by scooping up inexpensive stamps, and waiting on the pricey ones until that's all they've got left.

Well, let's take a longer look at this. Maybe we've got our reasons. After all, we're stamp collectors, and you know what that means; we may be crazy, but we're not stupid.

Here's one reason: Until I've acquired a substantial number of a country's stamps, I'm not sure how much they'll interest me. When a country is just a sea of blank pages in my album, I'm not much inclined to shell out a lot of dough just to fill one of those spaces. It's more of a commitment than I'm eager to make so early in the game.

And is it less of a commitment to spend the same amount of money on ten stamps, or a hundred? I'm hard put to explain why, but I think it is. Common stamps may never be worth much in dollars and cents, but each one adds value to my leisure time. I take a good look at it, I check it off my list, I cut a mount for it, I find the designated space for it, and I put it where it belongs. That process is pleasurable in and of itself—if it weren't, I'm in the wrong hobby—and the more stamps I obtain for my hundred bucks, the more times I get to repeat it.

That sounds like an argument for collecting nothing but low-priced stamps, and indeed there are plenty of ardent philatelists who pick areas in which they can buy no end of stamps without ever paying more than pocket change for a specimen. At the August APS show in Richmond, I heard a fascinating presentation on perfins, and one argument the speaker advanced was that not even the most elusive perfins ran into serious money. You could have a lot of fun, be entirely absorbed in your pursuit, and indeed amass an impressive collection— and never shell out very much money.

I've heard the same point made in respect to precancels and cinderellas. There are innumerable other reasons to collect them, but their wide availability and low prices are part of the attraction.

"Have fun—add thousands of stamps to your collection!" I still remember that line from a classified ad that ran sixty years ago. The man who ran it sold stamps on approval at one or two cents apiece, and I suspect he sold quite a few of them. I know he sold a good number to me. And the line stayed with me because the promise is so inviting. Having fun and adding stamps to my collection—isn't that what I'm here for?

That said, let me add that I find a special satisfaction in adding a hard-to-find (and hard-to-afford) stamp to my collection—especially when the space that awaits it is the last empty one on the page. By then I've already established that I'm interested in the stamps of the Philippines (or Peru or Poland, or Ponta Delgada). I know something about them. I've probably had my eye on C17 for a while, passing it up on various occasions, until the right example came along at the right price and caught me in the right mood. And now I get to go through the same ritual I've already performed no end of times with less costly stamps, checking it off my list, cutting a mount to fit it, and fixing it in the place where it belongs.

By this time I'll have learned a bit about Philippine stamps, and about my feeling for them. I'll know whether I care about gum, for example; it seems to matter more to me with some countries than with others, for reasons I couldn't begin to explain.

In a sense, I'll have spent enough time with Philippine stamps, and acquired enough of them, to have earned the right to spend $100 on a single stamp.

There's another reason I'll wait on the more expensive stamps. That way I have a chance to get the best stamp at the best price.

With cheap stamps, that's less important. Does it matter whether I spend ten or twenty or thirty cents to fill a particular space? It doesn't, not really.

But if I wait, I may scoop up C17 at a bargain price. One dealer I know sends out a wholesale list a few times a year, with everything at 25–30% of catalog. I never know what I'll find there—there are often a lot of broken sets, which may or may not work out well for me. But if C17's there, I'll probably get it for $60 or $70 instead of $100.

I actually own a copy of Philippines C17, but there are plenty of stamps I've been tracking for a long time. Austria 380, the Dollfuss memorial. Belgium B47, the high value of the 1918 Red Cross set. France C14 and C15. These aren't necessarily hard to find, but they command steep prices, and I'm biding my time.

What's the rush? I'm in no hurry. My albums don't lack for empty spaces.

19

MY FIRST COVER

Some months ago, I was browsing the new listings of my favorite eBay dealer. I saw right away that the day's offering consisted of covers, and was ready to click away, perhaps to see what Gail Collins had to say in the *New York Times*, or eavesdrop on my fellow citizens at overheardinnewyork.com.

Because, while I have great respect for covers and postal history, that's not what I collect. My philatelic interest is pretty much limited to unused pre-1940 worldwide stamps. I'll expand this a little for the British Commonwealth to include King George VI issues through 1952, and I can foresee a time when I might stretch my cutoff date for the rest of the world to the end of the Second World War, but we're still talking stamps, not covers.

At least half the time, this particular dealer's listing will consist of covers. And what he puts on the block each morning will generally be either stamps or covers; he rarely mixes them up. So, as I said, I was ready to move on to some other Internet landing spot, when something made me sift through the first page of his new listings, where one particular black-bordered envelope caught my eye.

His description identified it as a mourning cover, but I'd have known that instantly from the accompanying photograph. While I knew little enough about covers in general and mourning covers in particular, I was at least aware of what they looked like, with their black-bordered envelopes. I saw them offered for sale often enough, and thought them an interesting curiosity.

I've since learned that there's an American Philatelic Society affiliate, the Mourning Stamps and Covers Club, devoted to the study of just this sort of material. (Their website, www.mscc.ms, is well worth a visit. That's where I learned that a prolific writer on the subject, and a prizewinning exhibitor of the material, has the name Paul Bearer. I have to say I feel the richer for knowing that.)

I could imagine forming an absorbing collection of mourning covers—but never considered doing so, as what I already collect is more than enough to keep me busy and broke.

This mourning cover, though, had been mailed from France to an address in Buffalo, New York. And that destination, cited in the lot's description, was enough not only to catch my eye but to keep it from wandering.

I was born in Buffalo, toward the end of philately's first century, and lived there until I finished college—or, more accurately, until college was finished with me. I was a frequent visitor until my mother died ten years ago, and still get back from time to time.

Over the years, my wife and I have devoted ourselves to the eccentric occupation of collecting other towns and hamlets and wide places in the road named Buffalo—or Buffalo Gap, or Buffalo Hart, or perhaps New Buffalo. When our wanderings had brought us to more than fifty such places, each visit documented with Polaroids showing us in our Buffalo shirts ("Buffalo, City of No Illusions"), I wrote it all up for *American Heritage*. That fine publication has since moved on to the great newsstand in the sky, but in the meantime our personal Buffalo count has increased to 84.

So I clearly have an enduring relationship with my birthplace. But would that move me to snap up a mourning cover addressed to a Buffalonian?

No, not really. Buffalo postal history might be an interesting field, for Buffalo NY and for its lesser siblings, but I haven't felt a strong pull in that direction. The late Charles Peterson, the fine gentleman and distinguished philatelist who was one of my sponsors for membership in the Collectors Club, made me the generous gift of a stampless cover with a Buffalo postmark, thinking it might turn me into a postal historian, or at least a postal hysteric. I was grateful for the gift and treasure the cover, but felt no urge to seek out others of its ilk.

But it got me to look at the thing. I noted its stamp, which looked to be France #168, the 25-centime blue depicting a woman sowing seed. The stamp's a common one, first issued in 1906 and part of the regular issue that prevailed for three decades. I have a mint copy myself, and it's not at all expensive; the used specimen on the mourning cover is valued at Scott minimum.

And the address? It was written by hand, naturally enough; one wouldn't expect to encounter a typed address on a mourning cover. A handwriting analyst could very likely tell us more than we need to know about the character, diet, and inner life of the person who addressed the envelope, but all I could say was that it looked like a woman's hand to me, and that she'd taken the trouble to write neatly.

The Severance Family, she wrote. *150 Jewett Parkway. Buffalo, New York. U.S.A.*

Whereupon I sat up and took notice.

I attended Buffalo's Bennett High School, as in fact did my mother before me. In my first year there I took a required freshman course called Economic World, with global geography as its focus. It was taught by one Miss Severance, whose primary service was as a teacher of French, and I suspect she had as little interest in teaching the economic world curriculum as we did in studying it.

There's only one thing I recall from that class, but I recall it vividly. Miss Severance read aloud from the textbook—which, I seem to remember, was itself called *Our Economic World:* "'The religions of the world may be divided into Christian and non-Christian.'" She put the book down and sighed. "Now isn't that brilliant? If a Zoroastrian had written this book, he'd be telling us that the world's religions can be conveniently divided into Zoroastrian and non-Zoroastrian."

Come to think of it, that class may not have been the huge waste of time I thought it was . . .

Miss Severance, as I said, taught French, and had been at Bennett since the school opened in 1925. She was one of two French teachers; the other was Mlle. Jassogne, who had in fact been born and raised in France. Miss Severance and Mlle. Jassogne lived together, and I don't suppose there are five high school students in a thousand nowadays who would fail to draw the obvious inference from this fact, but the early 1950s were a more innocent time. While some of my fellow students may have been better than I at putting two and two together, or even one and one, most of us simply assumed that the two teachers lived together, and in fact spent all their time together, so that they might better practice their language skills.

The Severance Family.

Severance is not a rare name, but it's hardly a common one. There was a Leigh Severance a year behind me at Bennett, and it may have occurred to me to wonder if Miss Severance was his aunt, but I didn't know him and was never moved to inquire. (He's now the prominent owner of a capital management firm based in Denver. Thank you, Google.)

150 Jewett Parkway.

There are two streets named Jewett in Buffalo—or one street, with two different names. Jewett is in Buffalo's Central Park section, and west of Main Street it's Jewett Parkway, while east of Main it's Jewett Avenue. The address on the mourning cover is a block from Delaware Park at the corner of Woodward Avenue, on the same block with a famous Frank Lloyd Wright house. You could walk from there to Bennett High, although you probably wouldn't want to. It's a little over a mile.

Hmmm.

Had the mourning cover been sent to the family of the Miss Severance I remembered? It seemed a very strong possibility. Miss Severance and Mlle. Jassogne summered in France every year, and the Jassogne family would surely have known Miss Severance, and would want to express their sympathy upon the death of a close relative of hers. They wouldn't pick up the phone, not in those days. They'd send a note, very likely in a black-bordered envelope.

And what would be the opening bid on this cover? A mere ten dollars. I bid either the minimum or not much more, and forgot about it until I got an email a few days later informing me that I'd won the lot. And in another couple of days it turned up in my mailbox.

Now what?

Back to Google. It didn't take too much surfing to establish that a prominent Buffalo resident named Frank Hayward Severance was very likely the inspiration for that black band on the mourning cover. Born in 1856, he graduated from Cornell University in 1879, worked at the *Gazette* in Erie, Pennsylvania, "and then was hired by the *Buffalo Express* in 1881 as its marine editor. Before long he was named editor for the *Illustrated Sunday Express*, a position he left when hired by the Buffalo Historical Society at age 45. By that time, he had become a Buffalonian and deeply interested in the early history of Buffalo and the Niagara Frontier. Before joining the Society, he published a book called *Old Trails of the Niagara Frontier*, in 1899, which he dedicated to the school children of Buffalo."

Clearly a man of substance. He'd died in January of 1931, I learned, and was still Secretary-Treasurer of the society at his death. His survivors, I learned on another site, included two daughters, Edith and Mildred.

Mildred! That was Miss Severance's name, which I'd known once but had long since forgotten. I Googled "Mildred Severance," added "Jassogne" to the mix, and found a few pages of listings. Bennett High's two French teachers, I discovered, had collaborated after hours as writers, editors, and translators, and several Internet antiquarian booksellers would be happy to sell me copies of their work. Mlle. Jassogne's first name turned out to be Florentine, and that was something I'd never known. I'd never really known anything about Mlle. Jassogne. I'd assumed she spoke with a French accent, but I don't know that I ever heard her say a word, in French or English.

But I did find out that Miss Severance had been born in 1892, that she died in 1966, and that she was buried with her parents and a brother in the family plot in Isle La Motte, Vermont. Frank Severance, I learned from his gravestone, had been born in Massachusetts, but Miss Severance's mother, Lena Lillian Hill, was born in North Hero, Vermont, in 1855.

Mlle. Jassogne was born the same year but outlived her by a decade, dying in 1976. I don't know where she was buried, although a more Net-savvy person could no doubt find out without much effort, but she doesn't seem to have been buried with Miss Severance, and that seems somehow wrong to me. But what do I know?

The Severance Family, 150 Jewett Parkway, Buffalo, New York.

I decided that it was almost certainly Frank Severance's death that prompted the French mourning card or letter. His widow, Lena Hill Severance, lived until 1942, by which time a letter mailed in France would have borne a different stamp.

I'd be more certain if the postmark enabled me to date the cover, and I wouldn't be surprised if somebody with a knowledge of French postmarks could do just that. A knowledge of mailing rates might also be useful, and I suspect that information's readily available, but haven't bothered to chase it down.

It's a pity the letter was no longer in its envelope. Mourning covers, their black bands notwithstanding, were by no means certain to have mournful contents. Sometimes, I'm told, the letter itself would be newsy and chatty, and not funereal in tone at all.

Would this one have been in English or in French? Hard to say, and of course I'll never know.

But look how much I do know, that I didn't know before this particular cover came into my life. I never did study French, so after Economic World I doubt that I said another two words to Miss Severance, or she to me. (I took three years of Latin with Miss Florence Daly, who had also been one of my mother's teachers, and two years of Spanish with Miss Eleanor Sherman.)

My mother was Miss Severance's star pupil, but then she made a habit of that sort of thing; her piano teacher and her art instructor both wanted her to pursue those disciplines professionally. Miss Severance invited her to join her and Mlle. Jassogne in France for a summer, but she didn't go, and I wonder how her life might have changed if she had.

Frank Severance attended Cornell, and I'll bet his daughter did as well. Was it at Miss Severance's suggestion or with her encouragement that my mother went to Cornell? That's where she met my father, so it's entirely possible that I owe Miss Severance far more than I ever would have imagined.

All this from a single black-bordered envelope franked with an exceedingly common stamp. It serves to demonstrate, of course, the remarkable power of philately to open windows onto the world. And it shows, too, how much information is available to us instantly, and without our having to leave our desks. Data that not too long ago would have required months of investigation (and travel and correspondence and all the attendant expense) now takes minutes. You don't even have to be particularly good at online research to find out a huge amount about almost anything.

"The past is a foreign country," wrote Leslie Poles Hartley. "They do things differently there." Well, that may be, but it's a far more accessible country than it used to be. Things don't disappear within its borders as they once did.

So will this lead me to collect mourning covers? Or covers with a Buffalo connection?

I don't know. But any time I spot a cover that rings the sort of bell this one rang for me, rest assured that I'll be on it like a mongoose on a cobra.

Keller's Swedish Classics

—From *Hit & Run*

Keller drew his pair of tongs from his breast pocket and carefully lifted a stamp from its glassine envelope. It was one of Norway's endless Posthorn series, worth less than a dollar, but curiously elusive, and missing from his collection. He examined it closely, held it to the light to make sure the paper hadn't thinned where a hinge had once secured it to an album page, and returned it to the envelope, setting is aside for purchase.

The dealer, a tall and gaunt gentleman whose face was frozen on one side by what he had explained was Bell's Palsy, gave a one-side-of-the-face chuckle. "One thing I like to see," he said, "is a man who carries his own tongs with him. Minute I see that, I know I've got a serious collector in my shop."

Keller, who sometimes had his tongs with him and sometimes didn't, felt it was more a question of memory than seriousness. When he traveled, he always brought along his copy of the Scott Classic Catalog, a large 1100-page volume that listed and illustrated the stamps of the world from the very first issue (Great Britain's Penny Black, 1840) through the initial century of philately and, in the case of the British Empire, including the last of the George VI issues in 1952. These were the stamps Keller collected, and he used the catalog not only for its information but as a checklist, deliberately circling each stamp's number in red when he added it to his collection.

The catalog always traveled with him, because there was no way he could shop for stamps without having it at hand. The tongs were useful, but not indispensable; he could always borrow a pair from whoever had stamps to sell him. So it was easy to forget to pack tongs, and you couldn't just tuck a pair in your pocket at the last minute, or slip them in your carry-on. Not if you were going to get on an airplane, because some clown at Security would confiscate them. Imagine a terrorist with a pair of stamp tongs. Why, he could grab the flight attendant and threaten to pluck her eyebrows . . .

It was surprising he'd brought the tongs this time, because he'd almost decided against packing the catalog. He'd worked for this particular client once before, on a job that took him to Albuquerque, and he'd never even had time to unpack. In an uncharacteristic excess of caution, he'd booked three different motel rooms, checked into each of them in turn, then wound up rushing the job on an impulse and flying back to New York the same day without sleeping in any of them. If this job went as quickly and smoothly he wouldn't have time to buy stamps, and who even knew if there were any dealers in Des Moines?

Years ago, when Keller's boyhood stamp collection rarely set him back more than a dollar or two a week, there would have been plenty of dealers in Des Moines, as there were just about everywhere. The hobby was as strong as ever these days, but the street-level retail stamp shop was on the endangered species list, and conservation was unlikely to save it. The business nowadays was all online or mail order, and the few dealers who still operated stores did so more to attract potential sellers than buyers. People with no knowledge of or interest in stamps would pass their shop every day, and when Uncle Fred died and there was a collection to sell, they'd know where to bring it.

This dealer, James McCue by name, had his store occupying the ground floor front of his home off Douglas Avenue in Urbandale, a suburb whose name struck Keller as oxymoronic. An urban dale? It seemed neither urban nor a dale to Keller, but he figured it was probably a nice enough place to live. McCue's house was around seventy years old, a frame structure with a bay window and an upstairs porch. The dealer sat at a computer, where Keller figured he probably did the greater portion of his business, and a radio played elevator music at low volume. It was a peaceful room, its manageable clutter somehow comforting, and Keller picked through the rest of the Norway issues and found a couple more he could use.

"How about Sweden?" McCue suggested. "I got some real nice Sweden."

"I'm strong on Sweden," Keller said. "At this point the only ones I need are the ones I can't afford."

"I know what that's like. How about numbers one to five?"

"Surprisingly enough, I don't have them. But then I don't have the three skilling orange, either." That stamp, catalogued as number 1a, was an error of color, orange instead of blue green, and was presumably unique; a specimen had changed hands a few years ago for three million dollars. Or maybe it was euros, Keller couldn't remember.

"Haven't got that fellow," McCue said, "but I've got one through five, and the price is right." And, when Keller raised his eyebrows, he added, "The official reprints. Mint, decent centering, and lightly hinged. Book says they're worth $375 apiece. Want to have a look?"

He didn't wait for an answer but sorted through a file box and came up with a stock card holding the five stamps behind a protective sheet of clear plastic.

"Take your time, look 'em over carefully. Nice, aren't they?"

"Very nice."

"You could fill those blank spaces with these and never need to apologize for them."

And if he ever did acquire the originals, which seemed unlikely, the set of reprints would still deserve a place in his collection. He asked the price.

"Well, I wanted seven-fifty for the set, but I guess I'll take six hundred. Save me the trouble of shipping 'em."

"If it was five," Keller said, "I wouldn't have to think about it."

"Go ahead and think it through," McCue said. "I wouldn't really care to go lower than six. I can take a credit card, if that makes it easier."

It made it easier, all right, but Keller wasn't sure he wanted to take that route. He had an American Express card in his own name, but he hadn't used his own name at all this trip, and figured he'd just as soon keep it that way. And he had a Visa card he'd used to rent the Nissan Sentra from Hertz, and to register at the Days Inn, and the name on it was Holden Blankenship, which matched the Connecticut driver's license in his wallet, on which Blankenship's middle initial was J., which Keller figured would help to distinguish him from all the other Holden Blankenships in the world.

According to Dot, who had a source for credit cards and drivers' licenses, the license would pass a security check, and the cards would be good for at least a couple of weeks. But sooner or later all the charges would bounce when nobody paid them, and that didn't bother Keller as far as Hertz and Days Inn and American Airlines were concerned, but the last thing he wanted to do was screw a stamp dealer out of money that was rightfully his. He had a feeling that wouldn't happen, that the credit card company would be the one to eat the loss, but even so he didn't like the idea. His hobby was the one area of his life where he got to be completely clean and aboveboard. If he bought the stamps and avoided paying for them, he was essentially stealing them, and it hardly mattered if he was stealing them from James McCue or Visa. He was perfectly comfortable with the notion of having official reprints on the first page of his Swedish issues, but not stolen reprints, or even stolen originals. If he couldn't come by them honestly, he'd just as soon get along without them.

Dot would have a snappy comeback for that one, he supposed, or at the very least roll her eyes. But he figured most collectors would get the point.

But did he have enough cash?

He didn't want to check in front of an audience, and asked to use the bathroom, which wasn't a bad idea anyway, after all the coffee he'd had with breakfast. He counted the bills in his wallet and found they came to just under eight hundred dollars, which would leave him with less than two after he bought the stamps.

And he really wanted them.

That was the trouble with stamp collecting. You never ran out of things to want. If he'd collected something else—rocks, say, or old Victrolas, or art—he'd run out of room sooner or later. His one-bedroom apartment was spacious enough by New York's severe standards, but it wouldn't take many paintings to fill the available wall space. With stamps, though, he had a set of ten large albums, occupying no more than five running feet of bookshelf space, and he could collect for the rest of his life and spend millions of dollars and never fill them.

Meanwhile, it wasn't as though he couldn't afford six hundred dollars for the Swedish reprints, not with the fee he was collecting for the job that had brought him to Des Moines. And McCue's price was certainly fair. He'd be getting them for a third of catalog, and would have cheerfully paid close to full catalog value for them.

And did it matter if he wound up short of cash? He'd be out of Des Moines in a day or two, three at the most, and aside from buying the occasional newspaper and the odd cup of coffee, what did he need cash for, anyway? Fifty bucks to cover a cab home from the airport? That was about it.

He shifted six hundred dollars from his wallet to his breast pocket and went back to have another look at the stamps. No question, these babies were going home with him. "Suppose I pay cash?" he said. "That get me any kind of a discount?"

"Don't see much cash anymore," McCue said, and grinned. One side of his mouth went up while the rest stayed frozen. "Tell you what, we can skip the sales tax, long as you promise not to tell the governor."

"My lips are sealed."

"And I'll throw in those Norway stamps you picked out, though I don't guess that'll save you much. They can't come to more than ten dollars, can they?"

"More like six or seven."

"Well, that'll buy you a hamburger, if you don't want fries with it. Call it an even six hundred and we're good."

Keller gave him the money. McCue was counting it while Keller made sure he had all of the stamps he'd bought, tucking them away in an inside jacket pocket, adding the pair of tongs, closing the stamp catalog, when abruptly McCue said, "Oh, holy hell! Hold everything."

Were the bills counterfeit? He froze, wondering what was the matter, but McCue was on his feet, walking over to the radio, turning up the volume. The music had stopped and an agitated announcer was interrupting with a news bulletin.

"Holy hell," McCue said again. "We're in for it now."

20

Every Stamp has a Story

There's nothing like a due date for a column to make a month fly by. For fifteen years, starting in 1976, I contributed a monthly column on fiction writing to *Writer's Digest,* and during the first year I often worried that I would run out of things to write about. Sometime during the second year I learned to take the process on faith; something, I came to realize, would always pop up in my reading or writing, just in time for me to discuss it in my column.

This is the twentieth installment of *Generally Speaking,* and up to now I've never had a problem coming up with subject matter. And why should I? It is, after all, a general column by a general collector. That gives it a focus as wide as the whole world of philately, and that's a very wide range indeed.

And then this month, with the column's delivery date approaching, I found myself fresh out of ideas. The mental cupboard was bare.

Then the mail came, and I found myself saved—well, not by the bell, as our postman doesn't ring once, let alone twice. But he does put the mail in the mailbox, and this particular delivery included an order of stamps from a favorite dealer. I sorted through them, made note of them in the Scott Classic Catalogue that serves as my checklist (and bible, and encyclopedia, and window on the world), and while I was doing this a phrase popped into my head.

Every stamp has a story.

And here I'd just received an envelope chock full of stories. If I had a column to deliver, why not tell one of them?

One of the stamps that caught my eye was New Zealand Scott 126, the 3p orange brown of 1907–8. It pictures a pair of Huia birds, and is the fourth stamp of this particular design.

The Huia birds made their first appearance on the 3p orange brown of the 1898 pictorial issue, which was itself something of a milestone in British Empire philately. While a few countries (Portugal, the United States) did produce pictorial sets during the 19th Century, those portions of the world under Queen Victoria's rule largely limited their stamp output to representations of Her Royal Majesty. The exceptions include New South Wales (Scott 77–82, with a view of Sydney, an emu, a lyrebird, and a kangaroo, along with Captain Cook and the queen), Tasmania (Scott 86–93, showing mountains and waterfalls) and British Guiana (Scott 152–6, a mountain and a waterfall).

Sometime in 1894, sentiment arose in New Zealand for a stamp issue that was symbolic of the country, and a public competition drew over two thousand designs. The entries of William Rose Bock of Wellington were chosen for the 2p, 9p, and one shilling stamps—and for our 3p orange brown stamp as well.

The 2p (Scott 72) depicts Pembroke Peak, on the west coast of the South Island. The 1/- (Scott 81) shows two species of native parrots, the Kea and the Kaka. And the 9p (Scott 80) has a view of the Pink Terrace at Rotomahana, which, like the White Terrace shown on the 4p rose (Scott 76), had ceased to exist some twelve years before the stamp was issued. (The pink and white terraces were destroyed in 1886 when a volcano erupted, and their subsequent representation was based on paintings and photographs.)

Every stamp really does have a story, and I haven't even mentioned the two versions of the 2-1/2p blue, with the pictured lake spelled Wakitipu on one and Wakatipu on the other. But let's stick with our timbre de jour, the 3p orange brown.

In its initial appearance in 1898, as Scott 75, the stamp was unwatermarked, and perforated 12 to 16. A year later finds it still unwatermarked, but perf 11, and designated Scott 89. (The rest of the series has some additional changes, with a new design for the 4p and some color changes here and there.)

The 1902 reissue is watermarked (NZ and star close together). The 3p orange brown, otherwise unchanged, is listed at Scott 112.

And then, finally, in 1907, William Rose Bock's design for the 3p orange brown had its final incarnation. The color is unchanged, the perfs continue to vary a bit (Scott lists 14, 14 x 13, and 14 x 14-1/2), and the watermark is the same.

But the new stamp (Scott 126) is smaller. Earlier versions were 23 mm tall, and the new stamp is 21 mm.

Why?

Well, the printing plates for the series were worn, and it was time for them to be replaced. For the sake of uniformity, it was decided to reduce the 3p, 6p, and 1/- stamps to the size of the 1p carmine. (This latter stamp, showing an allegorical female figure—"Zealandia" or "Commerce," depending which source you consult—was issued in 1907 to replace Scott 85, a 1p stamp showing the extinct White Terraces previously shown on the 4p stamp; Scott 85 had itself replaced the 1p bicolor with a scene of Lake Taupo which migrated to the 4p value in 1900.)

I'm not sure why uniformity of size was important, but perhaps it facilitated the perforation process. While they were at it, the postal authorities redrew the 1p carmine, so that it could be surface printed; this would result in lower production costs.

A few months before the four redrawn 21mm stamps appeared, New Zealand issued a set of four pictorial issues commemorating an exhibition in Christchurch, and depicting the arrival of the Maoris, Maori art, Captain Cook's landing, and the formal annexation of New Zealand. And a little later, in 1909, the large pictorial issue gave way to a set with a portrait of King

Edward VII, although Zealandia retained her spot on the 1p carmine.

And was that the end of the 3p orange brown? We've noted four major listings in Scott (75, 89, 112 and 126), and the back of the book offers a pair of Officials. In 1902, Scott 89 was handstamped O.P.S.O. in violet, to create Scott O12. (The letters stand for "On Public Service Only.") And in 1907, Scott 112 was overprinted OFFICIAL and is listed as Scott O26.

We might also note that Scott 112 was overprinted in 1903 for Aitutaki (Scott 4), Niue (Scott 10) and Penrhyn Island (Scott 10).

After that, Bock's Huia bird design becomes extinct. Which, ironically enough, is precisely what happened to the stamp's subject.

The Huia, or *Heteralocha acutirostris*, probably became extinct shortly after it made its last appearance on a stamp. The last confirmed sighting was in December of 1907, although plausible reports of sightings continued near Wellington until 1922. (There were alleged sightings in a national park in the early 1960s.)

And why did this beautiful bird become extinct? Two reasons—hunting and destruction of habitat. The Huia was hunted extensively so that it could be mounted and displayed in museums and private collections; it was also hunted so that its long tail feathers could adorn fashionable hats. (While the latter folly is plausible enough, it's harder to believe that a species could be wiped out in the name of science. It's worth noting that the naturalists of the time were given to wholesale slaughter, and a glance at the diary entries of John James Audubon reveals a man who spent most of his waking hours killing birds. His motivations notwithstanding, it seems a curious role for one who has since become a patron saint of conservation.)

The Huia was a creature of the forest primeval, and the lowlands of the North Island were largely deforested to create agricultural pasture. The Huia were unable to flourish in secondary forests.

Our stamp shows a pair of the birds, and that was a wise decision on Bock's part, because the male and female, while similar in their plumage, have the most different beaks in all of ornithology. The female's beak is long and thin, and curves downward; the male's is short and thick, like that of a crow. This allows them to feed in different fashion, as one might imagine, but why they should have evolved in this manner is not all that clear.

One thing our stamp fails to show is the considerable beauty of the Huia. For that, color reproduction would be required, and a larger canvas than the small stamp affords. The birds had black plumage with a green metallic cast to it. The wattles were bright orange. (Those wattles affirm the Huia's membership in a small family, the Callaeidae, or New Zealand Wattlebirds; the other two species, the Saddleback and the Kokako, still exist, although the Saddleback is endangered.)

The Huia had brown eyes, a white beak, blue-gray legs and feet, and light brown claws. Its twelve long black tail feathers were each tipped with a broad white band.

The Maori regarded the Huia as sacred, and its feathers were to be worn only by chiefs and other high-status individuals.

Unlike the kiwi, the flightless bird that has become symbolic of New Zealand, the Huia was capable of flight. But it doesn't seem to have been particularly good at it. Huia mated for life, and were generally seen in pairs, hopping along the ground or from branch to branch, and only taking flight when they had to. And this very likely made them easy prey to their hunters.

The islands of the South Pacific have been home to a good many endemic species of flightless birds, and for the longest time I couldn't imagine how in the world they got there. What I found out was that they flew there—and, in the absence of ground-based predators, they evolved into flightlessness. That may seem counter-intuitive, but when the ability to fly is not essential to one's survival, it means devoting much of one's energy to the development and maintenance of an unnecessary musculo-skeletal system.

That's fine, until someone or something comes along and changes the game. Consider the flightless Stephens Island wren, widespread throughout New Zealand until the coming of the Maori. By the time British settlers arrived, the bird was confined to Stephens Island, and there it survived until a lighthouse keeper arrived, and brought along a cat. And that, alas, was the end of the Stephens Island wren.

But from a philatelic standpoint, the Huia wasn't finished yet.

There are no additional empty spaces for it in my collection, which cuts off in 1940. But the nations of the world didn't cease issuing stamps at that date, and the Huia, extinct or not, has had a number of curtain calls in recent years.

Seven of them have been furnished by Aitutaki, one of the larger Cook Islands. Aitutaki began by overprinting New Zealand issues, including our Huia 3p in 1903. The island issued nine of its own pictorial stamps from 1920 to 1927, then used Cook Islands stamps for forty-five years. Then Aitutaki re-emerged as a stamp-issuing entity, producing a run of pictorial issues.

In 1974, a stamp and souvenir sheet marking the centenary of the Universal Postal Union shows two early stamps, the 1903 Huia overprint and the 1920 1/2p. Five years later, Sir Rowland Hill joins those two stamps, along with the Penny Black, on a stamp and a pair of souvenir sheets. Finally, there's a stamp-on-stamp-on-stamp issued in 1984, showing three Aitutaki stamps, one of them the 1974 UPU issue. (And, along with the stamp there's a souvenir sheet.)

In 1996, New Zealand brought out a set depicting seven extinct birds, and the $1.20 stamp shows a pair of Huia to great advantage. Two years later the Huia shows up again, in a 14-stamp set reproducing the pictorial issue of 1898. The Huia looks much as it did a century earlier, but the price has gone from 3p to 40¢. New Zealand Post issued two souvenir sheets that year as well, and one of them shows the Huia stamp, along with a pair of the 80¢ Lake Wakitipu-Wakatipu stamps.

And is that it for the Huia? Well, no—because in 2009, the island nation of Sao Tomé e Princípe issued a souvenir sheet purportedly showing the parrots of New Zealand. Three of the six birds shown are parrots, but the others are the Huia and its fellow New Zealand Wattlebirds, the Saddleback and the Kokako. It's hard to know what these birds have to do with Sao Tomé e

Príncipe, those two islands being situated in the Atlantic off the west coast of Africa, but I'm not going to quibble. Where else are you going to see all three of the Wattlebirds up close?

Every stamp has a story, and one story leads to another. I should probably point out that I didn't take a lot of time picking a stamp with a story. The one I chose, New Zealand Scott 126, was simply the first one to catch my eye. I might have found just as much to ruminate about had my eye—and my tongs—fastened on any of the other stamps in that envelope.

And, if I hadn't had this column to write, I'd very likely have mounted that 3p orange brown stamp without giving it a second thought. I might have quickly noted (and as soon forgotten) the name of the bird, but I wouldn't have known anything about it.

Half a century ago there was a TV series called *Naked City,* set in New York and written by Stirling Silliphant. Each episode concluded with these lines: "There are eight million stories in the naked city. This has been one of them."

And how many stories do you suppose there are tucked within the pages of my Scott Classic Catalogue? Too many to count, I suspect.

And this has been only one of them.

21

STRICTLY FOR THE BIRDS

"That's a Blue-crowned Motmot," Guillermo announced, and four pairs of binoculars, mine among them, promptly swung around to aim themselves in the direction he was pointing. My companions evidently found the bird without difficulty, and told each other what an attractive fellow he was.

I saw a lot of leaves and twigs.

"Can't you see it? It's right there," someone said helpfully. "It's on the branch, the one sticking out from the tree. About, oh, two feet away from the other tree. Do you see it now?"

I didn't.

"Right there! See the blue on its head? See the long tail?"

"Oh, there he is," I said, just to bring this little farce to an end. I couldn't see the bird, and I knew I wasn't going to see the bird, and I was rapidly tiring of the whole enterprise.

"Beautiful, isn't he?"

"Gorgeous," I agreed. "I'd have hated to miss him."

It was on the Caribbean island of Tobago that I failed to see the Blue-crowned Motmot. I was on a small-ship cruise with my wife and our eldest granddaughter, along with sixty other passengers. We'd boarded at Sao Luis, in Brazil, and stopped in Suriname and Guyana on our way to a four-day cruise of the Orinoco in Venezuela. Now we were in Tobago, on a walk to the Argyle Falls; next would be Trinidad, and two days later we'd be flying home from Curaçao.

And who could say how many birds I'd be unable to see by then?

This is not to say that our trip so far had yielded nothing but invisible birds. I'd seen Great Kiskadees in Suriname and Guyana, and from a Zodiac in the Orinoco I'd looked at a Pied Water Tyrant, a Lesser Kiskadee, a Green Ibis, and a number of toucans and parrots. One tree held a flock of *Opisthocomus hoazin,* the Hoatzin, an extraordinary leaf-eating bird with a digestive process not unlike that of a cow; this internal fermentation endows the Hoatzin with a powerful stench that keeps predators at bay. It is, as Sherlock Holmes would tell us, "Alimentary, my dear Hoatzin."

And, on the same walk that failed to show me the Blue-crowned Motmot, I'd had a good look at a Rufous-tailed Jacamar and a couple of other fine feathered friends. I still would have liked a glimpse of that Motmot, but I didn't get all broody over my failure.

It's all right, I told myself. One way or another, I'll get that bird.

I'd always liked birds, finding them both beautiful and interesting. One of my earlier childhood memories is of a break-of-day visit to Buffalo's Forest Lawn Cemetery with my Uncle Jerry, where we watched the early birds in pursuit of the worms. I remember that he pointed out a Prothonotary Warbler and told me that it was an uncommon bird locally. I don't know that I actually saw it, but its name has somehow stayed with me for over sixty-five years.

(And, it pains me to confess, it wasn't until I was writing this very column that I learned what the word *prothonotary* means. It doesn't have much to do with either stamps or birds, so I'll leave you the fun of looking it up on your own.)

While that was my sole childhood birding experience, I learned a fair amount about birds from a favorite book, *The Burgess Bird Book for Children*, with vivid color illustrations by Louis Agassiz Fuentes, and my library also contained one of Roger Tory Peterson's field guides. I spent a lot of time with those books, and I came to know the birds.

Knew them on the page, that is to say. But then when I went out in the open air and looked up at the sky, I didn't have a clue what I was looking at.

In recent years I've been on any number of cruises and nature walks, and I love being out in the open air and relish the opportunity to see birds. But here's what happens: the trip leader, or someone else with a little ornithological expertise, points off into the distance.

"A Speckle-tailed Rabbit Snatcher," he announces, and I look where he's pointing. There's a dot out there, about the size of the floaters that appear in my field of vision in any bright room with white walls, and every bit as elusive to pin down. I try to aim my binoculars at it, and on the rare occasion when I manage this feat, I get a quick glimpse of a slightly larger dot, which wastes no time in darting out of sight.

"Note the field marks," he says. "See the vivid golden eye?"

My own eyes, neither golden nor terribly vivid, were not made for spotting birds at a distance. Lenses help correct my lifelong myopia, but nothing can change the fact that one of my eyes is sufficiently dominant to keep me from having true binocular depth perception.

See the vivid golden eye? All I saw was the hopelessness of the enterprise. I couldn't swear that the creature had an eye, let alone guess its color.

The pictures in the books were a lot easier to deal with, let me tell you. They were right there in front of me, not hundreds of yards away, and they stayed put. No flying away, no blending in with their surroundings. They held their position perfectly, just like—well, like stamps in an album.

When I contemplated a return to philately some fifteen years ago, I had to figure out what to collect. Various possibilities suggested themselves before I settled on Worldwide 1840–1940, and one of the first was topical; I'd been a writer since college, and a reader for longer than that, so what would be more natural than for me to collect Writers on Stamps?

I took a stab at it, and wound up buying fifty or a hundred stamps from various countries, all depicting writers of one sort or another. But I just didn't get interested. The great majority of the stamps showed portraits of their subjects, so they weren't terribly interesting visually. And most of the writers were men and women I'd never heard of, and I was content to leave it that way. I decided I wasn't really geared to collect topically. I had the greatest respect for topical or thematic philately, and enjoyed viewing such displays at shows, but it just didn't seem to be my thing.

Well, you see where this is going, don't you? Blinking away at the birds like Mr. Magoo, I had one of those *Aha!* moments. I could collect birds on stamps, and would thus be able to inspect up close and at my leisure the creatures who proved so elusive in real life. Tongs and a magnifier would do what binoculars could not, and I could see my fill of birds without leaving my desk.

I could find fulfillment as a topical collector after all, just by shifting my focus from writers whose work I'd never read to birds whose field marks I'd never spotted.

That's it in a nutshell. But how I got there, and what effects it had, is a little more complicated. And, I have to hope, a little more interesting.

In a sense, my most recent *Linn's* column got me started. You may recall that, acting on the premise that every stamp has a story, I chose a recent acquisition at random and wrote a column about it. The stamp was New Zealand Scott 126, which pictures a pair of the now-extinct Huia bird. I wrote about the stamp and its several philatelic permutations, and then I wrote about the bird itself. It was a pretty interesting creature, and a very attractive one, and it's a shame it's not still around to ornament the woodlands of New Zealand. Hunting (for decorative plumage and for museum specimens) combined with habitat destruction to kill off the Huia, though philately has given it an afterlife, not only on the century-old stamp I had chosen to write about, but on more recent issues of New Zealand, Aitutaki, and Sao Tomé e Princípe.

I found those later issues on a pair of web sites devoted to bird stamps, and a little browsing acquainted me with extraordinary quantity of issues depicting birds. And the stamps were interesting and attractive in the bargain. I knew that birds were one of the most popular of philatelic topics, and I could understand why.

But it didn't yet occur to me that this might be a direction I wanted to take.

I wasn't thinking about birds when we prepared for our trip. But I was in fact thinking of stamps. I have a pocket-sized album I've written about before, in which my wife and I endeavor to obtain a stamp from each country we visit, affixing it to the page and getting the postal clerk to cancel it. This isn't always possible, as we often find the local post office closed or otherwise inaccessible, but we've been successful a fair amount of the time, and the little book provides a vivid if incomplete record of where our travels have taken us.

I packed the book, and when we boarded our ship I took it out and paged through it. When our post office visits give us some choice in the matter, I tend to pick out stamps depicting living creatures, and I noted a bat from Moldova and a wombat from Australia, wild cats from Spain and Kazakhstan, butterflies from Macedonia, New Zealand, and the Marshall Islands, and a hooded cobra from Turkmenistan.

And there were birds in fair supply: a Song Thrush (Ireland), a Copper-rumped Hummingbird and Violaceous Euphonia (Trinidad & Tobago), a Formosan Blue Magpie (Taiwan), a Loon (Canada), a pair of Cranes (Lithuania), Gentoo Penguins (Falkland Islands), Adelie and Emperor Penguins (British Antarctic Territory), two Magellanic Penguins (Argentina and Nicaragua), a Bahama Woodstar (Bahamas), Peruvian Boobies (uh, Peru), a Gray-crowned Palm-tanager (Haiti), a Polynesian Triller (Aitutaki), a Barn Owl (Niue), a Red-shining Parrot (Tonga), a Common Tern (Sint Maarten), and a Hoopoe (Gibraltar).

The two birds from Trinidad & Tobago were acquired on two separate visits—to Tobago in early 2000 and to Trinidad three years later. They're from a 12-stamp set issued in 1990, and I wondered if I could add a third in 2011. I couldn't count on getting to a post office on either island, or indeed anywhere else, but if I did I decided to try for bird stamps, as I especially liked the ones I already had.

In Suriname we walked through Peperpot, an old plantation reborn as a nature reserve. I couldn't see any of the birds the guide pointed out, but looked them up later in a booklet we were given. It contained good color photos and descriptions of fifty endemic birds, and listed around 200 more. Back in our cabin, I familiarized myself with the birds I hadn't managed to see, and decided I'd get as many as I could at the post office.

The next morning, we were shown around Paramaribo, Suriname's capital, and in the park I did get a good look at the Great Kiskadee. It's a pretty yellow bird, and to be found in great profusion throughout the country, but I doubt I'd have found it at the post office. It was on one of the country's first bird stamps, back in 1966, and they've shown at least 180 bird species since then and haven't yet had to repeat themselves. I might not find the Great Kiskadee, but I'd have plenty of other bird stamps to acquire.

But it was Saturday, and the post office was closed.

Never mind. I had already taken a big step, even if I hadn't spent a cent or acquired a stamp. I was a collector of bird stamps. I'd crossed the line in my own mind if nowhere else, and that's really all it takes.

In Guyana we flew to a spectacular jungle waterfall, and some other members of our party got a good look at the spectacular Cock-of-the-rock. The following morning we had a city tour of Georgetown, and the highlight for my granddaughter and me was a chance to slip off to the post office. I left their philatelic window with five souvenir sheets showing toucans and parrots and hummingbirds—along with a duplicate sheet of a parrot (Jendaya Conure), pasted in our album and duly canceled.

In our days on the Venezuelan Orinoco, I never set foot on land, and the villages we passed were too small to have post offices. We went out a couple of times a day in Zodiacs, looking for howler and capuchin monkeys and, especially, for birds.

And something interesting happened. I was still myopic, and lacking in binocular depth perception, and ill-equipped by nature for the task of spotting birds in the wild. But I was somehow better at birding now than I had been a few days ago.

I suspect motivation had something to do with it, but the result was that my ability to spot the birds improved, and I took longer and closer looks at the ones I managed to see. And took inordinate delight in sitting there and staring at them.

After the Blue-crowned Motmot escaped me in Tobago, we moved on to Trinidad and the Asa Wright Nature Centre. Their screened-in veranda looked out at a sort of Bird Heaven. Hummingbirds hovered at the feeders, while no end of other birds took their turn at the banquet table. All I had to do was sit there and watch them, and I could have happily devoted the whole day to that occupation.

Now I suppose this was the ornithological equivalent of shooting fish in a barrel, but it was a great opportunity for the visually challenged, and took advantage of it. I'd seen a picture of a Crested Oropendola in the Peperpot book, and now I got to watch one, bright blue eye and all.

Then we walked the pathways of the Asa Wright Centre, and saw more birds. We finished up in the lodge, where I moved from the veranda to the gift shop, where a clerk was able to sell me a stamp. Trinidad & Tobago has issued several sets of bird stamps in recent years, but she didn't have any of them, and I settled for one celebrating local herbal medicine, and showing an herb called

Wonder of the World. (That's a name frequently given to Asian ginseng, but the Trinidadian version, *Kalanchoe pinnata*, is something else entirely.) I put it in my book, she canceled it for me, and I went back for another look at the birds.

Later that day, in another part of the island, we took a boat ride through a swamp to view the glorious Scarlet Ibis returning to their roosting grounds.

Back home, I darted around the Internet, investigating possible birding tours, acquiring a monocular (since I close one eye when using binoculars, why not go for simplicity?), and joining the American Topical Association.

I'm not sure where any of this will lead me. There were, according to Wikipedia, over 10,000 bird stamps as of 2003, and I don't know that I'd want to collect them all, even if I were in a position to make the attempt. Should I pursue stamps of the birds I've actually seen? Or ones I'd been in the presence of, even if I haven't quite managed to see them?

Or could I widen the field to birds I'd like to see, given the chance? (That way I could include the extinct ones, and I've already got the Huia.)

We'll see. I don't know how much actual birding I'll do, nor can I guess if this new passion for bird stamps will last. Some years ago a cousin of mine announced that he'd long resisted the urge to collect something, and had finally decided to collect giraffes. He'd always enjoyed looking at the animal in zoos, and decided a few months back that a collection of giraffe figurines would be just the thing.

"It's enriched my life," he confided. "Things haven't been the same since I started collecting giraffes."

And how many giraffes had he so far acquired?

"None," he said. "I haven't yet found any that meet the standards of my collection. But I'll keep on looking."

22

DRINKING MYSELF TO BOLIVIA

Some years ago in Florida I overheard a fellow talking about the life he used to live. "I'd spend every day at the office," he said, "shoving papers around, and then on my way home I'd pick up a bottle of blended whiskey. Every single night I'd sit in front of the TV with the sound off and drink myself to Bolivia."

I love the image: The fellow takes that third or fifth or seventh drink and—poof!—the next thing he knows he's in La Paz, thirteen thousand feet above sea level, staggering down Sagamaga Street, haggling over fetal llamas at the Witches' Market, and continuing his search for the perfect Pisco Sour. (What he meant, of course, was that he used to drink himself to *oblivion*, but somewhere along the way he'd misheard the expression, and thought the landlocked South American nation was where one went, at least metaphorically, when one had a little too much.)

The expression came back to me the other day when I was paging through one of my albums. Without ever paying a great deal of attention to Bolivia, I've managed to acquire unused examples of 275 of the 361 stamps issued through 1940. (That's the cutoff date of my worldwide collection; however rich the country's post-1940 philatelic history may be, I'm entirely out of the loop.)

I'd picked up Bolivian stamps when they turned up on dealers' lists, and I'd been philatelically well disposed toward the country. Bolivia wasn't beset by an excess of minor varieties, nor did one have to contend with a glut of Seebeck reprints. There were enough surcharged issues to make it interesting, but not so many that they gave you a headache. You didn't have to check watermarks, because Bolivia never used them. Few of the stamps were so cheap as to be essentially worthless, while none were prohibitively expensive. You could complete the country without robbing a bank.

And the stamps, now that I took a moment to look at them, were attractive, too. Most of the early issues were portrait stamps, depicting some handsome chaps whose names meant nothing to me, but many of those were bicolor, with the portraits in black, and they certainly looked nice enough in my album. Later on Bolivia moved toward pictorial stamps, culminating in 1939 with a set of eighteen stamps (Scott 251–268) showing a variety of indigenous birds and animals. I own that set, and am happy to have it, but I added it to my album without paying much attention to it and have barely glanced at it since.

It struck me that I had somehow continued to equate Bolivia with oblivion, that I'd collected the country with what amounted to little more than benign neglect. And, coincidentally enough, this revelation came when I had a column to write.

So why not take a good look at my Bolivian stamps? Why not find out who those good-looking gentlemen might be, and just what they're doing in my album?

The first living creature to appear on a Bolivian stamp was a condor; Big Bird's Andean cousin may be seen on Scott 1–6, issued in 1867–8. One could make a philatelic career out of this issue, as my Scott Classic Catalogue mentions a total of 414 varieties, along with some fairly common reprints. The first human being granted philatelic recognition is Tomás Frías (Scott 147, 1¢ pale yellow green of 1897). He was 68 when the congress chose him as president after the death of dictator Agustín Morales in 1872. His charge was to call free elections, and he did so, transferring power to the victor, Adolfo Ballivián, who fell ill and died after nine months in office; as head of the Council of State, Frías succeeded him and thus had a second term as president.

He made one mistake, signing a treaty with Chile that proved contrary to Bolivian interests; a later government annulled it, and the result was the disastrous War of the Pacific, as a result of which Bolivia lost access to the sea and much of its mineral wealth. Before then, Frías's term ended prematurely in a coup in 1876. He left the country and died eight years later in Italy.

Scott 48, the 2¢ red, shows one of Frías's predecessors, José Maria Linares, who became Bolivia's first civilian president in 1857. He introduced many reforms, abolished governmental abuses, and then a year later had himself proclaimed Dictator for Life and was overthrown in 1861 and soon died in exile.

The same series shows Simón Bolívar and his close friend, José Antonio de Sucre. Both led the fight for independence from Spain, and each served a term as president of Bolivia, and of other neighboring countries as well. The new republic took its name from Bolívar, while one of its two capitals bears the name of Sucre.

Pedro Domingo Murillo (Scott 47, 5¢ dark green) joined the rebellion against Spain in 1805, and was hanged for it in 1810. Bernardo de Monteagudo (Scott 50, 10¢ brown violet) was an associate of Bolivar's, assassinated in 1825 for reasons that remain unclear. And José Ballivián (Scott 51, 20¢ lake and black) was a Bolivian general during the war with Peru and Bolivia's eleventh president (1841–1847); he was also the father of the chap Tomás Frías installed as president, and subsequently succeeded.

Both Balliviáns, José and Adolfo, turn up on the 1901 series, along with Eliodoro Camacho (the loser in three fraud-riddled elections), Narciso Campero (whose failures on the battlefield were supplanted by a Golden Age of Bolivian politics), and Andrés de Santa Cruz (who fought against San Martin's rebel force in 1820, and, having been beaten and captured, switched sides with a smile and fought rather more successfully against the Spanish.)

Bolivia issued its first two commemorative sets in 1909. The first (Scott 78–81) marks the centenary of the Revolution of 1809. One stamp shows the departmental coat of arms of La Paz, while the others picture two patriots of that war—Murillo, who as we've seen was hanged, and José Miguel Lanza, who was not; Sucre complained to Bolívar that Lanza was an inept administrator, unable to control the greed and corruption that surrounded him. Also honored, on the high value 2 bolivianos stamp, was Ismael Montes, who wasn't even born until 1861. But he happened to be president of the country when the stamp was issued, and I can only guess that's what got his face onto it.

The movement to throw off Spanish rule began in 1809, and the War of Independence lasted until the royalists' capitulation after Sucre's forces defeated them in 1924 at the battle of Ayacucho. Even then a General Olañeta refused to accept the peace agreement and continued fighting, proclaiming himself "the only defender of throne and altar." He went on waging his hopeless fight until his own men displayed rare common sense and killed him themselves.

Don't look for Olañeta's picture on a stamp.

Having just issued four stamps to mark the rising against Spain, Bolivia brought out a second set that same year to commemorate the sixteen-year war. The stamps show some familiar faces—Murillo, Monteagudo, Sucre and Bolívar—along with Esteban Arce, Manuel Belgrano, Miguel Betanzos, and Ignacio Warnes.

I found out interesting things about two of them. Belgrano (Scott 89), born in Argentina, was a general with important victories in the battles of Tucumán and Salta, and a number of defeats as well; he died of dropsy in 1820, and his last words were either "Alas, my poor country!" or "I don't feel so good," depending on sources.

Warnes (Scott 83), an Argentinean general under Belgrano's command, had an up-and-down military career himself; in his final battle he defeated the royalist cavalry but was himself shot dead, and his opponent, a Colonel Aguilera, entered the city of Santa Cruz with Warnes' head on a pike.

Now it's entirely possible that Señores Acre and Betanzos had equally checkered careers, and came to ends every bit as colorful as Belgrano and Warnes, but Arce had the bad luck to bear the same name of a Mexican television entertainer, while a latter-day namesake of Betanzos is a novelist in Buenos Aires. And wouldn't you know it? It's these Juanos-come-lately that draw the attention of Google and Wikipedia, thus making it a fool's errand to find out anything about their predecessors.

A year later, in 1910, Bolivia issued a sort of addendum to this series. Scott 92–4 show three of the chaps of the preceding series—Warnes, Betanzos, and Arce. They shifted denominations, and the colors are different, but the only significant change in the design is to be found in the scrolls on either side of the portraits. The scrolls in the original set are dated 1809 and 1825, presumably to mark the beginning and end of the war. The three stamps of 1910 retain "1825" in the scroll at the lower right, but the left-hand scroll is dated "1910."

As far as I can make out, 1910 is significant only in that it was the year the stamps were issued. You'd think there'd be a more cogent reason for the date, but it might require a specialist's knowledge of Bolivian philately to supply it.

A specialist would probably also be able to explain why the three stamps of 1910 were issued in the first place. They were not needed to create new denominations, or to honor new heroes.

Bolivia's first pictorial stamps, mentioned but unlisted and unvalued in Scott, were printed in 1915 to commemorate the Guiqui-La Paz railroad, but were never issued. The catalogue illustration is of the 10¢ violet, showing a crude native boat on a river. The set's denominations range from one centavo to 5 Bolivianos and show various views of pre-Columbian ruins, a boat on a lake, a ship in port, a church at Tiahuanacu, the national coat of arms, and, not surprisingly, a locomotive. One source says they are "not uncommon," while another states that they're listed in the Bolivian "Cefilco" catalogue at around $100, and occasionally turn up on eBay for $20 or so.

I'll have to look. I certainly wouldn't mind having a set.

A year later, Bolivia issued a scenic set, Scott 111–116. The 2¢ stamp, picturing Lake Titicaca (named, I suspect, by a potty-mouthed toddler) shows a native boat seemingly identical to the unissued Guiqui-La Paz stamp.

I'd heard of Lake Titicaca, but it's taken this more extensive look into Bolivian philately to inform me that it's the highest commercially navigable lake in the world, and the largest in South America. And, toddlers aside, I now know that the origin of the name Titicaca is unknown. Local people see the lake's shape as suggestive of a puma hunting a rabbit, and translate the lake's name as Rock Puma. I've had a look at a map, and I sort of get what they mean, but I'd have to say they're a pretty imaginative bunch. I can only wonder what they'd make of a Rorschach test.

My own sole venture into Bolivia took me to a couple of mountain lakes, though neither was a tenth so grand as Titicaca. Some years ago my wife and I spent several days at a lodge in the Atacama desert in Chile, and jumped at the chance to book a half-day excursion into the Andes and across the Bolivian border. It cost next to nothing, included a picnic lunch, and allowed us to see two lakes, each with a resident population of flamingoes. The birds at one site were a rich pink, while the others were snow white; with stamps, it's often exposure to the sun that makes for color changelings, but with flamingoes it's more a matter of what's in the water.

Flamingoes, pink or white, don't turn up on a Bolivian stamp until 2005, but Bolivian wildlife makes an appearance on a 1939 series, Scott 251–268. Subjects include a pair of llamas, a vicuña, two cocoi herons, a chinchilla, a condor, and a jaguar; there's also a toco toucan, and if it's the toco toucan of Titicaca, I think we've got a 1940s pop song just waiting for Carmen Miranda to come along and sing it.

I didn't see any of these fellows during my too-brief visit, but I did catch sight of a couple of vizcachas. The vizcacha's a close relative of the chinchilla, but its longer ears give it a more rabbit-like appearance. The Bolivians might well have chosen the vizcacha instead of the chinchilla for philatelic representation, as the chinchilla, prized for its fur, had been hunted almost to extinction by the end of the 19th century, and survives largely in captivity, on fur farms.

The vizcacha, on the other hand, seems to be doing nicely to this day. There's a 1987 Chilean air mail stamp that shows a handsome specimen, but I haven't been able to find it illustrated on a stamp of Bolivia.

After a brief look at the stamps, it's hard to imagine mistaking Bolivia for Oblivion. And yet they might have been one and the same for all the attention I paid to the country and its philately prior to writing this column.

And I'm sure I could have done the same for dozens upon dozens of the countries, living and dead, whose stamps I collect. It's all too easy to take each new acquisition from its glassine housing, assess its centering, hold it to the light to check for thins, make sure it's the particular variety it purports to be, and then cut a mount for it and fill the space assigned to it—all without paying the slightest attention to what's depicted on its face, or why.

After the hours I've spent looking deeply into my Bolivian stamps, I find myself more appreciative of the ones I have and more determined to acquire the ones I lack. Funny how it works, isn't it?

23

THE BEAUTY OF HOME-MADE STAMPS

Good morning, class.

Good morning, sir.

Today we're going to talk about the aesthetics of philately. Ask a roomful of collectors to name the most attractive stamps, and you'll get a roomful of answers. That's not terribly surprising, given that the question calls for a subjective judgment, and that there is such a profusion of stamps with a fair claim to the title.

Beauty is indeed in the eye of the beholder, and there are plenty of us out there, and no end of beauty for us to behold.

But if the question is posed to a roomful of classic collectors, unapologetic troglodytes who limit their focus to philately's first century, you may hear the same answer more than once or twice. In 1935, 44 colonies and protectorates of the British Empire marked the 25th anniversary of the reign of King George V with a set of four stamps, all with the same design: at the right, the monarch's crowned head in profile, facing left, and overlooking a distant view of Windsor

Castle. The stamps are bicolor, with the castle generally in a darker shade, and both the color combinations and the denominations vary from one colony to the next.

It's fitting, certainly, that the stamps issued for the silver jubilee of this particular king be attractive and philatelically interesting, because George V was a committed philatelist, spending his personal funds to enhance the royal collection. The story is often told of the time in 1904, when the then-Prince of Wales bought the Mauritius "Post Office" 2p blue (Scott 2) for £1450. News of the auction record got around, and the following day a courtier of his acquaintance announced indignantly that "some damned fool" had paid such a price for a postage stamp. "Yes," said the future king. "It was this damned fool."

The Silver Jubilee constituted the first British omnibus issue, but they were by no means the first guests at this particular party. Portugal got there 37 years earlier, with a well-designed series of eight pictorial stamps issued to commemorate Vasco da Gama's 1498 discovery of a sea route to India; stamps were issued for eight colonies plus the mother country. The first French omnibus series appeared in 1931, and 26 colonies issued four stamps each to herald an international colonial exposition in Paris.

Then, in 1935, the British honored their king—and most stamp collectors would say they got it right. The design is attractive, and the decision to vary the colors of the individual stamps from one colony to the other makes for a series that achieves uniformity while avoiding visual monotony. A single stamp looks good, a four-stamp set is undeniably attractive, and a whole album devoted to the royal philatelist's jubilee continues to please the eye all the way to the last page.

It's worth noting that 15 stamp-issuing entities of the British Commonwealth passed up the King-and-Castle design and found another way to commemorate the Jubilee. Great Britain chose a design unlikely to head anyone's list of beautiful stamps, and overprinted it for use in British Offices in Morocco. Australia issued three stamps showing the king on his horse, conveniently named *Anzac* for the Australian and New Zealand troops in the World War.

Canada's set is an attractive one, with one stamp showing the future King

Edward VIII, then Prince of Wales. India's seven stamps are an echo of the Common design, with various local edifices standing in for Windsor Castle, while New Zealand's three stamps show full-face portraits of the king and queen.

South Africa had its own design, as did South West Africa and Southern Rhodesia, but in the Pacific a more slapdash approach prevailed. For Cook Islands, Niue, Samoa, New Guinea, Nauru, and Papua New Guinea, postal authorities simply chose two or three or four regular-issue stamps and overprinted them accordingly. I somehow doubt they made the list of royal favorites.

The Silver Jubilee stamps were immediately popular, and not only with philatelists. Royal souvenirs have always found an appreciative audience in the UK, as one can tell by the profusion of Coronation and Royal Wedding plates and tea cups in Portobello Road, and the stamps made good souvenirs. While they did get used for postage, the greater portion seem to have survived uncanceled.

One result is that they're abundant without being dirt cheap. The least expensive sets list for five to ten dollars in Scott, while a few more elusive ones—Ascension, Hong Kong—may bring five or ten times as much. It may take some hunting to track down every set, and you'll have to spend some money, but everything's available and you won't need to take out a second mortgage to fill your collection.

Unless you make the issue a specialty, that is. These are engraved stamps, and the philatelist with an enthusiasm for die breaks has a world of opportunity here. Minor varieties abound, and if you're a Flyspeck Collector with a strong lens and a stronger imagination, you can find extra flags flying over Windsor Castle, and other curiosities to keep you squinting through your magnifier.

What you won't have a great problem with is condition, except to the extent that a particular stamp may have endured mistreatment after its release. I can't recall ever seeing a King-and-Castle stamp that wasn't well centered. (I'm sure there must be one, even as there must be off-center examples of the

Great Britain Seahorses issues, but if they exist they really ought to command a premium; they're that much the exception.)

Nor, as far as I know, have any examples turned up with the castle upside down. These are bicolor stamps, and had to make two trips through the printing presses, and what an opportunity that proved to be for postal authorities in Liberia and Somali Coast.

Ah, I see a hand raised. Do you have a question, Arnold?

Not a question, sir. I'm just guessing that you've just given us your choice for Most Attractive Stamp.

I think the stamp is beautifully designed and wonderfully executed. But "most attractive"? You can probably name a great many beautiful stamps. Ah, now I see a lot of hands in the air. Rachel? What's your pick?

Well, it's a U.S. stamp, sir. And you only collect the rest of the world.

That doesn't mean I can't appreciate my country's stamps. And your choice would be—

The $1 Trans-Mississippi of 1898, sir. "Western Cattle in Storm." I don't know if you're familiar with the stamp, sir.

Familiar enough to know they're Scottish cattle, Rachel, and the storm's in the Highlands of Scotland. The painting's by James McWhirter, but the post office didn't know any of that until the stamp had already been issued.

They used it without permission, sir?

They apologized to Mr. McWhirter. Arnold? Did you say something?

Just that I bet the apology meant the world to Mr. McWhirter.

I'm sure it was a comfort. The stamp, like all of the Trans-Mississippi set, was supposed to be a bicolor, and in this case a red frame was intended for the black vignette of the cattle.

The foreign cattle.

That's right, Rachel. But the Spanish-American War came along, and the post office decided to keep things simple and make the stamp all black, though it's hard to fathom how much a batch two-toned stamps could have complicated their wartime world.

I guess those were simpler times, sir.

I guess so, Arnold. But I agree it's a beautiful stamp, with the aesthetic appeal of a noir film in the days before Technicolor. I can see why it's your favorite.

Gwen?

Sir, speaking of Technicolor, there are some modern stamps in living color that put those Scottish cattle in the shade. All the French stamps reproducing famous paintings, and all the flora and fauna topicals.

Very true. I've been accumulating some beautiful bird stamps myself. And you don't have to cross the ocean for art on stamps; my wife's a big fan of the American painter series. She uses them whenever she mails a letter. Shaheen, you look agitated. Is something troubling you?

The title, sir.

The title?

"Home-Made Stamps." I don't get it. What is home-made about the stamps we have been discussing?

Nothing, Shaheen. But the stamps we've been discussing, while all examples that I greatly admire, aren't my absolute favorites. So shall I tell you what stamps I especially like?

I have a special fondness for home-made stamps. Now they aren't literally home-made, the work of enterprising forgers or freelance do-it-yourself postmasters, but you wouldn't know it from the way they look. They're crude and artless, with all the unsophisticated charm of a child's drawing, and you're not sure whether to reach for a hinge or a mount or a refrigerator magnet.

Some of the greatest rarities of philately fit this description. I've so often read newspaper stories where the unique British Guiana 2c black on rose (Scott 1) is mentioned, and more often than not the writer pauses to tell us how unattractive the stamp is. ("A quarter of a million dollars for a postage stamp, and it's not even a pretty one!")

Sir, isn't the only copy used? And don't you only collect mint stamps?

Rachel, I'd make an exception. I think I could force myself. But you don't have to run a hedge fund to be able to afford a home-made stamp from British Guiana. Consider Scott 103–6, produced by typesetting them twelve to a sheet. To keep enterprising counterfeiters from printing up their own postage, the authorities made perfins of them by perforating them with the word "specimen". (That would lead almost anyone to assume they're specimen stamps, but they're not, and the rare non-perfin of this issue commands a substantial premium.)

I own an unused example of one of these, Scott 104, illustrated here. Its design, as you can see, is quite pleasing in and of itself, and the home-made element enhances it for me.

A country's earliest stamps often have this home-made feel. Finland's very first issues, with a crowned coat of arms in a circle, are a costly example. (I have two of the reprints.) And the serpentine roulette stamps that followed have a special quality, challenging though it is to find one without a couple of broken teeth.

The first stamps issued for Epirus are home-made in appearance, as are many early Albanian issues. Malta, after having issued sophisticated engraved stamps from 1860 on, threw up a wonderfully home-made set of 10 imperforate typeset postage dues in 1925. An urgent need? How urgent could it have been? In any event, before the year was out they were replaced by a typographed and perforated set.

Stressful times and special circumstances are apt to spawn home-made stamps, too. A few months back I wrote about war as a moving force in philately, and wartime provisional issues often display the crude beauty I find so appealing. The Boer War of 1899–1902 may have been quite awful for the participants, but its philatelic legacy a century later is considerable.

The Boers in the field in the northern part of Transvaal printed some stamps (Scott 175–201), primitive in appearance and initialed by the postmaster, that never seem to have carried the mail; all "used" specimens are said to have been given favor-cancels.

For all that, they're not expensive. I have one, Scott 196, valued at $10, illustrated here. Isn't it pretty?

Even a well-designed engraved stamp can look home-made with enough overprints on it. The siege of Mafeking led to a number that qualify, listed in Scott as Cape of Good Hope 162–180. I have Scott 173, a 1p lilac, originally Great Britain 89, changed by a two-line overprint into Bechuanaland Protectorate 70, and then elevated by surcharge to a 3p value and overprinted "Mafeking / Besieged". (Excellent forgeries are known, my Scott Classic Catalogue assures me, and I can only hope mine's not one of them. But it looks pretty, doesn't it?)

Cape of Good Hope 178–180 were designed and printed specifically for use during the Mafeking siege; 178 is the 1p blue on blue, showing 13-year-old Warner Goodyear, Sergeant-Major of a group of boy cadets. The 3p stamp, also blue on blue, portrays General Robert S. Baden-Powell, at that time the British colonel in charge of the defense of Mafeking. Goodyear's young troops made an impression, and inspired Baden-Powell to create the Boy Scout movement in 1907.

Yes, Arnold? You seem to be humming.

Sorry, sir. It was unconscious.

So many things are. What song was that? It sounded familiar.

Blue on blue, sir. You know, like the stamp. "Blue on blue, heartache on heartache." I wonder if that's how they picked the color scheme.

It's probably the only paper and ink they had. The color of the paper varies from pale blue to deep blue, and there are two distinct varieties of the Baden-Powell 3p, one a full 2-1/2 mm wider than the other. All three stamps are expensive, and the wide 3p, Scott 180, costs a small fortune.

Or a large fortune. One sheet of twelve stamps was reverse-printed with Baden-Powell looking left instead of right. Three mint and seven used copies survive, and one of the latter, with a minor repair and a gorgeous sock-on-the-nose cancel, sold last month at Cherrystone; the before-sale estimate was $7500, the hammer price $12,500.

Is that the one you have, sir?

I don't have any of them, Gwen, and probably never will. But I live in hope.

I like stamps. I like to buy them, and I like to mount them in my albums, but I'm also able to appreciate the ones I don't collect. If I'm especially fond of stamps with a crude and improvised look to them, that doesn't keep me from admiring and cherishing the others. Really, what more can any person ask of a pastime? I was thinking just the other day—I'm sorry, did you have a question, Rachel?

About that last stamp you mentioned, sir. With the old guy looking to the left instead of to the right.

Robert Baden-Powell.

Whatever. Do you think that was a political statement, sir?

I'm sure I don't know, Rachel. You'd have to ask him yourself.

Is he still alive? I mean, he must be dead by now, sir.

You can ask him that as well. I'm out of here. Goodbye until next month, class.

Goodbye, sir.

24

A Book for a Desert Island

Good morning, class.

Good morning, sir.

There's a question I thought we might discuss today, and it's one that's not that often raised in a philatelic context.

What book would you want to have with you on a desert island?

It is, I'll be the first to admit, very much a hypothetical question. It's unlikely that any of you will wind up on a desert island, and even less likely that you'll have the opportunity ahead of time to pack for the occasion. Still, considering it might prove instructive, and—yes, Arnold?

Just to get the parameters straight, is this your basic cartoon desert island we're talking about here, sir?

That's correct, Arnold.

Not much more than some sand and a scraggly palm tree? And a guy in raggedy cutoff jeans? Plus a caption marked by the sardonic humor for which you're justly famous?

No caption, Arnold. And I don't know what the island's sole resident is wearing, and I don't much care. The question is what is he going to read. He's only got one book, and it's his sole diversion, because there's no TV on the island, and no Internet access, and—yes, Rachel?

Can he text people?

Uh, I'm afraid not. No phone, no computer, and no way on earth to send anybody a text message.

I would kill myself.

Let's move on, shall we? You're a stamp collector, and through no fault of your own, it's your destiny to finish out your days on one of those cartoon islands. Food and fresh water won't be a problem, but a single palm tree's all you've got for companionship and intellectual stimulation.

And you get to bring along one book. What'll it be? Seth?

I'd go for How To Build a Raft, *Mr. B.*

And then you'd cut down the only source of shade on the island, would you? No rafts, Seth. You're stuck on the island. Edna?

"One Hundred and One Great Seaweed Recipes."

Really? I think one great seaweed recipe strains the bounds of plausibility all by itself. Paula, did you have your hand up?

Oh, I was just going to say the Bible.

A natural thing to say. And, depending upon your particular faith, you might mention any of a number of holy books. But I'm going to rule out religious and spiritual books, as well as the various self-help guides charting the route to inner peace.

Did you say something, Arnold?

I was just telling Rachel that a blank book would be the natural choice for an atheist.

Or for those of you who've been saying for years that you'd write a novel if you could only find the time for it. No spiritual books for us today, class, and no blank books either. More seaweed recipes, Edna?

I was just joking before, sir. Seriously, I guess I'd go with The Complete Works *of Shakespeare.*

In a compact one-volume edition? It's hard to find fault with the Bard of Avon as a companion in exile, and if I had no one but him for company, sooner or later I might actually get through *Titus Andronicus.* I'm not sure I can say the same for Marcel Proust, though, in case any of you were about to bring up *In Search of Lost Time.*

Before we go further, I should point out that we're a philatelic bunch gathered here, so the answer ought to have some sort of philatelic spin to it. Rachel, you look troubled.

I just hope you're not suggesting we bring our albums to that desert island.

No, not at all.

My stamps would get ruined, sir. Tropical stains everywhere.

No albums, Rachel.

And it would just be frustrating anyway, wouldn't it? I'd page through my album, knowing that every blank space in it was destined to stay blank until the end of time. And I couldn't even tell anybody how I felt, because you won't let me send text messages!

Easy, Rachel. Everything's going to be okay. It's just an imaginary island. Paula, could you give Rachel a Kleenex? And, before I lose control of this classroom altogether, I'm going to cut to the chase and tell you my choice of a book for a desert island.

It's the *Scott Classic Specialized Catalogue of Stamps & Covers.*

Well, what a bunch of blank stares. Morgan, you look especially puzzled.

I am, sir. It seems so pointless.

Pointless?

I mean, if you're out in the middle of nowhere, and you don't have your stamps with you, or any opportunity to add more stamps to your collection, why would you want a book that tells you what they're worth?

Ah, but price information is such a small portion of what the catalogue provides! The book is a treasure trove of information, a virtual encyclopedia in a single volume. And you wouldn't sit down and read an encyclopedia all the way through, whereas—yes, Arnold?

I know somebody who did, sir.

Someone who read an entire encyclopedia?

Just one volume. See, there was this supermarket promotion where they offered the first volume for 49¢, and then each week there was a new volume available, but the price was higher. 99¢, I think it was, but it may have been as much as $1.98.

I'm sure there's a point to this, Arnold, but—

Bear with me, sir. His mother bought the first volume, but when they raised the price on the others she decided the hell with it. So my friend never got past the first volume, and it was the only book in the house, and he read it cover to cover, and went through it more than once. He may be the world's foremost authority on everything from Aardvark to Bathysphere, although in other respects he's a pretty ignorant guy.

I see. Well, there's much to be said for specialization, although as a generalist myself—Yes, Edna?

I know a woman who just collects A countries, sir. Everything from Aden to Azores and nothing else. I wonder if she knows Arnold's friend?

He doesn't get out much, Edna.

Neither does she, but—

All right, this seems to be getting out of hand, doesn't it? I'm going to put a damper on your questions for now and sing the praises of the Scott Classic Catalogue, my choice for a desert island.

It's pretty widely acknowledged that philately, in addition to being the king of hobbies and the hobby of kings, is remarkably educational. Perhaps the best thing about its educational aspect is that it's an unsought consequence of a pastime that is enjoyable in and of itself.

One's parents may rejoice to see their offspring with a magnifier in one hand and a pair of tongs in the other, knowing that the little darling will merge knowing more for the hours spent in this fashion. But what little darling ever picked up tongs out of a desire to increase his or her store of knowledge?

We collect stamps because it's fun. And, while we're busy having fun, we get an education in spite of ourselves.

A few years ago, Robert Fulghum climbed high on the bestseller lists with *All I Really Need to Know I Learned in Kindergarten*. The book's a good one, but in my own case I can't think of more than two things I learned in kindergarten. (One was how to make the number 9 correctly, and the other was how to skip. And I learned both of these indispensable skills outside of the classroom. My mother taught me, after Miss Ruth and Miss Joette got nowhere. I never did get very good at skipping, but I can make 9s to this very day.)

Well, all *I* really need to know I learned in the Boy Scouts, or by collecting stamps. And through philately I also learned no end of things I probably don't need to know, but my life is richer for knowing them.

An obvious example: I can name the presidents in order. I never set out to memorize their names or the order in which they served, but I collected the U.S. Presidential series of 1938, and absorbed the information effortlessly. This bit of knowledge, I should add, is hardly mine alone. I know quite a few people who share it. Every last one of them, I might add, is a fellow philatelist.

But let's open the Classic Catalogue and see what it has to tell us.

Shall we consider Latvia? My book just fell open to that page, so let's take advantage of serendipity. And what does my catalogue have to tell me about Latvia?

Well, it's in northern Europe, bordering on the Baltic Sea and the Gulf of Riga. It's known also at Lettonia and Lettland, has an area of some 25,000 square miles and a population, in 1939, of just under two million. It was then an independent republic, and its capital was Riga.

And we read: *Latvia was created a sovereign state following World War 1 and was admitted to the League of Nations in 1922. In 1940 it became a republic in the USSR.*

In 1918, the unit of currency was the Rublis, consisting of 100 Kapeikas. It was supplanted in 1923 by the Lat, which consisted of 100 Santims.

Now I might come across this information in any article on the subject, and I rather suspect my eyes would glaze over if I did. And the fact that it appears at the beginning of the Latvia section of my catalogue doesn't mean I'll necessarily study it closely and commit it to memory, and why should I?

But it's there, and my eyes will scan it now and then, and some of it will soak in. When mounting a stamp, I'll glance at the catalogue to find out what the Ks and Rs stand for. If I think about it, I might realize that the Kapeika is clearly a Latvian equivalent of the Russian Kopeck, while the Rublis is a remake of the Ruble. The 1923 currency change, then, would amount to an assertion of the new national identity, with the Lat replacing the Russified Rublis.

(And all of that is a connection I myself didn't make until just now, as I was writing this piece. But the information was right there all along, waiting for me to require it.)

It's evident that suitable paper was in short supply when Latvia achieved her independence. The earliest issues were printed on the backs of German military maps. "Values given are for stamps where the map on the back is printed in brown and black," we are told. Maps printed only in black are worth three times as much, while stamps with no printing at all are even more valuable. A later issue, Scott 63, was printed on the backs of unfinished 5 Rublis bank notes of the Workers and Soldiers Council of Riga, while Scott 68–9 used unfinished bank notes of the government of Col. Bermondt-Avalov "and on the so-called German 'Ober-Ost' money."

Now that's the sort of factoid that can send one rushing off to Google and Wikipedia. It had that effect on me, and I learned that Bermondt-Avalov, a Cossack warlord, led an army "which was meant to go to fight the Bolsheviks in the Russian Civil War, but, believing that communists would be defeated without his help, Pavel Bermondt-Avalov decided to strike against the newly independent nations of Lithuania and Latvia instead." And I'll spare you what I learned about the Ober-Ost currency, because we don't have Internet access on our desert island, so some of our catalogue's revelations will leave us wishing for more.

And the catalogue does tell us a bit more about Bermondt-Avalov. Toward the end of the Latvian section, we find first Scott 1N1–13, stamps of Germany overprinted "LIBAU" for use in German-occupied Latvia. And next we have Scott 2N1–36, issued under Russian occupation, with the note that the stamps "were issued at Mitau during the occupation of Kurland by the West Russian Army under Col. Bermondt-Avalov."

Kurland? Where did Kurland come from?

No Internet? No Google and no Wikipedia? No problem! A note after a Latvian commemorative issue of 1919–20, Scott 64–7, informs us that the stamps (which show a warrior slaying a presumably allegorical dragon) were issued "in honor of the liberation of Kurzeme (Kurland)." And, if we consult the catalogue's index, we're referred to Lithuania 1N1–12, where a note advises us that the stamps were used in the former Russian provinces of Suvalki, Vilnius, Kaunas, Estland, Lifland . . . and, yes, Kurland.

It's hardly a revelation that Latvia's stamps have a lot to tell us about the nation's history and culture. But sometimes the stamps require a word from the catalogue. Consider the 1932 semipostal issue, B82–6; just looking at the stamps, one would be hard put to know what was going on. The catalogue tells us what we're being shown: Kriva telling stories under the Holy Oak, enslaved Latvians building the city of Riga under a knight's supervision, Lacplesis the Deliverer, the death of the Black Knight, and the spirit of Lacplesis hovering over Riga. Another note translates the inscription "Aizsargi" as "Army Reserve," and we're told also that the semipostal's surtax aided the Militia Maintenance Fund.

Want more? Turn to Russia, and consider the back of the book issues designated L1–12. These are local stamps, issued from 1862 to 1884 for Wenden. And what, pray tell, is Wenden? Why, it's a former district of Livonia, a province of the Russian Empire, which became a part of Latvia under the name of Vidzeme.

Of course, while we're reading about Wenden (and thus Livonia, and Vidzeme), it's almost impossible not to move to the next entry for stamps issued under the 1919 Finnish occupation of Russia; they consist of Finnish stamps overprinted "Aunus," which turns out to be the Finnish name for the Russian town of Olonets. And next we have General Nicolai Yudenich's Army of the Northwest, and then the Army of the North, and—

One book for a desert island? In the main, I'd just as soon stay where I am. I like having my stamps close at hand, and I'd miss my Internet connection. But if I had to be stuck out there in the middle of the ocean, with only a single palm tree for company, and if I were limited to a single book, well, my Scott Classic Catalogue is the one I'd pick.

All right, Arnold. What is it?

I was just wondering, sir. The Scott Classic Catalogue *is published by the same people who pay you to write your column. Wouldn't you call that a conflict of interest?*

No, Arnold. I'd call it a happy coincidence.

25

MAINTENANCE

When Hurricane Irene was tearing up North Carolina's Outer Banks toward the end of August, I found myself remembering my own visit to those barrier islands in 1975. I spent the month of September in a motel in Rodanthe, and when I wasn't in my room writing short stories I was out on the long pier, pulling fish out of the Atlantic. I never went hungry, and those short stories are still in print, so is it any wonder I remember the time fondly?

September was an interesting time of year on the Outer Banks. The summer tourist season was over, but the motels and campgrounds got a heavy play from people who came for the fishing. There were some sport fishermen, chartering boats or casting from the shore. There were some idlers like me, enjoying the experience of living on what we caught.

But most numerous were the farm families, for whom a couple of weeks at the shore amounted to a working vacation. Their crops were in, and they had a respite from field work, but that didn't mean they could go off and lie in the sun. Instead they'd line the pier from sunrise to sunset, catching all the spot and croaker they could, gutting and cleaning and filleting their catch at the day's end, and filling the ice chests they'd brought with them. By the time they headed back west to their tobacco farms, they'd have caught the fish they'd be eating all winter long.

Arnold, did you want to say something?

I was just making an observation to Edna, sir.

Would you care to share it with the class?

I just said, "Wait for it."

Wait for what?

The connection, sir. Between farmers and fish and philately. I know you're going to draw one, sir, and I wanted to reassure Edna on that point.

I see. Your faith is comforting, Arnold.

And, as it happens, I was getting there. Around the time I found myself recalling those days on the Outer Banks, I myself had recently returned from Columbus, Ohio, where it was my pleasure to attend the American Philatelic Society's stamp show. I arrived Thursday afternoon and flew back on Sunday, and I can't tell you what the weather was like in Columbus that weekend because I never set a foot outdoors. There was a passageway from my hotel to the convention center, and I crossed it many times coming and going, but that was the extent of my explorations. If I wasn't in my room or at a restaurant, I was looking at stamps.

It struck me that I was displaying much the same single-minded devotion to the task at hand as did those farmers on the pier in Rodanthe. They spent their days filling their ice chests, while I spent mine filling in the gaps in my stamp collection.

And, while there was a certain amount of work involved for both of us, there was pleasure and satisfaction as well. Those autumn anglers obviously enjoyed catching fish, and not just because they'd get to eat them at some later date. They enjoyed the act of fishing, even as I enjoyed searching through boxes of stamps and selecting the ones I wanted.

Then I went home and spent the next ten days or so adding my purchases to my collection, and I suppose the folks from western North Carolina performed some equivalent task to keep their catch in good shape until they were ready to fry it up and put it on the table. I can but hope they enjoyed it as much as I did.

And the next season, for them and for me, is the season of Maintenance.

Now I don't know just what tasks occupy a farmer in the interval between harvest and planting, and I don't feel a need to enlist Google and Wikipedia in the service of what's no more than a metaphor to begin with. So let's just assume that our farmer, his annual fishing trip over, will devote the next couple of months to repairing his tools and mending his fences and all those endless chores that come under the heading of maintenance.

Well, the metaphor holds. Because as a stamp collector I'm also required to devote time and energy to maintenance. And, while it's less seasonal (because my hobby is after all a good deal less dependent than agriculture upon weather) there does seem to be a seasonal component to it. And my time of year for philatelic maintenance is fast approaching.

For me, you see, it's often tied to the appearance of the new edition of the Classic Catalog.

Yes, Rachel?

Sir, would that be Scott's Classic Specialized Catalogue of Stamps & Covers, 1840 to 1940?

Well, that's it's full name, Rachel. I hadn't felt the need to be quite so formal, but I'm glad to see you're able to reel it off like that.

It's the book you were talking about at our last class, sir. You said it would be the book you'd want to have with you on a desert island.

I did say that, didn't I?

Is that what you do in the winter, sir? Do you pack up your catalog and go to a desert island? Just you and the book and a palm tree?

No, actually—

I hope you remember sunscreen, sir.

I'm not going anywhere, Rachel. But this may be the year I buy a new Classic Catalog. It comes out in November, you see, and I could buy a new volume every year, as some collectors do. The subject doesn't change from one year to the next, because it's always limited to the same one hundred years worth of stamps, but the book grows every year as the editors expand their coverage of varieties, note more shades as minor varieties, add listings of covers and valuations for never-hinged stamps, and even find whole new categories of stamps to include.

Arnold, what do you know about Western Hungary?

I'm pretty sure it's located to the west of Eastern Hungary, sir.

That's a safe guess, Arnold, but can anybody tell us anything about Western Hungary as a philatelic entity. Paula, I haven't seen your hand in quite awhile. What do you know about Western Hungary?

Not too much, sir. Just that after the First World War, the Trianon Treaty of 1920 specified that four German-speaking districts of western Hungary be transferred to Austrian administration. Three of them joined Austria as the province of Burgenland.

That's correct, Paula.

Thank you, sir. The fourth district included the city of Sopron, where Hungarian militia resisted incorporation into Austria. In December of 1921, a plebiscite was held, and the citizens of the province, even though they were mostly German speakers, voted two-to-one to remain a part of Hungary.

And as far as stamps were concerned—

I was getting to that, sir. For three and a half months before the plebiscite was held, Hungarian partisans issued stamps for use in the territory under their control. There were 88 regular postage stamps issued, plus nine postage dues. Most of these were overprinted Hungarian stamps, but one set of eleven stamps, Scott 67–77, bears original designs, and the legend "LAJTABÁNSÁG POSTA." I'm not sure if I pronounced that correctly.

It sounded fine to me, Paula.

Oh, and there was also an unissued set of six stamps showing an eagle.

It's worth noting that two of the Lajtabánság stamps show Pal Pronay, the White Guard leader who seized control of the province. The Banat of Leita was the name he gave it, so that's probably where the name Lajtabánság come from. Pronay, if Wikipedia is to be believed, was a rabidly anti-Semitic terrorist, and the plebiscite voting may not have truly represented the wishes of the local populace.

But that's beside the point, which is that these stamps existed for almost ninety years, and were well known to Hungarian specialists, before the decision was made to list them in the Classic Catalog. At some point I began to see stamps of Western Hungary offered for sale in dealers' ads, and looked in vain for them in my catalog.

When I bought a new 2009 catalog, Western Hungary was to be found at the end of the Hungarian occupation listings. It had already appeared in at least one earlier edition, as I confirmed by checking the section in front that lists recent additions and deletions. 2009 saw the addition of 52 Canadian Air Post Semi-Official stamps, and an impressive lot they are—but the Hungarian section held nothing new.

And what has this to do with maintenance?

First of all, there's a big reason I don't buy a new catalog every year, in addition to a reluctance to spend the money. You see, I use my catalog as an inventory of my collection; whenever I add a stamp, I circle its number in red.

This works quite well. When I'm at my desk, working with my stamps, my catalog is certain to be there with me. And when I leave home on philatelic business—to drop in on a dealer or visit a stamp show—my catalog takes up residence in my backpack. (Each year it adds pages, 23 of them in 2009 alone, and I can only assume that 2012's total will substantially exceed the 1188 pages of 2009. So each year my backpack gets a tiny bit heavier.)

But whenever I buy a new catalog, I have to transfer all that personal information from the old volume to the new one. And I have to do it carefully and accurately, or I risk buying a stamp I already own, or passing up one I need. It is, to be sure, no backbreaking chore. I can do it sitting down. But merely contemplating this particular task leads me to envy that farmer, sharpening his scythe and mending his fences.

It sometimes occurs to me that there might be a better way to maintain my inventory—on my computer, say. All I would need to do is keep a running list of all the stamps I need; whenever I acquire a new stamp, a single keystroke would delete it from the list.

If I did this, I wouldn't need to schlep my catalog to stamp shows and on road trips. (One of my most harrowing philatelic experiences occurred on a book tour five or six years ago, when I brought my catalog along on the off chance that I'd visit dealers along the way, or want to buy stamps from online dealers. I left the book in one motel room and drove two hundred miles before I realized it was missing; I called the motel, spoke to the manager, couldn't persuade the moron to have someone check the room, and drove all the way back wondering what on earth I would do if the thing was gone. It was there, right where I left it, but what a nightmare until I laid hands on it!)

With a computerized list, I could print out as much or as little as I wanted and tuck a few sheets of paper in my pocket. And maybe I'll try it that way. But not just yet.

Because there's data I've entered in my catalog, data I duly transfer to each new volume, that I might find difficult to add to a computerized list. My set of albums, the Brown Album Reproductions, is capricious in respect to which minor varieties it does and does not provide spaces for. It omits most shades but includes a few, has spaces for most errors of color.

(There's even a designated spot for Sweden 1a, the unique 3 skilling orange. A VW Beetle I once owned had a wildly optimistic speedometer dial showing 120 miles per hour as its top speed. That car was a lot more likely to hit 120 than I am to own Sweden 1a.)

While I don't let my album make all my philatelic decisions for me, it does play a role. All things being equal, I'm more apt to spend a few dollars on a die variety or a shade if there's a space waiting for it. So whenever I become aware that my album has made room for a particular minor variety, I put a blue mark beside its listing.

And whenever a stamp I own is sufficiently damaged to constitute a blot on the landscape, I'll note it in my catalog as a candidate for replacement. One way or another, there's a lot of information in my catalog besides what was there when I bought it—and all of it has to be transferred from one volume to its successor.

It's all part of a very enjoyable hobby, so I really can't resent the hours I'm forced to devote to maintenance. And, while the task itself is tedious and essentially mechanical, in the course of performing it I acquire a fuller sense of the scope of my collection, of what I have and what I don't have. At the same time, I become familiar with the new catalog itself, its price changes and expanded listings.

So all in all—yes, Seth? Did you have a question?

It's not really annual maintenance, is it, sir? Not if you only buy a new catalog every two or three years.

That's quite true, Seth. But that's just catalog maintenance. We haven't even talked yet about album maintenance.

Album maintenance? You mean like changing the oil and rotating the tires?

Not exactly, but if I'd done those things for that Volkswagen Beetle, maybe it would have hit 120 mph after all. There are enough aspects to album maintenance to warrant giving it a column of its own, but I'll give you one quick example because it ties in with those stamps Paula was telling you about, the ones from Western Hungary.

I like the Hungarian occupation issues, and I have a general fondness for the stamps of post–World War One plebiscite territories, so as soon as Western Hungary came to my attention I began to acquire some of its stamps. I now have 27, none very costly and most of them quite inexpensive. (There are, as Paula has pointed out, 97 major varieties in addition to the unissued set. There are also a great many inverted overprints, which don't interest me, and one surcharged issue, 10 korona on 15 filler, upon which the surcharged value is "01" instead of "10". That one actually might interest me, were it to catch me in the right frame of mind.)

And where are these 27 stamps of mine? Why, they're in an envelope, waiting for me to create space for them. I'll have to lay out pages for all of Western Hungary, three or four pages should do it, and then I'll need to mount the ones I own, and then I'll have to disassemble the album that holds my Hungarian stamps and put it back together with the new pages included.

I'll tell you, I get out of breath just thinking about it. And it's just one item on a long list under the heading of album maintenance.

But it's something we'll have to consider next month.

ALBUM BULGE AND OTHER AFFLICTIONS

Good morning, boys and girls.

Good morning, sir.

Today I think I'll talk about the way we tend to compromise our standards on condition on the very stamps where it's most important. Just the other day I picked up an unused example of Scott 5, the 2 groschen ultramarine, imperial eagle with small shield, from Germany's first issue of 1872.

It's nice looking, but it has some serious thins, and while I'm by no means fanatical about gum or centering, I've always avoided buying thinned stamps. I'd never have given the purchase any consideration if the stamp had a catalog value of ten dollars, or even a hundred dollars, but it's listed in my catalog at $1350, and—Arnold, why are you waving your hand in the air?

I was hoping to get your attention, sir.

You seem to have succeeded. What is it?

Sir, would that be the 2009 Scott Classic Specialized Catalogue of Stamps & Covers?

It would. Why?

Well, sir, at our last meeting you were talking about replacing that catalog with the new one. And you told us all the maintenance that was required of you when you bought a new catalog, transferring the inventory of your catalog from the old book to the new one.

I'm not doddering, Arnold.

Certainly not, sir.

I'm capable of remembering what I say from one month to the next.

Yes, sir. So of course you remember that you promised to talk to us this month on another aspect of philatelic maintenance, specifically album maintenance.

I did, didn't I.

So I was just wondering how buying a thinned copy of Germany #5 would lead into a discussion of album maintenance. Sir.

Hmm. Well, Arnold, I could say that, if all my stamps sported thins in the manner of my latest acquisition, album maintenance might be a good deal simpler. And that should serve to lead us to the central element in the whole world of album maintenance.

And that, of course, is the dreaded condition known as Album Bulge.

Album bulge! The phrase alone leaves the seasoned philatelist with a dry mouth and a fluttering pulse. It's the state one's stamp albums achieve in the ordinary course of things, simply because one's collection grows.

And it always comes as something of a surprise, and even a shock. I tend to think of stamps as two-dimensional entities, and forget that they have depth as well as height and length. There are, of course, thick and thin paper varieties of some issues, but even the thickness of a thick-paper stamp doesn't seem like something one needs to take into account.

> *Little drops of water,*
> *Little grains of sand,*
> *Make the mighty ocean*
> *And the beauteous land . . .*

So wrote Julia Carney in 1845 (and if you want the rest of the verses, Google will surely supply them). Well, I'm here to tell you that little squares of paper will as surely have a cumulative effect as will those ambitious drops of water and grains of sand. Add stamps to an album and the album will inevitably expand in girth.

My own albums, the reprinted Scott Brown Albums covering philately's first century, have spaces for stamps on only one side of the page. Most albums for general collectors are designed to have stamps mounted on both sides of each page, and I suspect album bulge would occur more rapidly with such an album.

It's rapid enough with mine. While I don't mount stamps on the backs of the pages, I'll attach the occasional expertization certificate there, so that it's conveniently facing the stamp it calls genuine. And any space I save by using just one side of the page is more than offset by the fact that every stamp in my collection is housed in a mount.

Rachel, you look concerned.

Sir, every stamp? You put every single stamp in a mount?

That's right.

Even the cheapest ones? Even stamps with no gum?

I like the way they look in the black-backed mounts, Rachel. And I figure if a stamp's not worth the trouble and expense of a mount, then why am I bothering to collect it?

That's an admirable attitude, sir.

Thank you, Rachel. I'm glad you see it that way. Others, I'm sure, would see it as evidence of obsessive-compulsive disorder. Arnold, did you just put your hand up?

I took it down, sir, when you took the words right out of my mouth.

I see.

Well, then. Over the course of time, stamps added to an album expand its girth. My album pages are housed in Scott International binders, which in turn fit neatly into the slipcases designed for that purpose.

Or at least they did originally. As the albums expand, it becomes difficult to slip them in and out of their cases. Eventually it becomes impossible.

It's very easy to postpone dealing with album bulge. Procrastination has been defined as the gentle art of keeping up with yesterday, and I have to say it comes naturally to a philatelist. When the overwhelming bulk of the stamps I seek were issued before I was born, I have all I can do just to keep up with the distant past.

The first time album bulge made itself known, I knew right away what I would have to do about it. I'd have to get one or two additional binders, with slipcases to match, and I'd have to move pages from binder to binder; without adding any pages, my collection would occupy more albums and take up a few more inches of shelf space.

You'll note that it took me just one paragraph to say that. I knew, though, that actually doing it would take a good deal longer, and that it would be a thankless task that, based on past experience, would almost certainly involve a great deal of vituperative language.

I've found, too, that putting things off sometimes leads to their resolving themselves. Leave a letter unanswered for a couple of months and there comes a time when answering it is pointless; one can safely run it through the shredder.

How did that work for you, sir?

Not well, Edna. I told myself I could stand it the way it was, and would deal with it if and when it got worse. So of course it got worse.

And you dealt with it?

No, I found it easier to adjust to it. When an album bulged sufficiently to render it incapable of fitting into its slip case, I retired the slipcase to a closet and shelved the album uncased.

So I guess that solved the problem.

Not at all. It added the extra dimension of exposed and thus unprotected albums, sitting on the shelf where dust could get at them. Meanwhile, of course, I went on buying stamps, and the albums expanded surely if imperceptibly, and the problem got worse instead of better.

Eventually I had to deal with it. I bought two new binders and two new slipcases, and by the time I was done, what had stuffed ten binders to overflowing now fit quite properly into twelve binders, each tucked into its slipcase.

"By the time I was done . . ." That cheerful phrase makes the process sound so much simpler than it was. The hinged-post binders are a pleasure, until the day comes when you have to unhinge the posts and move pages around. Sometimes reinserting the length of wire that keeps the post in place is effortless, while at other times the act seems to require a graduate degree in mechanical engineering.

That was a few years ago. And I've continued to add stamps to my collection, with predictable results. Once again, my albums are bulging. And a couple of the binders are beginning to show the effects of wear and tear, with the covers beginning to separate from the spines. The message is fairly clear. It's time for me to acquire some new binders, time for me to repackage the contents of a dozen albums into fourteen.

I don't have to start today, or even tomorrow. The most overstuffed of my binders still fits its slipcase, though it's an increasingly tight fit. I can wait and allow the problem to grow worse, as it inevitably will. And, if history is anything to go by, I'll very likely hold out as long as I can.

When I do tackle the problem of my bulging albums, I'll have the opportunity to address some other aspects of album maintenance.

If I remember, I'll be able to shift some pages to where they properly belong.

The Brown Albums are a treasure, but by faithfully reproducing the originals, they manage to perpetuate some historic anomalies.

Consider, for example, the stamp-issuing entity of Eastern Rumelia. This autonomous unit of the Ottoman Empire, located in southern Bulgaria, overprinted nine Turkish stamps in 1880, and issued ten more stamps of its own in 1881 and 1884 by adapting a Turkish design.

Then, in 1885, the province revolted against Turkish rule and united with Bulgaria, a union confirmed a year later under the Treaty of Bucharest. Forty stamps (plus minor varieties) appeared during 1885, all of them created by overprinting the Eastern Rumelian issues of 1881 with the heraldic crowned lion of Bulgaria.

All well and good. The stamps are interesting to collect, and many of them are reasonable in price. They're all listed under Eastern Rumelia in my catalog, and that's how they turn up in dealers' lists, and almost anywhere else you might find them.

But not in my album. The first nineteen stamps appear on a page headed *Eastern Rumelia*. The 1885 issues have a separate page, *South Bulgaria*.

Well, that's easily corrected. It took me a while to discover it in the first place. But the day came when I bought a couple of the 1885 stamps and looked in vain for them in what I presumed to be the appropriate place. When they weren't there I consulted my catalog, found "South Bulgaria" preceding the 1885 listings (right above the disheartening announcement that counterfeits of all overprints are plentiful), looked in my album between South Australia and Southern Nigeria, and found the page I was looking for.

I ought to move it. It belongs with the rest of Eastern Rumelia, and all I have to do to put it there is take two albums apart and put them back together again.

Just last week I acquired a very nice example of Eastern Rumelia 29a, and I know it's not one of those plentiful counterfeits because it was accompanied by an expert's certificate. That would have been an opportune moment to move the South Bulgaria page, but I didn't feel I could spare the time.

Yes, Paula?

Sir, won't you be able to shift the South Bulgaria page when you expand from twelve albums to fourteen?

That's my plan, Paula. Unless is slips my mind.

Oh, I'm sure it won't do that, sir.

I hope you're right, Paula. But that's what happened a few years ago, when my albums grew from ten to twelve. I did remember to relocate the South Africa pages from the U volume (for Union of South Africa) to an appropriate place in the S volume, and I remembered a couple of other moves as well, but I didn't remember them all, and Eastern Rumelia was one I managed to forget.

There are other glitches to lay at the door of the Brown Album's publishers. Some stamps are unaccountably missing—Queensland 130–44, for example, the 1907–9 set. (Perhaps the page got omitted from the original Brown Album. Maybe it was left out when the albums were reprinted. Or, possibly, a snafu in the gathering phase of the printing process shorted my album and no one else's. It hardly matters; what's relevant is that I had to make up a page, and take the album apart, and add it.)

There are also pages I could do without. Because the original albums grew over time, with supplements supplied every few years, there are many pages supplied with designated spaces for only one or two stamps. This is especially true for back-of-the-book issues. If a given country issued a postage due stamp in 1928, say, and another in 1932, and a third in 1935, and two more in 1939, my album scatters the spaces for them over four pages. What is it, Rachel?

Couldn't you put them all on one page, sir? And reduce Album Bulge accordingly?

I could, Rachel, and it's an act I could perform without taking an album apart. But I'm a little hesitant to do it. It would, after all, be hard to undo. So we'll see.

My own collecting decisions account for some other album maintenance problems that I can't blame on the album designers. While the Classic Catalogue, like the Brown Albums, stops in 1940, it makes an exception for the British Empire and includes stamps issued through the reign of King George VI (1937–1952). I stayed with the 1940 cutoff for some years, and gradually began picking up post-1940 George VI stamps when I ran across them.

There was usually room for them in the margins of my album pages. The results were not as pleasing to the eye as I may have preferred, but at least they were displayed, and close to the right page if not precisely on it.

I'd been avoiding the omnibus issues—the Peace issue of 1946, the Silver Wedding and UPU issues of 1949. Then a dealer offered the complete Peace issue as a lot, at a decent price, and I scooped it up. And set it aside while I figured out what to do with it. Should I find room for each pair of stamps on the exiting pages? Add pages to each Commonwealth member for these and other post-1940 stamps? Or would I be better off with an entirely separate section just for the Peace issues, keeping them all in one spot?

While I was mulling this over, an auction offered the full set of Silver Wedding issues, a pricier proposition than the low-priced Peace set. I already had some of these, but not too many, and I adjusted my bid accordingly, and won the lot. And, a set at a time, I've been picking up the UPU issues as well.

And they're all in a big manila envelope, which may be found in a cardboard carton, while I (a) figure out what to do, and (b) do it. And I know full well that the best thing I can do is make up new post-1940 pages for all of the countries and colonies involved, and mount all of the stamps where they belong, and add all of the new pages to the appropriate albums.

Well, I can't do that until I'm ready to reorganize the albums altogether. If my albums are bulging already—and they are, I assure you—the last thing they need in their present overstuffed state is more pages.

I have to remind myself periodically that stamp collecting is a hobby and a pastime, a leisure-time pursuit. This does not absolve me of the need to take it seriously. Nietzsche defined the true maturity of man as regaining the seriousness one had as a child at play, and if I weren't serious about it I don't imagine it would be much fun.

But it's not a job, and I don't have to punch a time clock. If my albums bulge, if an imaginary line separates Eastern Rumelia from South Bulgaria, if half my stamps of George VI (for whom I feel a special fondness after watching *The King's Speech*) repose for now in a box in the closet, well, so what?

Album maintenance is something that has to be done sooner or later. But it's not like automobile maintenance, neglect of which can lead to brakes failing or an engine seizing or any number of awful eventualities.

And I'll get around to it sooner or later . . .

27

ALL PHILATELY IS LOCAL

It was Tip O'Neill who famously observed that "All politics is local." The influential Massachusetts congressman was underscoring the fact that basic bread-and-butter issues and direct personal relationships are as important on Capitol Hill as in the Fourth Ward.

Yes, Rachel?

Sir, why did his parents name him Tip?

I don't know that they did, Rachel. They named him Thomas Philip O'Neill, Jr. The fact that he had the same name as his father may have led them to search for a nickname, and the initials might well have suggested *Tip* as a logical choice.

On the other hand, there was a baseball player called Tip O'Neill who played for ten years in the later 19th Century. I've no idea why they called *him* Tip, given that his given name was James Edward O'Neill, while his soubriquet was "The Woodstock Wonder." He was still alive when the future Speaker of the House was born, and might have been enough of a presence in the collective consciousness so that a young boy named O'Neill stood a fair chance of being called Tip. In much the same way, the novelist Elmore Leonard is known as Dutch, so called after a baseball pitcher.

Arnold?

Sir, is Tip O'Neill portrayed on a stamp?

No, I don't believe so. As far as I know, there were only three men honored on U.S. postage stamps who had held the House Speakership—Henry Clay, James Knox Polk, and Sam Rayburn. (Polk, of course, got philatelic recognition because he went on to become the country's eleventh president.) There are no doubt Democrats who would like to see a Tip O'Neill stamp, even as there are surely Republicans who would not, but—

But he's not on a stamp.

No.

Then with all respect, sir, why are we talking about him?

Because I thought his oft-quoted remark might lead us into a discussion of Guanacaste. Edna, what can you tell us about Guanacaste?

Not very much, sir. Guanacaste is a Costa Rican province, located in the northwesternmost part of that country. It's bordered on the west by the Pacific Ocean and on the north by Nicaragua. It covers an area of almost 4000 square miles, and its population is either 69,531 or 264,238, depending on whether you believe the Scott catalog or Wikipedia. Either way, it's the most sparsely populated Costa Rican province. During the Spanish colonial period, Guanacaste was part of Nicaragua, but after independence the populace chose to join with Costa Rica.

Thank you, Edna. As Guanacaste has almost a hundred thousand people in its capital city, my guess is that the figure in the Scott catalog ought to have a 2 in front of it. But we're no more concerned today with population figures than we are with Tip O'Neill. Why is Guanacaste of philatelic interest? Seth?

Sir, they issued stamps. From 1885 to 1889, Costa Rican stamps were overprinted "Guanacaste" for use in that province. My Scott catalog lists over 60 varieties. And here's something interesting.

Oh? Do tell.

Well, evidently Guanacaste was remote and isolated, and the climate made it difficult to keep mint stamps there. So the overprinted stamps were sold at a discount from face value, but could only be used on letters mailed in Guanacaste.

That's very interesting. Yes, Arnold?

I like their reasoning, sir. "These stamps will probably stick together and become useless, so you can have them at a discount." Or maybe someone in San José felt folks in Guanacaste weren't writing enough letters, and wanted to encourage them. Isn't it wonderful, sir, the way philately seems to ask two new questions every time it answers an old one?

It's wonderful, all right. But there are some other points to note about the Guanacaste overprints. They were extensively counterfeited, and one can only assume the counterfeits were philatelic in nature, as it's hard to imagine someone going to the trouble of forging an overprint in order to create a stamp that would be sold at a discount, and only valid in a remote province. Among stamp collectors, on the other hand, the overprinted stamps command a premium, with many of them quite scarce.

A complete collection of Guanacaste stamps wouldn't have much eye appeal for a non-collector. Three designs served for the first 54 stamps, which are distinguished by the font and color of the overprint, and whether it is horizontal or vertical. The stamps of the last Guanacaste series, Scott 55–67, all show the same portrait of the mustachioed President Soto Alfaro, but with different frames. Four of these exist with the province's name misspelled as "Guagacaste."

Does anyone know why they called the place Guanacaste? Rachel?

I don't suppose it had anything to do with guano, did it, sir? And, uh, throwing it?

No, but I like your thinking, Rachel. The province is named for the Guanacaste tree, *Enterolobium cyclocarpum*, also known as the Elephant Ear tree, so-called for the shape of its seed pods. It's the national tree of Costa Rica, and if you're going to have a national tree you almost have to show it on a stamp, but Costa Rica seems to have held off at least until 1940, so you won't find it in my catalog or my collection.

I've found some photos, sir. One of the tree itself, and one showing the seed pod.

Thank you, Shaheen. It's still hard to know where the word "Guanacaste" comes from, but it may have been a native name, though it does have a Spanish sound to it. It was also the name of the capital city of the province, but in 1854 the name was changed to Liberia.

Was it named for the country in Africa, sir?

Well, it could have been, Rachel. That West African nation was first colonized by freed American slaves in 1820, and the Republic of Liberia was established in 1847. The first Liberian stamps weren't issued until 1860, however, six years too late to inspire the change of name on the other side of the Atlantic.

And those first Liberian stamps might leave one wondering where they were from. The country's name appears in small type beneath an idealized female figure, suggesting that either she or the clipper ship behind her is in fact Liberia. The first twenty Liberian issues bear that design, while Scott 21, issued in 1881, says simply "INLAND" and lets it go at that. It wasn't until 1882 that a Liberian stamp made it clear where it was from.

Sir, wouldn't it be nice if the Costa Rican city and the West African country got together? They could proclaim themselves twins, and have an exchange program.

I suppose they could, Paula.

And they could issue one of those philatelic joint issues, too. All philately may be local, but at the same time philately can let us reach out to one another, across both oceans and national boundaries, uniting us in bonds of fellowship.

Rachel, give Paula a tissue, will you? Thank you, Paula, that's a lovely idea, and perhaps the respective governments will take steps in that direction. But meanwhile here we are taking a look at Liberia, and while we are at it we can see another instance of local philately on display.

Sir, I don't believe Liberia issued any local stamps. If they did, my Scott catalog doesn't know about them.

Oh, they exist, Arnold. There are 34 that have a definite local aspect to them, although they're not locals as such. They're listed by Scott as F1–F34, and they're registration stamps, used to frank a registered letter.

They were sold at five post offices in five Liberian cities—Buchanan, Greenville, Harper, Monrovia (the capital), and Robertsport, and the city's name was prominent on each stamp. Indeed, on the first issue of 1893, the city name and "REGISTERED" was the only information the stamp conveyed. (The following year, a surcharge supplied the 10¢ denomination, previously unspecified.) And there was a space where the registration number could be added by hand.

Later issues include the country's name, and omit the space for numbering. But all of Liberia's registration stamps include the name of the locality where they saw use, presumably as an aid in record-keeping and tracking.

The great majority of these stamps are quite reasonably priced. It's only the first issue, F1–5, that gets a little expensive, with mint and used stamps priced alike. F4, the Monrovia stamp, is only $30, but Buchanan is $250, Robertsport $1000, and Greenville and Harper $2250 each.

But let's talk about Greenville.

About Greenville? Is it twinned with Greenville, South Carolina, sir? Or Greenville, Texas, or Mississippi, or Ohio, or any of the many other Greenvilles?

Not that I know of, Paula, but perhaps you can suggest something to them, and a joint philatelic issue might yet be the outcome. No, I thought we might talk about Greenville because in 1903 (F11) and again in 1919 (F16) it was spelled "Grenville."

This was clearly a mistake, as the city, located on the coast some 150 miles southeast of Monrovia, was named after Judge James Green, a Mississippi Delta plantation owner who was among the first to repatriate former slaves to Liberia.

Was it only misspelled on those two stamps, sir? F11 and F16?

A good question, Seth, and one I had some trouble answering. I don't have a copy of the 1893 Greenville stamp, nor do I have a spare $2500 to spend on one, I'm sorry to say. I do have mint copies of all of the 1894 stamps, which vary in color from the all-black stamps of 1893, and are surcharged with the denomination. But, while Buchanan and Harper and Monrovia and Robertsport were all included in the 1894 set, Greenville evidently didn't get the memo. No Greenville stamp was issued that year.

My Scott catalog lists F2 as Greenville, spelled correctly, but illustrates the Monrovia stamp, so the catalog listing isn't necessarily the final word on the subject. I don't suppose it's terribly important in the overall scheme of things, but half the charm of any hobby is its unimportance, and I really wanted to know whether the "Grenville" spelling was an original error ultimately corrected in 1921, or if it was a brief lapse in 1903 and 1919.

I did determine that Grenville was a distinguished name, belonging to several prominent English politicians, including one who served as Prime Minister. The ranks of prominent Grenvilles include military men and an historian, and one Kate Grenville is at present a well-known Australian novelist.

But none of that, so far as I could determine, had anything to do with Liberia. So what do you suppose I did?

You went to the Internet, sir.

I did, and saw for myself, and it's my pleasure to include a photo of Liberia F2, with the city's name correctly spelled. They got it right originally, and someone's mistake in 1903 was repeated in 1919, and then they got it right again.

It's an inspiring story, sir.

I'm glad you think so, Arnold.

And it shows how everything's connected, even when it's local. And how a city named for a Mississippi planter can lead all the way to a woman in Australia. Isn't it marvelous, sir? Isn't it extraordinary?

Indeed it is, Paula. It's philately, at once local and universal, and I think Tip O'Neill would find it all very illuminating. Paula? Get a grip, Paula. Arnold, give Paula your hanky, will you?

28

YOU SAY YOU WANT A REVOLUTION?

In the course of his ground-breaking visit to China, Richard Nixon had a question for his host, foreign minister Zhou En-lai. His aides had prepped him with the information that Zhou was a student of French history, so Nixon floated one over the plate. What, he asked, had been the impact of the French Revolution of 1789 on world history?

Zhou thought about it, smiled. "It's too early to tell," he said.

Isn't that terrific? I love that story, and I've retold it any number of times, and I suspect I'll go on doing so even though I've just learned that it's probably not strictly true. The revisionist conventional wisdom now holds that Zhou understood Nixon to be referring to the Paris student riots of 1968; that was only four years before Zhou and Nixon met, and it really *was* too early to tell what might be the uprising's lasting effects.

But I much prefer it the way I heard it the first time. This French Revolution of 1789? The one that took place almost two centuries ago? And what was its overall impact?

"It's too early to tell."

Arnold, I think I know what you're about to ask. You're wondering what all this has to do with philately.

How well you know me, sir.

So let me ask you a question instead, Arnold. What was the impact upon philately of the 1789 French Revolution?

Let me see, sir. How's this? "The events of 1789 set in motion a chain of events that culminated in the issuance of the first French postage stamps a mere sixty years later."

Seems like a stretch, Arnold. Great Britain's Penny Black preceded the first French issues by nine years. And it's not as though those Ceres heads had been severed by Dr. Guillotin's remarkable machine. Edna?

Perhaps postal history shows an impact, sir. There were no stamps, but surely there would have been stampless covers. Would mail delivery have been delayed?

There may have been less mail to deliver, what with most of the country's literate population suddenly rendered a head shorter. But let's limit ourselves to the first century of postage stamps, shall we?

Now 1889, the centennial year, would have been a perfect opportunity for a commemorative issue, but the French were not to issue their first commemorative stamp until 1923, when the centennial of Louis Pasteur's birth was thus recognized. The first philatelic reference to the Revolution comes on the regular issue of 1900, with several stamps bearing an allegorical representation of Liberty, Equality, and Fraternity—the battle cry of 1789—and others illustrating the Declaration of the Rights of Man.

In June of 1939, for the 150th anniversary of the Revolution, France issued Scott 390, a 90 centime stamp depicting Jacques David's representation of *The Oath of the Tennis Court*, a pivotal event in the early days of the Revolution. The following month, 24 French colonies (but not France itself) issued a five-stamp semipostal set to commemorate the storming of the Bastille, and—yes, Rachel?

Sometimes it was six stamps, sir. Some colonies added an airmail semipostal as well.

And where would we be without knowing that, Rachel?

Less knowledgeable, sir.

Indeed.

Rouget de Lisle composed the stirring *La Marseillaise* in 1782, and two stamps (Scott 309–10) were issued in 1936 to mark the 100th anniversary of his death. And no end of post-1940 stamps are thematically linked to 1789, with such key figures at Robespierre, Danton, and Saint Just portrayed.

But in none of these examples do we see the impact of the French Revolution. The events of 1789 have done little more than provide philately with subject matter.

But imagine, if you will, if the storming of the Bastille had been postponed for a century and a quarter. Imagine the same popular uprising, the same Reign of Terror, the same Napoleonic aftermath, occurring not when it did but 128 years later. What would that have done to the philately of France, and indeed all of Europe?

1789 plus 128 would be—

1917, Paula.

Well, how could you have a French Revolution in 1917, sir? That would put it smack in the middle of the First World War.

Paula, you're absolutely right.

Maybe you could move it up to, oh, 1900. Or hold it off until 1930. That might be interesting, if the French Revolution happened during the Great Depression, but—

I don't think so, Paula. I kind of like the date I selected, 1917. But how could we get all those Germans and Englishmen out of the trenches, to make room for a revolution? I'll tell you what, Paula. Let's head northeast and pace off 1800 miles, and wherever we wind up, that's where we'll have our revolution. Can anyone tell where we'd be? Seth?

That would put us in St. Petersburg, sir.

St. Petersburg. In Florida? Near Tampa and Clearwater?

In Russia, sir.

Ah, *that* St. Petersburg. Now how's that for coincidence, class? Because they had a couple of revolutions there in that very year, one in February and another in October, and the world has not been the same since.

The impact, let it be said, was seismic. And philately felt and recorded it, aftershocks and all.

A look at the stamps of Russia provides quick evidence of the change of government. The portrait series of 1913, marking the tercentenary of the Romanov dynasty, disappeared along with the tsar and his family. In 1918, the Russian Empire was supplanted as a stamp-issuing entity by the Russian Soviet Federated Socialist Republic, which gave way five years later to the Union of Soviet Socialist Republics—the USSR, or, in Cyrillic, CCCP. 1922's surcharged issues show evidence of financial instability and inflation, with the high-water mark reached by Scott 210; the 250-ruble dull violet of the previous year is revalued at 100,000 rubles.

Russian back-of-the-book issues go further to show the impact of the revolution and the civil war that followed it.

In 1919, eight Finnish stamps were overprinted "Aunus" for use in Russian territory under Finnish occupation. The overprint is the Finnish name for a town the Russians call Olonets, the oldest settlement in Karelia. Does that ring a bell? Edna?

Sir, two years after the Finnish occupation, Karelia rebelled against the Soviets. The rebellion didn't last long, but they issued a nice set of stamps in early 1922. And during the Second World War, the Finns took Karelia back and overprinted some more stamps.

Right you are, Edna. Russian back-of-the-book issues also include several sets issued for contingents of the White Army, which seems to have been a collective term for those anti-Bolshevik forces in the field.

Nikolai Yudenich commanded the Army of the Northwest, and almost captured St. Petersburg in 1919. The fourteen stamps issued under his aegis are all overprints of stamps of imperial Russia. Seven other stamps were overprinted but never placed in use, and along with five trial printings, they make for an interesting series.

Counterfeits abound, sir.

So I understand, Arnold, and I wouldn't be surprised if they're every bit as abundant in my own collection. I feel a little more confident about my Army of the North stamps, which don't seem to have been as extensively counterfeited, but on the other hand I've been unable to learn much of anything about them. There were five issued, each with its own original design, and they were in use for the last three months of 1919—though it's unlikely many of them saw postal duty. Most used stamps were canceled to order.

They bear the inscription OKCA, for "Special Corps, Army of the North", but where that army contended, which general commanded its troops, and what fate befell it is something I've been unable to determine.

I tried researching it, sir, and Google just sent me to one stamp site after another. The Army of the North seems to have been entirely forgotten by history—except for philatelists.

Who remember it, Arnold, but have no idea what it is, or where it fought, or what became of it.

We do know a little about General Evgeny Miller, who commanded a White army in the area of Archangel, Murmansk and Olonets. (You remember Olonets, right?) A set of seven stamps was prepared for Miller's army, but the stamps were never issued.

Miller had British support, but the British left in the summer of 1919, and some months later Miller fled to Norway. He moved from there to Paris, where he played a role in anti-communist activity. Then in 1937, Russian NKVD operatives posing as German Abwehr agents lured him to a meeting, drugged him, stuffed him into a steamer trunk, and shipped him back to Russia, where he was summarily executed in 1939.

Well over a hundred stamps were issued under the authority of General Pyotr Wrangel, commander of the White forces in the Crimea. In the fall of 1920, facing certain defeat, Wrangel organized an evacuation en masse to Turkey. The Wrangel issues consist of overprinted and surcharged pre-Soviet Russian stamps, presumably for use by Wrangel's soldiers and the civilian refugees who accompanied them. Few were ever sold to the public, fewer still ever carried letters, and Scott tells us that reprints abound.

Wrangel himself wound up in Belgium, where he died suddenly in 1928.

His family believed that he'd been poisoned by his butler's brother, who was presumed to have been a Soviet agent.

All that in Russian back-of-the-book issues, and we've barely scratched the surface. The Russian Revolution and Civil War were responsible for a profusion of dead countries—the philatelic term for entities which have ceased to issue stamps. Who can tell us about one of them? Rachel?

Transcaucasian Federated Republics, sir. Armenia, Azerbaijan, and Georgia, united to form the TFR in 1923. They began by overprinting eight Russian and five Armenian stamps, then issued seventeen of their own design. And stopped issuing stamps when each became a republic in the USSR.

Some very interesting stamps, too. Ah, I see a whole bunch of hands. Yes, Shaheen?

Before they joined together, each of those countries issued stamps on their own. They all had their first issues in 1919, and continued until they became dead countries in 1923. But here's the thing, sir. They're not dead anymore. With the dissolution of the Soviet Union, all three of them became independent and resumed issuing stamps. Isn't that great?

I do like your enthusiasm, Shaheen. Margo, I haven't seen your hand in a while.

I was thinking about Batum, sir, or Batumi, as it's generally now known. Russian after the Treaty of San Stefano in 1878. Then Turkey took it during the World War, and the British occupied the city from shortly after the 1918 Armistice until July of 1920.

And it was the British who issued stamps.

That's right, sir. The first series consisted of six stamps designed and printed for Batum, and showing a tree. I don't know what kind of tree it is.

I'm not sure we need to know, Margo.

Perhaps not, sir. All the succeeding Batum stamps are overprints. Russian stamps were overprinted "Batum" in Cyrillic, and some of the overprints included the phrase "British Occupation."

Not in Cyrillic.

No, sir. In English. And stamps with the tree design were also overprinted "British Occupation." And then there was a final nine-stamp series in 1920 with the tree design and the "British Occupation" overprint. The stamps are in different colors and denominations from before, and they are known without the overprint, so it all adds up to a fertile field for collectors.

I'll bet it does. And I suppose counterfeits abound, don't they?

It doesn't say so in my Scott catalog, sir. But it wouldn't surprise me if they do. When all it takes is an overprint to turn a common stamp into one with a three- or four-figure value, well—

It's a nasty old world out there, Margo. Yes, Paula?

South Russia, sir.

South Russia indeed. And what can you tell us about South Russia, Paula?

It's in the southern portion of Russia, sir, and—

Who could have possibly guessed?

Well, it's philatelically complicated, sir. General Denikin was in command of the White forces there, and there were different factions, the Don Cossacks and the Kuban Cossacks. One stamp of the Don government, Scott 10, shows Yermak Timofeyevich, the Cossack leader.

How did he get along with Denikin?

They never met, sir. Yermak was wounded while fighting in Siberia. He tried to escape by swimming across the Wagay River, but the weight of his own chain mail dragged him under and he drowned. That was in 1585.

Oh.

Scott 61–71 is known as the Denikin issue, for use in all the areas of South Russia held by his forces, and the inscription reads "United Russia."

Optimistic, I'd say. Seth?

I just realized no one mentioned Far Eastern Republic, sir. Of all the countries that sent troops to Russia after the Revolution, Japan sent the most—70,000, to establish a buffer state in Siberia. After the White leader Admiral Kolchak was killed in 1920, the Red government set up the nominally independent Far Eastern Republic to the east of Siberia's Lake Baikal. In late 1922, as soon as the Civil War ended, it was merged with the RSFSR.

That's the Russian Soviet Federated—

Socialist Republic, sir. The stamps are pretty interesting. The overprinted Russian issues, Scott 2–32, bear an elaborate script monogram that looks like

DBR, and stands for Far Eastern Republic in Russian. And there are some stamps with original designs, and four occupation stamps, Russian stamps overprinted with new values for use by the forces of General Semenov. He'd been occupying Chita, and that city became the capital of the province after his troops were ousted.

Very good, Seth. Did you have something to add, Rachel?

I was just wondering if it was the birthplace of Chita Rivera, sir.

I don't believe so. I have to say you all have done an estimable job here. I'm somewhat surprised that no one thought to mention Siberia, where two different anti-Soviet governments issued stamps. And, speaking of Siberia, the Czechoslovak Legion saw service there, and can boast a very interesting philatelic history. But we're running out of time, aren't we? I so hate to keep you here after the bell . . .

Sir, we wouldn't want to skip over the Siberians, or give the Czech Legionnaires short shrift. Perhaps we could turn our attention to them next time the class meets.

That's not a bad idea, Arnold.

And then we can give them long shrift, sir. Long shrift for the Czech Legionnaires! Doesn't that sounds like a battle cry?

An inspiring one, Rachel. And that will do for now, boys and girls. I'll see you all next month, at which time we can take up the matter of Siberian philately, and the Czechoslovak Legion Post.

Unless you get distracted, sir, and turn the discussion in another direction entirely.

Always a possibility, Arnold. Either way, we'll meet again a month from now.

Keller Comes Up Empty
—From *Hit & Run*

Keller and his stamps had a complicated history.

He'd collected as a boy, which was hardly remarkable. Many boys of his generation had childhood stamp collections, especially quiet introspective types like Keller. A neighbor whose business involved a lot of correspondence with firms in Latin America had brought him a batch to get him started, and Keller had learned to soak them from their paper backing, dry them between sheets of paper towel, and mount them with hinges in the album his mother had bought him at Lamston's. He'd eventually found other sources of stamps, buying mixtures and packets at Gimbel's stamp department, and getting inexpensive stamps on approval from a dealer halfway across the country, picking out what he wanted, returning the rest along with his payment, and waiting for the dealer to send the next selection. He'd kept this up for a few years, never spending more than a dollar or two a week, and sometimes forgetting to return the approvals for weeks on end because other pursuits intruded. Eventually he lost interest in the collection, and eventually his mother sold it, or gave it away, as there wasn't enough there to interest a dealer.

He was dismayed when he eventually found out it was gone, but not devastated, and he forgot about it and went on to other things, some of them more suspenseful than stamp collecting, though less socially acceptable. And time passed and the world changed. Keller's mother was long gone, and so were Gimbel's and Lamston's.

For decades, he rarely thought of his stamp collection unless his memory was triggered by some bit of knowledge he owed to those childhood hours with tongs and hinges. There were times when it seemed to him that the greater portion of the information stored in his head had got there as a direct result of his hobby. He could, without any great difficulty, name all of the presidents of the United States in order, and he owed this ability to the series of presidential stamps issued in 1938, with each president's head on the stamp with a value corresponding to his place in the procession. Washington was on the one-cent stamp, and Lincoln on the 16-cent stamp. He remembered this, even as he remembered that the one-cent stamp was green and the 16-cent stamp black, while the 21-cent stamp, picturing New York's own Chester Alan Arthur, was a dull blue.

He knew that Idaho had been admitted to the union in 1890, because the fiftieth anniversary had been commemorated by a stamp in 1940. He knew that a group of Swedes and Finns had settled at Wilmington, Delaware, in 1638, and that General Tadeusz Kosciuszko, the Polish general who served in the American Revolution, had been granted American citizenship in 1783. He might not know how to pronounce the man's name, let alone spell it, but he knew what he did about him because of a blue five-cent stamp issued in 1933.

Occasionally a memory might turn him wistful, wishing he still had that essentially worthless collection that had filled so much of his time and turned his head into such a wonderland of trivia. But it never occurred to him to try to recapture those days. They were part of his youth, and they were gone.

Then, when the old man started slipping mentally, and when it was becoming clear that he was beginning to lose it big-time, Keller found himself contemplating retirement. He had some money saved up, and while it had amounted to less than ten percent of what he'd eventually have in Dot's online account, he'd managed to sell himself on the notion that it was enough.

But what would he do with his time? Play golf? Take up needlepoint? Start hanging out at the senior center? Dot pointed out that he would need a hobby, and a bunch of childhood memories popped into his head, and the first thing he did was buy a worldwide collection 1840–to–1940, just to get himself started, and before he knew it he had a shelf full of albums and a subscription to *Linn's* and dealers all over the country sending him price lists and approvals. And he'd also spent a surprisingly substantial portion of his retirement fund, so it was just as well when the old man was out of the picture entirely and he could go on working directly with Dot.

When he thought objectively about his stamps, he couldn't avoid concluding that the whole enterprise was nuts. He was spending the greater portion of his discretionary income on little pieces of paper that were worth nothing except what he and other like-minded screwballs were willing to pay for them. And he was devoting the greater portion of his free time to acquiring those pieces of paper, and, having done so, to mounting them neatly and systematically in albums created for that purpose. He put a lot of effort into getting them to look just right on the page, this in spite of the fact that he never intended for any eyes but his to see them. He didn't want to display his stamps at a show, or invite another collector over to have a look at them. He wanted them right there on the shelves in his apartment, where he and only he could look at them.

All of which, he had to admit, was at the very least irrational.

On the other hand, when he was working with his stamps, he was always entirely absorbed in what he was doing. He was expending considerable concentration on what was essentially an unimportant task, and that seemed to be something his spirit required. When he was in a bad mood, his stamps got him out of it. When he was anxious or irritable, his stamps took him to another realm where the anxiety or irritation ceased to matter. When the world seemed mad and out of control, his stamps provided a more orderly sphere where serenity ruled and logic prevailed.

If he wasn't in the mood, the stamps could wait; if he was called out of town, he knew they'd be there when he got back. They weren't pets that had to be fed and walked on a regular schedule, or plants that needed to be watered. They demanded his entire and absolute attention, but only when he had it to give.

He wondered sometimes if he was spending too much money on his collection, and perhaps he was, but his bills were always paid and he wasn't carrying any debt, and he'd somehow managed to accumulate two and a half million dollars in investments, so why shouldn't he spend what he wanted to on stamps?

Besides, decent philatelic material always increased in value over time. You couldn't buy it one day and sell it the next and expect to come out ahead, but after you'd owned it awhile it would have appreciated enough to cover the dealer's mark-up. And what other pastime worked that way? If you owned a boat, if you raced cars, if you went on safari, how much of what you spent could you expect to get back? What, for that matter, was your net return on bottles of Cristal and lines of cocaine?

And so he'd returned to New York for his stamps. There was nothing else to come back for, and ample reason to stay away. If he was a person of interest to the police, in addition to entering his apartment and sealing his bank accounts, they might very well have posted somebody to watch the place on the slim chance that he'd be fool enough to return.

If the cops weren't waiting for him, what about Call-Me-Al? The people who'd pulled the strings in Des Moines weren't willing to sit back and let nature take its course. They'd proved that in White Plains, because it wasn't the old man's chickens that had come home to roost, it was the turkeys on Al's team who'd shot Dot dead and burned the place down around her.

They might have already known his name, and where he lived. If not, they'd have asked Dot, and he could only hope she'd answered right away, and that two quick bullets in the brain were all the punishment she'd been forced to endure. Because she'd have talked sooner or later, anyone would, and in this case sooner was better than later.

But maybe nobody had the place staked out, not the cops and not Al's boys, either. Maybe all he had to do was figure out a way in and out without being spotted by the doorman.

It would probably take two trips, though, or even three. His collection was housed in ten good-sized albums, and the best plan he could come up with, sitting in the movie house in East Stroudsburg with his eyes on the screen, was to load up the oversize wheeled duffel that he'd bought on QVC a few years ago. He had never once used it, it held far more stuff than he ever wanted to drag on any trip, business or pleasure, but the pitchman on the shopping channel had caught him at just the right moment, and before he knew what was happening he'd picked up the phone and bought the damn thing.

You could get four albums in it for sure, and possibly five, and the handle and wheels would enable him to get it to the car. Dump the albums in the trunk, go back for another load—two trips might do it, or three at the most.

There was some cash in the house, too, unless someone had found it by now. Not a fortune, just an emergency fund of somewhere between one and two thousand dollars. If this didn't constitute an emergency he didn't know what did, and he could definitely use the cash, but it wouldn't have been enough to draw him back to the city, not if it had been ten or twenty times as much as it was.

The stamp collection was something else. He'd lost his first collection all those years ago. He didn't want to lose this one.

If anyone was watching the place, Keller couldn't spot him. He spent a full half-hour looking and never saw anybody suspicious. Nor could he find any route into his building that didn't lead past the doorman. The closest thing to a possibility would involve finding a six-foot ladder somewhere and using it to reach the fire escape in the rear, from which he might be able to break into one of his fellow tenants' apartments. He'd have to be awfully lucky to pick an empty apartment, and even if he did, how was he going to get back down the fire escape with a king-size suitcase loaded with stamp albums?

The hell with it. The first thing he did was take off the Homer Simpson cap, which was all wrong for what he had in mind. He might need Homer soon enough, so he didn't just toss the cap but folded it as best he could and put it in his pocket. Then he crossed the street, shoulders back, arms swinging slightly at his sides, and walked right up to the doorman and into the lobby.

"Evening, Neil," he said as he entered.

"Evening, Mr. Keller," the doorman said, and Keller saw his blue eyes widen.

He gave the fellow a quick smile. "Neil," he said, "I bet I've had a few visitors, haven't I?"

"Uh—"

"Nothing to worry about," Keller assured him. "Nothing that won't get itself straightened out in a day or two, but right now it adds up to a lot of aggravation for me and a batch of other people." He dipped a hand into his breast pocket, where he'd put aside two of Miller Remsen's fifties. "I have to see to a few things," he said, palming the folded bills into Neil's hand, "and nobody needs to know I was here, if you follow me."

There was nothing like the air of self-assurance, especially when it was coupled with a hundred dollars. "Sure, and I never saw you, sir," said Neil, with that slight Irish lilt to his speech that was rarely present outside of moments like this one.

He rode up in the elevator, wondering if there'd be one of those seals on his door, proclaiming it a crime scene. But there was nothing like that, not even a paper band assuring him that the apartment had been sanitized for his protection. Nor had anyone changed the locks; he used his key and the door opened. Things were not as he'd left them, he saw that right away, but he didn't waste time on any of the unimportant stuff. He went straight to the bookcase where he kept his stamps.

The albums were gone.

29

IF YOU TURN ME DOWN ONCE MORE I'LL JOIN THE CZECH FOREIGN LEGION

Ah, good morning, boys and girls.

Good morning, sir.

Last month, as I trust you'll recall, we talked about the considerable philatelic fallout of the Russian Revolution of 1917. Overprints for the Finnish occupation, issues of the Army of the North and the Army of the Northwest, short-lived stamp-issuing entities like South Russia and Far Eastern Republic and the Transcaucasian Federated Republics, General Wrangel's overprints for use in exile in Turkey—even as the overthrow of the Romanovs resounded throughout the world, so was its echo heard throughout the shadow-world of philately.

Well put, sir.

Thank you, Arnold. Today we're going to consider further philatelic effects of 1917, some that we didn't have time for when last we met. So let's consider Siberia. What do we know about Siberia? Rachel?

It's vast, sir. It extends east from the Ural Mountains to the Pacific Ocean, and includes most of Northern Asia. And it includes Lake Baikal, the world's oldest and deepest lake, containing around 20% of the world's unfrozen fresh water.

That's interesting, Rachel, not least because it's unusual to find the word *unfrozen* in a paragraph about Siberia. One tends to think of it as an enormous frozen wasteland, but the Russians found it worth colonizing, and moved there in greater numbers with the 1892–1916 construction of the Trans-Siberian Railway.

Just in time for the Revolution, sir.

That's how it worked out, Seth, although I don't suppose anybody planned it that way. After the Revolution, Admiral Aleksandr Kolchak formed a counter-revolutionary provisional government in the Siberian town of Omsk, and in 1919 issued a series of ten stamps by the simple expedient of overprinting Russian stamps of the 1909 series with new values. They're all relatively inexpensive, though used stamps are valued higher than mint ones; there's some question as to whether used copies ever saw actual postal service.

Kolchak evacuated Omsk in November of 1919, and the Red Army moved in. In 1921, elements of the White Army in Vladivostok staged a coup aiming to break away from the Far Eastern Republic. We talked about the Far Eastern Republic last month.

They have that pretty script monogram that stands for Daine Vostochnaya Respublika, sir.

I'll take your word for it, Paula. There were a couple of factions, including what was left of Vladimir Kappel's army, known as Kappelevtsy, and the Cossacks under Grigory Semyonov, known as Semyonovtsy. The two groups despised each other.

Probably because neither couldn't pronounce the other's name, sir.

That might explain it. In July of 1922 they proclaimed a reinstituted monarchy under the Grand Duke Nikolai Nikolayevich Romanov, called for all Russian people to repent for having overthrown the czar, and renamed the territory Priamursky Zemsky Krai.

And did they issue stamps, sir?

If they hadn't, Edna, we wouldn't be paying attention to them, would we?

They issued over fifty stamps, and none of them are cheap. Many run to three figures. The first series, Scott 51—72, consists of Russian stamps handstamped with the initials of "Nikolaevsk-on-Amur Priamur Provisional Government" and, in most cases, new values. The Scott catalog values all of these in mint condition only, noting that no evidence exists that any were ever used as postage.

Next came four stamps of the Far Eastern Republic, with an oval overprint commemorating the first anniversary of the overthrow of the local Bolsheviks. More overprints followed—on stamps of Russia and of Far Eastern Republic, and on a couple of Russian stamps already surcharged in 1919 as Siberian issues. These later issues, Scott 78–118, did see postal use.

But not for long. After the Japanese withdrawal from Siberia, Far Eastern Republic troops quickly retook the province. The Civil War was over.

What was that, Arnold?

Nothing important, sir. Just a little joke.

Oh?

I said, "Save your Confederate rubles, boys. Siberia will rise again."

You did, eh?

It was just a little joke, sir.

Indeed. But let's move on to the stamps of the Czechoslovak Legion, a particularly interesting example of the philatelic fallout of the Russian Revolution.

The Legion, as it happens, was formed well before either of the 1917 revolutions, and had its origins in the desire of Czechs and Slovaks for independence from the Austro-Hungarian empire. There were units fighting in the West under the direction of the French, but it's the troops serving in Russia who had our best interests in mind—and showed as much by issuing stamps.

In 1914, a Czech company was formed as a part of the Russian Army, and its ranks swelled with the addition of Czech and Slovak prisoners of war and deserters from the Austro-Hungarian army. Early in 1917, Thomas Masaryk, destined for the presidency of the future republic of Czechoslovakia, came to Russia and succeeded in establishing the Czech units as an independent Czechoslovak army.

In March of 1918, the Bolshevik government made peace with Germany via the treaty of Brest-Litovsk. They arranged to repatriate the Czech Legion, with its members either going home or continuing the fight in France. Russia's European ports were not safe, so the Czechs were dispatched on the Trans-Siberian Railway, to be evacuated from Vladivostok.

But that didn't work. The Germans put pressure on Leon Trotsky, who re-scinded his offer of safe passage and ordered the Czechs disarmed and arrest-ed. In May the Czech legionnaires revolted, and attempted to fight their way to Vladivostok.

They were fighting against the Red Army, sir?

They were, Edna, and when various Western nations sent counterrevolu-tionary troops to Siberia, the Czechs were enlisted in that effort. The military history gets complicated at this point.

It wasn't that simple to start with, sir.

Good point, Seth. But we don't have to follow all its twists and turns, though if you're interested you might want to explore the topic further on your own.

Did you say something, Arnold?

No, sir.

I could have sworn—

It must have been the wind, sir.

It sounded suspiciously like *Fat chance,* Arnold. But never mind. The mili-tary ins and outs of the affair aside, we can concentrate on what's really import-ant. Who can tell us what that is? Rachel?

The stamps, sir.

Exactly. Battles come and battles go. Stamps endure. And the Czech Legion issues hold much to interest us.

The first stamp, Scott A1, was issued in 1918 and sold for just a few days in Chelyabinsk, the town occupied by the legionnaires when they rose against the Red Army. The 10 kopeck stamp, Russia #78, was overprinted "Czech Post" in Cyrillic characters—but it was withdrawn from sale because they left out a letter, rendering the top line CZESZKJA instead of CZESZKAJA.

Sir, couldn't they get some more Russian stamps and overprint them correctly?

I was wondering the same thing myself, Paula, but I guess they had other things on their minds. The stamp's rare, and the Scott catalogue prices it in mint condition only. The same overprint was also applied to 17 other Russian stamps, but they're regarded as trial printings and were never sold to the public. I suppose the same typographical error that led to the withdrawal of A1 kept the others from ever being placed on sale.

Are they all expensive, sir?

Well, I don't think you're likely to see any of them in a dealer's bargain box. Scott A1 is listed at $2500; its 17 fellows, while mentioned, are neither listed nor priced.

I'd like to own one, sir.

As would I, Seth. Issued stamp or trial printing, an example would find a welcome spot in my collection. But I've steeled myself to the likelihood that it'll never happen.

But I do own nice-looking copies of Czechoslovak Legion Post 1–3. The 25 kopeck stamp shows an urn in front of the cathedral at Irkutsk, where the stamps were printed in December, 1919. An armored railway car appears on the 50 kopeck stamp, perhaps in reference to the revolt of the legionnaires, which was touched off when some of them stopped a Hungarian train at Chelyabinsk and shot a soldier. And the high value, the 1 ruble red brown, shows a sentinel with a rifle.

The printer delivered the stamps, imperforate and ungummed, to the Czech Field Post, where a crackled yellow gum was applied before the stamps were sold. In January, some of those sheets were perforated.

Later on, remainders were shipped—imperforate and ungummed— to Prague. By this time that city was the capital of the new nation of Czechoslovakia, as established under the Versailles Treaty. The remainder sheets were perforated and gummed for sale to collectors, no doubt as souvenirs of a heroic episode preceding the nation's birth.

My stamps, perforated 13-1/4, with gum that is neither crackled nor yellow, can be identified as Prague remainders, valued at $3 for the set of three, or $6 never-hinged.

That's a bummer, sir.

Oh, I don't know, Shaheen. It's hardly a tragedy. The imperfs aren't expensive—$10 each for 1 and 2, and $19 for the high value, and the ones gummed and perforated in Siberia (Scott 1a–3a) are not much more than that. I'd add them if I had the chance, but I'm not unhappy with what I've got. They certainly look good in my album, and bear witness to an interesting historical episode.

There are some very interesting overprints on these Irkutsk issues, and one would love to know where they were applied, and why. One announces: "Packages to the Homeland—50 Rubles," while others proclaim "First Jugoslav Regiment in Siberia" and "Train of the Czechoslovak Red Cross."

Czech Legion Post issues 4–14 are interesting as well. The design, which at a glance reminds one of stamps of Imperial Russia, are blue, with the heraldic lion of Bohemia in a red oval. These stamps were printed in Prague and shipped to Siberia for sale and use there. They bear the date "1919" at the bottom, although they didn't reach the Czechs in Siberia until the following year.

Thus Scott 4 is the stamp as printed, and Scott 5 is the same stamp overprinted "1920".

Though no face value appeared on them, both 4 and 5 were 25-kopeck stamps. This lack was remedied by surcharging copies of #5 with values ranging from two kopecks to one ruble, thereby creating the stamps Scott lists as 6 to 14.

There were three printings, and only the first two were sent to Siberia.

Were they being punished, sir?

Arnold—

Sorry, sir. Just a little joke.

Indeed. The first and second printings differ in color; the first printing stamps (6–14) are steel blue and carmine, the second's (6a–14a) gray-blue and red. The value's the same for both, $35 per mint stamp.

The third printing, which never did go to Siberia, has a deep blue frame and a carmine center, described as heavily inked at the top of the oval. These stamps were produced in Prague well after the Legion's departure from Siberia, and were made for sale to collectors. They're neither listed nor valued in Scott, and a notation explains that examples of this philatelic printing are much lower in price.

Yes, Edna?

Sir, couldn't you say that all of the Czech Legion Post stamps are philatelic? Not a single one of them is priced in used condition, and most of them don't even have that horizontal line in the price column that indicates that they exist, even if a price can't be determined. I get the impression that, aside from favor cancels and forgeries, none of these stamps ever turned up on an envelope.

You may be right, Edna.

So why call the third printing philatelic and list the others as legitimate postal issues?

That's a very interesting question, Edna, and one that applies to far more stamps than ever came out of Prague—or Irkutsk, or indeed all of Russia. Maybe we'll take a closer look at it next month, but right now we're out of time.

Some days it really flies, doesn't it?

That's enough, Arnold.

30

THE LONG FLIGHT OF THE QUETZAL

Good morning, class.

Good morning, sir.

Here's a question to get us started. How far is it from Guatemala to Iceland. Seth?

From Guatemala to Iceland, sir? Uh, would that be from capital city to capital city? In other words, from Ciudad de Guatemala to Reykjavik? Or would you want to know the distance from the northeastern corner of Guatemala's El Petén province, bordering Belize and Mexico, to the southwestern-most point in Iceland, which would be a few miles west of Grindavik?

Either figure will do, Seth.

I make it 4650 miles, sir.

Thank you, Seth. I assume that's as the crow flies. Yes, Rachel?

Sir, I don't think it would be a crow.

Oh?

The national bird of Guatemala is the quetzal, and they're so attached to it that in 1927 they changed their currency unit from the peso to the quetzal. So maybe it should be "as the quetzal flies."

But would it fly all the way to Iceland, Rachel? The avifauna there runs to sea birds—puffins, skuas, and kittiwakes. A quetzal would freeze its tailfeathers off.

I didn't think of that, sir.

And why should you, Rachel? Because I'm looking for a more philatelic measure of the distance from Guatemala to Iceland, involving a route no bird would be likely to choose—and no airliner, either. The distance, I submit, is embodied in a single letter.

A letter, sir?

That's right, Edna. And the letter is H.

Late last year, I bought the 2012 edition of the Scott Classic Catalogue. It has 75 more pages than my 2009 volume, and no end of price changes and new listings. I'm happy to have it, but it means work.

I use my catalog as a checklist, circling in red the number of each stamp in my collection, and indicating with a blue dot those minor varieties for which my albums provide spaces. If my new catalog is to serve me, all of this information has to be copied into its pages.

In certain respects, I welcome this task; it allows me to familiarize myself with the new volume, to refresh my memory of what I do and don't own, and to absorb a little more of the nearly infinite stock of philatelic knowledge within its pages.

But it's work, and tedious work at that. So I do a little at a time. And I skip around—if the mail brings me some stamps from North Borneo, say, when I add them to my album I take a few minutes to transfer all my North Borneo data to the new catalog—and while I'm at it, I might do the same for Northern Nigeria, Northern Rhodesia, North Ingermanland, and North West Pacific Islands.

And Norway, sir?

Norway's already done, Paula. As I said, I skip around. And just the other day I took up my red fineline marking pen, and the catalogue fell open to

Hungary. I'd updated Hungary some time ago, but I paged back and there was Horta, which needed my attention. But I kept on paging back all the way to the beginning of the H's, and do you know what I found?

Just off the top of my head, sir, I'd guess that you found Haiti, Hatay, Heligoland, Honduras, Hong Kong, and Horta.

Right you are, Paula. There they all were, and in precisely that sequence, all through the miracle of alphabetical order.

You think alphabetical order is a miracle, sir?

I'm inclined to think order of any sort is miraculous, but alphabetical order strikes me as particularly wondrous. Numerical order is natural and inevitable, in that the sequence of numbers derives from their value. But for an alphabet to be arranged in a particular order is wholly arbitrary. Why should B follow A and precede C? The letters could perform their assigned task of coalescing into words without occupying specific places in a list.

But very early on some unsung genius put A and B and C (or Alpha and Beta and Gamma, or Aleph and Beth and Gimel) in a particular sequence, and roughly two thousand years ago some other genius realized that the order of the alphabet afforded a perfect way to organize lists. And now, owing to their efforts, I can find the stamps of Hatay after those of Haiti, and before those of Heligoland.

All because of alphabetical order, sir.

Exactly.

Well, after giving thanks to those unacknowledged heroes, I bent to the task of updating my catalog. And, of course, I learned a few things—about these six countries, about their stamps, and about my own collection.

Haiti's first stamps weren't issued until 1881. Before that, however, Great Britain operated post offices in seven Haitian cities, beginning in Jacmel in 1830. Pre-stamp postmarks from 1843 exist for both Jacmel and Port-au-Prince. From 1859 into the 1880s, British stamps were used in both those cities, and can be identified by their cancels—C59 for Jacmel, E53 for Port-au-Prince.

(This information, filling two columns in the 2012 catalog, was not included in 2009.)

Haiti's history makes unsettling reading; it has had one appalling government after another, with earthquakes and other natural disasters added to the mix. The stamps, however, are in the main quite attractive, and easy to collect, with no great rarities and relatively few that are dirt cheap.

And there are some interesting anomalies. On the last day of 1903, Haiti issued six stamps, Scott 82–8, to mark the country's centenary of independence. The catalog notes that they exist imperforate, and that the five bicolored stamps, 83–8, are to be found with the centers inverted, and even omitted altogether.

"Forgeries exist both perforated and imperf," Scott notes, "and constitute the great majority of Nos. 83–88 offered in the marketplace . . . Many forgeries exist with the heads lithographed instead of engraved."

Do you have the set, sir?

I do, Arnold.

Are your stamps forgeries?

I have no idea. Another attractive bicolor set, and one I don't have, was to be issued in 1914. While the stamps were in transit from the printers, a large quantity were stolen. As a result, the stamps were never placed on sale, although a few were canceled "through carelessness or favor." Scott values the set at $8.50, and I'd add it to my collection if the opportunity were to come along.

Haiti had a rare period of stability when the U.S. Marines occupied the country from 1915 to 1934. A 1929 stamp commemorates the signing of the Frontier treaty with the Dominican Republic; U.S. forces had established the boundary by taking land from the D.R., and after U.S. withdrawal, Rafael Trujillo drew up another treaty to reposition the border.

The Dominican Republic commemorated the new 1935 treaty with an issue of stamps, and then celebrated in fine style with the Parsley Massacre; Trujillo's army slaughtered some 20,000 Haitians living on the D.R. side of the new border.

What did parsley have to do with it, sir?

To determine if someone was a native Spanish-speaker, the soldiers would hold up a sprig of parsley and ask what it was. The word in Spanish is *perejil*, and a speaker of French or of Haitian Creole couldn't pronounce it correctly. Isn't your life richer for knowing that, Edna?

Sort of. Did anybody issue stamps for the Parsley Massacre, sir?

Not yet, but 2012 is the 75th anniversary, so perhaps there's time for a joint issue. But I wouldn't count on it.

But let's move on. Seth, what do you know about Hatay?

It's pretty interesting, sir. After the first World War, the treaty of Versailles mandated the Turkish province of Surya to France. As Syria, it remained under French mandate, but Kemal Ataturk found French rule over one portion of Syria to be unacceptable. That part was the Sanjak of Alexandretta, and in 1938 the French separated that portion from the rest and called it "Alexandretta", and issued stamps for it.

And how do we get from there to Hatay?

The French changed the name in 1938, and a year later they handed it back to Turkey. Hatay's first stamp issue, in 1939, consists of overprinted Turkish stamps. Later that year there was a 13-stamp pictorial series, showing the map and flag of Hatay, the post office, and the lions of Antioch. On June 30 of the same year Hatay was formally annexed to the Republic of Turkey, and the pictorial issue was overprinted to that effect.

So the province, taken from Turkey at the end of one war, was returned just in time for the next one. That's interesting, Seth, and—yes, Rachel?

The lions of Antioch, sir. I understand the flag and the map and the post office, but how did your college's football team get onto the stamps of Hatay?

Um . . .

You did go to Antioch College, didn't you, sir? And their football team must be called the Lions.

We didn't have a football team.

Oh.

And the city of Antioch was the capital of Hatay. I'm not sure how the lions got there, but St. Ignatius was the Bishop of Antioch; he was transported to Rome, where he was fed to the lions in the Coliseum. He is usually shown as a bishop surrounded by lions. From the look of the stamp, Rachel, I'd guess that there's a pair of stone lions in Antioch in his honor.

Shall we move on to Heligoland?

That's probably a good idea, sir.

Heligoland's pretty interesting. It's hard to find a philatelist who hasn't heard of it, or anybody else who has. Arnold, what do you know about Heligoland?

I know the song, sir.

The song?

A World War I song, sir. "We'll knock the Heligo-into Heligo-out of Heligoland!"

I don't suppose it got a lot of air play. Seth?

A pair of islands in the North Sea, sir. In 1714 Denmark took it away from the duchy of Schleswig, and a century later, during the Napoleonic Wars, Denmark ceded the island to Britain. Thousands of Germans massed there to form the King's German Legion, fighting Napoleon under the colors of the British king.

And the islands remained British after Napoleon's defeat, but it was largely Germans who came there. It was a tourist resort, popular with artists and writers, and a refuge for German revolutionaries in 1830 and 1848.

That explains a unique aspect of the stamps, doesn't it? The early stamps, issued from 1867 to 1874, are denominated in schillings. From 1875 on, Heligoland's stamps have dual values shown, both British sterling and German marks. If you stopped at the local post office and picked up Scott 14, for example, it would cost you either one farthing or one pfennig. (Scott 16, on the other hand, was valued at three farthings or five pfennigs. Scott 18 is three pence, which is to say twelve farthings, or 25 pfennigs.)

And they didn't even have calculators, sir.

It resolved itself in 1890, with the signing of the Heligoland-Zanzibar Treaty. And no, that wasn't to resolve a border dispute; Germany and Great Britain sorted out various African matters, and while they were at it shifted

Heligoland from British to German hands. It was all handled quite peaceably, too. Parsley didn't enter into it, and nobody got massacred.

Now the overwhelming majority of Heligoland stamps are reprints. They're not counterfeits, they were made from the original dies, and were produced for sale to collectors. Most old worldwide collections have a representation of Heligoland stamps, and they're almost always reprints.

It's possible to distinguish between originals and reprints. The Scott Classic Catalogue has some information, and online sites have a good deal more, and sometimes I look at my own Heligoland stamps and try to figure out what I've got, and after a few minutes I put down my magnifier and close my album and reach for the aspirin. It's easiest to assume they're all reprints and let it go at that.

Oh, dear. Look at the time! And we haven't even touched on Honduras or Hong Kong yet, not to mention Horta. While copying data into my new catalog, I was struck by how spotty my holding of Honduras is; I could fill a lot of spaces at low cost. There are a lot of gaps in Hong Kong, but that country's stamps climbed in price as newly-prosperous Chinese collectors entered the field. As for Horta, a group of four islands in the Azores, I own two-thirds of the 34 stamps, and could own the others without going deeply into debt. But they can be tough to find.

I'd like to leave you with an interesting fact, but I can't seem to think of one offhand, and—yes, Rachel?

I know one about Heligoland, sir.

Oh?

In 1890 a man named Heinrich Gätke published "Heligoland, an Ornithological Observatory" in which he described an astonishing array of migrant birds on the island. The book appeared in English five years later, and was a major influence on British studies of avian migration. Sir?

Yes, Rachel?

Do you suppose he had anything to say about quetzals? Do you think maybe they passed over Heligoland on their way to Iceland?

I think you should investigate the matter, Rachel. Let us know what you find out . . .

31

OF DODOS, LEMURS, PIRATES, AND STAMPS

Good morning, class.

Good morning, sir. It's so good to have you back.

Well, it's good to *be* back, Arnold. Vacations are a pleasure, but there's no place like home.

What a pertinent observation, sir. I'll have to write that down. But may I say we're pleased to have you back safe and sound? You might have been seized by pirates, gripped by malaria, or devoured by lemurs.

But I wasn't, Arnold. Still, that does let everyone know where I spent the past three weeks, doesn't it? Pirates, malaria, lemurs—where would we have had to have been? Rachel?

The San Diego Zoo, sir.

Pirates in San Diego, Rachel?

Let me think, sir. Pirates, pirates. I guess it would have to be the Pittsburgh Zoo, but I don't think they have malaria there. Still, with global warming—

Seth?

The Indian Ocean, sir. With Somali pirates and Anopheles mosquitoes. Lemurs are the giveaway, as they're endemic to Madagascar. My guess is you boarded a cruise ship in Mauritius with stops in Réunion, Madagascar, Mayotte, Ngazidja, and disembarked in Zanzibar.

Quite an itinerary, isn't it? And the common denominator here is that these are all places I knew only through stamp collecting. If you've never heard of Ngazidja, well, neither had I, but it's the largest island in the Comoro group, and has also been known as Grand Comoro. Under that name, it issued 29 stamps between 1897 and 1912.

I don't suppose many of your fellow passengers knew that, sir.

Probably not, Paula. You may recall my discussion of the way travel and philately tend to inform one another. I thought today I might review some of the philatelic aspects of our cruise.

I hope you took plenty of pictures, sir.

Not a one, Paula. We didn't even bring a camera. But let's get to it, shall we? Seth, what can you tell us about Mauritius.

Together with Réunion and Rodrigues, it's part of the Mascarene Islands, a name supplied by Don Pedro Mascarenhas, one of the Portuguese sailors who visited the uninhabited island in 1507. They didn't stay, and the next visitors were the Dutch in 1598. The Dutch didn't attempt to settle the island until forty years later. They gave it a name, Mauritius, in honor of Prince Maurits of Nassau, introduced deer and domestic animals, planted sugar cane, and sailed away after twenty years, their chief accomplishment being the extermination of the dodo.

A large flightless bird, whose name has survived as a label for people who are not terribly bright. I'm not sure that's fair; the bird was doing fine before people showed up, adapting to a predator-free island by giving up flight and adding mass. And it has survived as the national bird of Mauritius, where it shows up on T-shirts, souvenir key chains, and, yes, postage stamps.

Who showed up after the Dutch?

The French, sir. They came in 1715, changed the name to Ile de France, established plantations with slaves imported from the African mainland, and wound up using the island as a base in the Napoleonic Wars with England. Then in 1810 they surrendered the island to the British. Under the terms of surrender, the settlers were allowed to keep their land and property and to continue using the French language. From that point on Mauritius was British, until it became independent. But that didn't happen until 1968, sir, and we know you're not interested in anything that happened after 1940.

That's when my philatelic interest stops, Seth. But let's have a philatelic look at Mauritius. I'll take a moment to mention the "Post Office" issues, Mauritius 1 and 2, as they're high on the list of the hobby's greatest rarities; *Blue Mauritius,* Helen Morgan's remarkable book, tells the whole story.

By the time the first Mauritius stamps appeared in 1847, the currency system had for years been the pounds and shillings and pence of Great Britain. But one effect of British sovereignty was an end of slavery on the island in 1835. Slaveholders were financially compensated and the Creole-speaking slaves emancipated; from that time on, planters brought in indentured laborers from the Indian subcontinent instead—and one result of this was a subcategory of 15 collectible stamps.

By 1878, so many Indians had moved to Mauritius, and so many Indian rupees had come with them, that the decision was made to join Mauritius in a common monetary union with India. The new Mauritian rupee was divided into cents, not annas and pies like its Indian counterpart, and the first stamps in the new currency, Scott 50–58, appeared promptly in 1878.

Not surprisingly, the local post offices had on hand a good supply of the stamps denominated in pence and shillings. There were two perfectly natural things the authorities might have done with them; they could have overprinted them in the new currency, or they could have destroyed them.

Instead they remaindered them, overprinting them "CANCELLED" and selling them for less than face value. I haven't been able to determine just how the sale was managed. My guess would be that they offered the stamps to dealers and collectors in the UK, as it seems unlikely they could have sold many over the counter to postal patrons in Mauritius, but I'm just guessing, and couldn't even guess at the ratio of price to face value. Perhaps one of you could help me out. Yes, Arnold?

I'd be glad to, sir. Which way did you come in?

Ahem. I didn't really expect any of you boys and girls to have the answer, but perhaps there's a *Linn's* reader who does.

It seems worth noting that the Mauritius remainders get more philatelic respect than similar issues from other places. They're listed as mint rather than used, and priced about a third lower than ordinary mint stamps. (Scott 44 and 45 are exceptions; the stamps were never placed in use and are rarities with four-figure price tags, while the "cancelled" stamps are much cheaper, at $325 and $140 respectively.)

Contrast that with the bar-canceled remainders of Labuan and North Borneo; they'd seem to fall in the same category, but instead are regarded as used stamps, and priced below postally used specimens. The same is true of Costa Rica's bar-canceled remainders of 1914; Scott 68, for example, is pegged at $160 mint, $100 used . . . and a mere three bucks with a remainder cancel.

Why is it different for Mauritius, sir?

I don't know, Paula. But maybe one of my readers has the answer. Meanwhile, why don't you tell us something about Réunion?

I'd be happy to, sir. It's just west of Mauritius, and the French settled it in the mid-17th century, at which time they named it Ile Bourbon.

I guess we know what they were drinking.

Probably vin ordinaire, sir. They named the island for the royal house of Bourbon, not the Kentucky whiskey, and the name lasted until 1793, when French revolutionaries changed it to La Réunion to mark an event in Paris the previous year. Then in 1801 the name was changed to Ile Bonaparte, and the British captured it in 1810, and in 1815 the French got it back at the Congress of Vienna. It was Ile Bourbon until 1848, when it went back to being Réunion. In 1942, Free French forces took the island from the Vichy government.

And in 1946, Réunion became an overseas department of France. This was the equivalent of statehood status in the United States, and it had great positive effects on the island's economy and the welfare of its inhabitants, but it meant the end of Réunion as a stamp-issuing entity.

In much the same way, Martinique and Guadeloupe became philatelic "dead countries" with their absorption into the mother country. When the same thing happened to St. Pierre and Miquelon in 1976, the citizenry found themselves deprived of their most reliable industry, the sale of stamps to collectors; in 1985 they successfully petitioned to have their territorial status restored, and resumed printing and selling stamps.

Not Réunion, where the post office will sell you the same French stamps you could buy in Paris. But a near-century of its own stamps gives the island an interesting philatelic history. If you've got a spare $75,000, you can pick up Scott 1 and 2, issued in 1852. (Or you can fill those spaces with the reprints, a bit more affordable at $55 apiece.)

Réunion 3–33 consist of overprinted French Colonies stamps. The denomination plus the initial R appeared on the eight stamps issued in 1885, but in 1891 the colony's name appeared; unfortunately, the overprinters suffered from the worst case of philatelic dyslexia yet recorded. The accent on the É is sometimes omitted, but that's the least of it. Scott lists the following variations on the theme: RUNION, RÉUNIONR, REUNIOU, REUNOIN, RUENION, EUNION, ERUNION, and REUNIN.

Réunion's first airmail stamp, Scott C-1, consists of a 50-centime stamp from the regular issue of 1933 overprinted to commemorate the 1937 flight from Réunion to France of the airplane *Roland Garros*. M. Garros, born in Réunion's capital of St. Denis, was a French aviator and war hero, shot down and killed a month before the 1918 Armistice (and the day before his 30th birthday). In Réunion they've named the airport after him; in France his name survives on the clay courts where they play the French Open tennis tournament.

But let's move on. From Réunion, our small ship sailed on to Madagascar, and—yes, Rachel?

What about Rodrigues, sir? Seth said there were three islands in the Mascarenes, and you went to two of them. Did you get to Rodrigues?

No, I'm afraid we didn't. A couple of our shipmates paid a pre-cruise visit to Rodrigues. One was a Travelers Century Club members eager to check another country off her list, and the others were birders hunting for endemic species.

Does Rodrigues issue stamps, sir?

They're a semi-autonomous region of Mauritius, Rachel. And no, they've never had their own stamps.

And you didn't pay them a visit. Coincidence, sir?

It never occurred to me. I'm a TCC member, and might have made the trip if I'd thought of it, but I didn't. Of course you could argue that philatelic familiarity with Rodrigues might have made me more aware of it, and while I was there I might have had a glimpse of the Rodrigues Warbler or the Rodrigues Fody, both of them endangered—

But not the Rodrigues Solitaire, sir. It was a flightless pigeon the size of a swan, and a close relative of the dodo. And I'm afraid it's long since lost the battle with extinction.

That's true, Edna, and I regret the loss, but its role has been largely subsumed by the Computer Solitaire. Can we move on?

Thank you.

We'll move to Madagascar, a long narrow island off the east coast of Africa. It's sometimes called the Eighth Continent. Shaheen, would you happen to know why?

Because it sort of is, sir. It separated early on from Gondwanaland, the protocontinent of the southern hemisphere, and drifted to where it is now. That was before mammals evolved, and it explains why all the mammalian species on Madagascar are endemic.

Lemurs, for example.

And the fossa, and the tailless tenrec. Most of the reptile and insect species are found nowhere else, and the same is true of most plant species. In terms of its biodiversity, it's about as different from every place else on earth as is Australia.

Thus the Eighth Continent. Well, it's pretty interesting philatelically, too. After a day at sea, devoted to lectures and the consumption of great quantities of food, we made our first landing at Ile Ste. Marie. Does that ring a philatelic bell with any of you?

Sainte-Marie de Madagascar, sir. They issued thirteen stamps of the French colonial Peace-and-Commerce design in 1894. Then two years later they were re-placed by Madagascar stamps, and Sainte-Marie de Madagascar became a dead country.

Quite right, Paula. But Ile Sainte-Marie had an interesting history well before Rowland Hill thought up the Penny Black. For thirty-five years, from 1690 to 1725, it was a hotbed of piracy. It had all the requirements for that pastime—a good harbor with sheltered bays and inlets, proximity to rich shipping routes, and no strong local government to speak of. Pirates, mostly English, lived on an island in the bay and preyed on merchant ships, selling their wares in the American colonies. There are sunken pirate vessels in the bay to this day.

And, if it ever existed, the utopian pirate republic of Libertalia was in or around Ile Sainte-Marie. It's supposed to have been founded during those years by one James Misson, and was all written up in *A General History of the Pyrates*, by one Captain Charles Johnson. But the good captain may well have been a pen name of Daniel Defoe, and the book seems to be at best a mixture of fact and fiction. He may have invented Libertalia out of the whole cloth.

It's a shame they didn't issue stamps, sir.

It is, Arnold.

And I don't suppose Gondwanaland had stamps either.

I'm afraid not. But just the other day I saw a bumper sticker that read *Reunite Gondwanaland!* Now isn't that a cause to stir the blood? And if it ever happens—

You'll be first in line at the post office, sir.

Well, one of the first. But we're out of time, class, and we've only made our first landing in Madagascar. We'll get to the rest of the trip next month.

32

A SLOW BOAT TO ZANZIBAR

Good afternoon, boys and girls.

Good morning, sir.

Oh, is it morning still? It's hard to keep track when one keeps crossing time zones. When last we met, we were talking about Ile Sainte-Marie, known in the philatelic community as Sainte-Marie de Madagascar. It was, as you'll recall, the first place our ship landed in after we sailed from Réunion.

Our ship, sir?

Well, my ship, then. Mine and my wife's, and around a hundred fellow passengers on the *Clipper Odyssey*. The French issued thirteen Sainte-Marie de Madagascar stamps in 1896, some two centuries after the island served as a base for pirates.

And it may have been the legendary Pirate Republic of Libertalia.

Quite right, Rachel. If Libertalia was more than a figment of Daniel Defoe's fertile imagination, if it did in fact exist, Ile Sainte-Marie is where it would have been. But there are a lot of ifs in that sentence, aren't there?

Let's raise our sights from that sheltered harbor to the eighth continent as a whole. Seth, can you give us an overview of the philately of Madagascar?

Gladly, sir. The first Madagascar stamps were issued in 1884 by the British to carry consular mail. Scott lists 58 major varieties, but they're all essentially the same design, with the hand-stamped shield of the British Vice-consulate at Antananarivo. They were gummed in one corner only, and used stamps are frequently damaged at that corner. Many of the stamps are known only in mint condition, and none of them are cheap. The least expensive varieties are just under a hundred dollars, and Scott 57 is valued at $12,000.

Very good, Seth. Antananarivo, we should note, is the sesquipedalian capital of Madagascar, and—yes, Edna?

Just an observation, sir. Sesquipedalian is just that.

I beg your pardon, Edna?

It's an adjective used to describe a word of six syllables, and is has six syllables itself. I thought that was interesting.

Did you. Well, Antananarivo (which the locals generally shorten to Tana) is reasonably concise by Madagascar standards. They had kings named Andriamasinavalona and Andrianampoinimerina, not to mention the long-ruling prime minister, Rainilaiarivony. Madagascar's about as polysyllabic a place as you'll find anywhere.

Early in the 19th Century, British missionaries transcribed the Malagasy language into the Roman alphabet, but neither Scrabble nor crossword puzzles ever caught on in a big way.

Nor did the British, sir. In 1885 the French established a protectorate over the island, and first issued stamps in 1889. Scott 1–7 consist of numerically surcharged French Colonies stamps, similar to the early issues of Senegal. Then in 1891 the French produced half a dozen imperforate ungummed typeset stamps. They have a home-made look about them, and were printed on frail paper. In 1895, stamps of France were overprinted "Poste / Française / Madagascar", and the following year saw the issuance of a Peace & Commerce series, inscribed "Madagascar et Dependences."

That inscription, indicating that the stamps were for use in Madagascar and its dependencies, continued on the country's stamps until 1930. Along with Sainte-Marie de Madagascar, the dependencies in question include Diego Suarez, Nossi-Be, Anjouan, Mayotte, Moheli, and Grand Comoro. The three entities located on Madagascar (Diego Suarez, Nossi-Be and Sainte-Marie) ceased issuing their own stamps upon the emergence of Madagascar's Peace & Commerce stamps; the others, islands in the Comoro group, did not—as we shall see.

If you have a Peace and Commerce stamp, specifically Scott 37, 43, 44, or 46, stuck to a square of cardboard with animals printed on the back, you may want to transfer it to your coin collection; such creations served as emergency coinage in the Comoros in 1920.

Madagascar's first pictorial stamps, Scott 63–77, appeared in 1903, showing three indigenous life forms—a zebu, one of the humped cattle originating on the Indian subcontinent; a Traveler's Palm, so-called because the sheaths of its stems hold an emergency supply of rainwater for the passerby; and an example of the island continent's endemic (and irresistibly cute) primate group, the lemurs.

In recent years, Madagascar postal authorities have had the good sense to make use of their greatest asset, the endemic flora and fauna. Before 1940, however, that first issue was alone in showing a lemur. Another zebu has a supporting role on some stamps of the 1933–40 series, and the only other animal depicted is the horse shown on five stamps of 1931. Astride the horse we may see—

I don't suppose the horse is endemic to Madagascar, sir.

No, Paula. Nor is the animal's rider, General Joseph Simon Gallieni, who was born in France in 1849. He served as Governor of Madagascar from 1895 to 1905, suppressed a monarchist revolt there, and died in 1916.

But let's move on—and we'll do so without leaving Madagascar. The *Clipper Odyssey* anchored, you may recall, at Ile Sainte-Marie, and from there we sailed north to the city of Diego-Suarez. Remarkably enough, we'd docked at another erstwhile stamp-issuing entity.

He means a dead country.

Thank you, Arnold. Would you like to tell us something about this particular dead country?

I'll leave that to Seth, sir. He's better at sucking up.

Um . . .

I'm also better at conveying information in a concise and entertaining fashion, Arnold. Sir, Diego-Suarez is located at the very northern tip of Madagascar. It's named for Diogo Soares, the Portuguese navigator who found the place in 1543.

Why did they use a Spanish version of his name, Seth?

I have no idea, sir. Locally, guides cite an additional source of the town's name, a pirate called Diego Diaz. Now there was a pirate by that name, though I don't know that he was in the area, and there was also a Portuguese navigator named Diogo Dias who was the first European to sight Madagascar. He named it São Lourenço because he spotted it on St. Lawrence's Day in 1500, and—

What happened to "concise and entertaining"?

There's no call for that, Arnold. Please go on, Seth.

Thank you, sir. The name didn't stick, but the name of the town, Diego-Suarez, endures to this day, although it was officially changed to Antsiranana in 1975. It was the first place in Madagascar with stamps, with five French Colonies stamps overprinted "15" in violet. Counterfeits exist.

There's a surprise.

I know it's hard to believe, sir. Counterfeits also of another five-stamp 1890 issue, consisting of line drawings of a ship flying the French flag, an effigy representing France, and two conjoined female figures representing the union of France and Madagascar. They're very distinctive in appearance, sir.

And attractive, I'd say. Diego-Suarez was one of the first places to issue stamps because it was among the first to be under French hegemony. (Our final landing in Madagascar, just to round things out, was at Nossi-Be, the source of 61 stamps issued between 1889 and 1994).

When one hears that the French established a protectorate, one might assume that they were altruistically protecting the local inhabitants. But it was their own interests they were protecting, and toward that end they invaded Madagascar in 1883 and began what we know as the first Franco-Hova War, at the end of which Madagascar ceded three territories, Diego-Suarez along with Ile Sainte-Marie and Nossi-Be, to France.

Then France asserted dominion over the whole of Madagascar. That was fine with the British, but not with the royal government, and war resumed;

by the time it ended in 1896, the royal family had been exiled to Réunion and Algeria and the whole of Madagascar was under French administration.

We could talk more about Madagascar and its stamps, but it's time to move on . . . even as our ship moved on to Mayotte.

Edna, let's give Seth a rest. What can you tell us about Mayotte?

It's one of the Comoros, sir. Or it's not. It depends how you look at it.

Oh?

The Comoros consist of volcanic islands in the Mozambique Channel, the four principal ones being Anjouan, Grand Comoro, Moheli, and, yes, Mayotte. The French spent half a century establishing control over the island. They issued a series of Peace & Commerce stamps for each of the islands in 1892. By 1908 the Comoros were French colonies attached administratively to Madagascar, and they ceased to issue their own stamps by 1912.

And used the stamps of Madagascar?

Yes, sir. I guess that's what they had in mind when they printed "Madagascar et Dependences" on the pre-1930 stamps.

But what sets Mayotte apart from the other islands?

It set itself apart, sir, but not until 1974. That's when the French held a referendum throughout the Comoros to see if the people wanted to be independent. And the residents of Anjouan, Grand Comoro, and Moheli voted overwhelmingly for independence.

And the folks in Mayotte?

Voted almost unanimously against independence. They wanted to remain with France. Mayotte was more prosperous than its fellows, and French influence was greater, so that may have had something to do with it. France agreed to retain the island as an overseas territory, to the dismay of the rest of the Comoros, and ultimately the French used a Security Council veto to kill a UN resolution recognizing Comoro sovereignty over Mayotte.

And Mayotte's current status—

Has changed as the result of a 2009 referendum, sir. Over 95% of the population chose to become an overseas department of France, and this status was granted in 2011.

Like Réunion. So I suppose they must use French stamps, the same as Martinique and Guadeloupe.

That's the plan, sir. When the people of Mayotte voted themselves separate from the rest of the Comoros in the 1970s, they resumed issuing their own stamps. Perhaps you have some of their bird stamps in your topical collection.

I don't believe I do, Edna.

Your loss, sir. They're very attractive. And, like so many of the world's birds and animals, the stamps of Mayotte are an endangered species, soon to be replaced by the stamps of France.

That's a pity, but I don't suppose the World Wildlife Federation's likely to get their knickers in a twist over it. We saw a colony of lemurs on Mayotte, and a good number of fruit bats. And from there we sailed on to Grand Comoro, only they weren't calling it that. It's known as Ngazidja, while Anjouan is called Ndzwani and Moheli is Mwali. The chief city of Ngazidja is Moroni, which is the name of the angel who helped Joseph Smith translate the gold plates he found and later lost, from which he obtained the text of the Book of Mormon.

A coincidence, sir?

Probably, unless the angel turned up in the Comoros before he found his way to Wayne County, New York. We didn't spend much time in Moroni, nor did we get to Anjouan or Moheli, but set sail instead for Zanzibar.

Zanzibar! If you didn't want a country to be wrapped in mystery in romance, why would you give it a name like Zanzibar?

The Portuguese took control of the island during the 16th Century. Then it came under the Sultanate of Oman, and an Arab ruling class was established, with Zanzibar emerging as the main port of the East African slave trade.

This in turn led the British, committed as they were in the 19th Century to the abolition of slavery, to establish a protectorate over Zanzibar. We discussed Heligoland a couple of months ago, and you may recall that we mentioned the Heligoland-Zanzibar Treaty of 1890; even as the British returned that North Sea island to Germany, that nation—the nearest colonial power in East Africa—recognized British primacy in Zanzibar.

Arab sultans continued as Zanzibar's nominal rulers, but the British called the shots. In 1896, the death of a pro-British sultan and his succession by one Khalid bin Barghash led to the shortest war in history. On the morning of August 27, two days after the change in regime, British warships turned their guns on the royal palace. The new sultan fled, and a ceasefire was declared 38 minutes after the first shots were fired. Slavery was abolished the following year.

The first stamps of Zanzibar were overprinted stamps of British India in 1895–6, followed by similar overprints of British East Africa. Subsequent Zanzibar issues showed portraits of the various sultans, with some pictorial stamps, most of them showing a dhow, the characteristic sailboat of the region. I'm particularly fond of the postage dues of 1931; their wonderfully home-made look is enhanced by the phrase "Insufficiently prepaid". Most of the dues are reasonably priced, but a couple are genuine rarities, with five-figure price tags.

Zanzibar was granted independence in 1963 as a constitutional monarchy, but that didn't last; a month later, thousands of Arabs and Indians were slaughtered, thousands more fled the country, and a republic was established. The following year it was incorporated into the former British colony of Tanganyika (which in turn had previously been German East Africa). The combined nation soon had a combined name: Tanzania. Zanzibar retains a degree of autonomy, but its letters carry the stamps of Tanzania.

And it was in Zanzibar that we disembarked from the *Clipper Odyssey*. The Tanzanian stamp in my travel album is an ideal souvenir; it shows the Old Fort, an imposing building we walked past en route to the Zanzibar post office.

But I've kept you long enough. Good morning, boys and girls.

It's afternoon, sir.

Already? How time flies!

When you're having fun, sir. And even when you're not.

33

GOBBLE, GOBBLE

Good morning, boys and girls.

Good morning, sir.

I was flipping through my Scott Classic Catalog yesterday, hoping to find a subject for today's discussion, and I stopped when I got to page 1176. I trust you all brought your catalogs to class this morning.

We never leave home without them, sir.

I'm glad to hear that, Arnold. I'm the same way myself. After all, one never knows when one will require information that can be found nowhere else. Open your catalogs to the designated page and tell me what you find there. Rachel?

Turkey, sir.

True enough, Rachel, but that would be equally true of any page from 1174 to 1188. Can anyone be more specific? Yes, Seth?

Sir, there are several interesting elements on that page. First are the four sets of 18 stamps each that were overprinted in 1911 to celebrate the Sultan's visit to Macedonia. The Monastir overprints are Scott 165–182, Pristina is 165a–182a, Salonique is 165b–182b, and Uskub is 165c–182c. Some of the stamps are *valued at as little as a dollar, while others are priced as high as $100. It's a pretty interesting series, sir.*

It is indeed, and there are another 52 newspaper stamps, four sets of thirteen, a few pages further on along. The four cities were all in territories within the Ottoman Empire, so the sultan would have been welcome there—except perhaps by those factions seeking independence, who very likely longed to heave a paving stone at him.

There was a lot of pro-independence sentiment in the Balkans, and my guess is that the sultanic visit—and the stamps overprinted to commemorate it—had as a chief purpose the affirmation of Ottoman hegemony over the region. From what I know of groups like the Internal Macedonian Revolutionary Order, I doubt it proved terribly effective, for all that some 100,000 loyal subjects made their way to Pristina; that's where the Sultan visited a small mosque holding a relic of an earlier sultan, Murad, who'd expanded the Ottoman Empire into the Balkans.

Locating the four cities on a modern map might pose a challenge. Pristina still bears that name, but it's neither Turkish nor Macedonian now; it's the chief city of Kosovo. Salonique, in northern Greece, shows up on maps as Thessaloniki. Uskub was the Turkish name for what the Macedonians know as their capital city of Skopje. And Monastir, also in Macedonia, is now called Bitola.

Edna, did you have a hand up?

Sir, the overprints are all in Arabic except the city names. Isn't that interesting?

It is.

And I was going to say they're the first Turkish stamps with inscriptions in the Western alphabet, but they're not. Some earlier issues had the currency in Roman letters, and an 1876 issue is inscribed "EMP. OTTOMAN."

That's interesting, too, Edna. But that's not what caught my eye. Anybody want to guess what made me stop turning pages when I reached Page 1176? Paula?

The pictorial stamps, sir. Earlier Turkish issues showed either a crescent and star or a tughra. You know, I always thought that image was an old-fashioned oil lamp, or possibly the head of a bird. But it turns out it's a tughra.

And a tughra is . . .

The monogram of Sultan Abdul-Aziz, sir. I can just imagine what his full signature must have looked like. But in 1913 there was a 14-stamp set, Scott 237–50, showing the General Post Office in Constantinople.

You mean Istanbul, Paula.

No, Arnold, Paula's right to call it Constantinople. They didn't change the name officially until 1930. There's a song about the name change, with lyrics by Jimmy Kennedy and music by Nat Simon, and the Four Lads had a big hit with it in 1953. I could sing it for you, but I won't.

You're a good man, sir.

Thank you, Arnold. Paula, the set was pictorial in that it depicted something, but it was hardly a riot of color.

No, sir. They were small monochromatic stamps, four of them overprinted with the Arabic character for B, to indicate they were sold at a discount. That was to encourage the use of Turkish stamps on foreign correspondence, instead of stamps from European countries that maintained post offices in Turkey. I've seen that overprint for years, sir, and I never used to know what it was for.

That's interesting, and—yes, Seth?

Like Stampazine, sir. The New York firm that mailed their auction catalogs at the United Nations post office, because dealers discounted UN postage even more sharply than U.S. issues.

I remember Stampazine. I spent many a pleasant Saturday afternoon at their auctions. Paula, what came after the stamps showing the Constantinople Post Office?

The first true commemoratives, sir. Scott 251–3, showing the mosque of Selim. The stamps commemorate the recapture of Adrianople by the Turks. The Russians had seized the city in 1829, and the Turks won it back in the First Balkan War in 1913.

And issued these three stamps to mark the occasion.

Yes, sir. Adrianople is in Thrace, and Scott 252, the 20 paras red, was overprinted by the Greeks during their occupation of Thrace in 1920. Scott lists it as Thrace N84. And I should probably add that Adrianople is now known as Edirne, but I don't believe the Four Lads ever sang about it.

Then neither will I, Paula. But I'll have to admit something to all of you. Just as I overlooked the Monastir-Pristina-Salonique-Uskub overprints when my eyes first landed on page 1176, so did I somehow skip right past both the Post Office and the Mosque of Selim sets. Can anyone guess why? Shaheen?

Scott 254–70, sir. Seventeen stamps, each with a different pictorial design, and four of them bicolors. The 200 piastres high value, Scott 270, bears the portrait of Sultan Mohammed V, and even that's noteworthy because he's the first person ever pictured on a Turkish stamp.

The price alone would make the stamp noteworthy; it's listed at $550 mint, $400 used, with all but two of the other stamps in the set valued at well under ten dollars. And the sultan, known also as Mehmed V, is an imposing figure, with his mustache and his fez. Shaheen, what do we find on the other stamps in the series?

There are two mosques, sir. Scott 260 shows the Mosque of Sultan Ahmed, better known as the Blue Mosque for the blue wall tiles of its interior. It's one of Istanbul's chief tourist attractions, and was built at the beginning of the 17th century. The Mosque of Suleiman was built fifty years earlier by Suleiman the Magnificent. It's also in Istanbul and also a tourist attraction, but it was damaged by fire in 1660, and an earthquake toppled the dome in 1766. Then during the First World War, not long after it was pictured on Scott 267, it was used as a weapons depot, and some of the ammunition exploded. It wasn't fully restored until 1956.

There are some scenic stamps as well. Edna, you're a fan of stamps with landscape views, if I remember correctly.

What a memory, sir!

Why, thank you, Edna.

Scott 268, the 50 piastres carmine, shows the Bosphorus, the strait in Istanbul that serves to divide Europe from Asia. The 2-1/2 piastres olive green and orange, Scott 264, is another very attractive view of the Bosphorus, showing the town of Kandilli on the Asian or Anatolian side. And the 20 paras red (Scott 259) depicts the Castle of Europe. I'm not sure, sir, but I think this has to be the Rumelihisarı, a castle on the European side of the Bosphorus; the castle on the

Asian side, Anadoluhisari, was built at the same time, and both were designed to keep Genoese ships from relieving the Siege of Constantinople.

I see Leander's Tower is on one of the stamps. That's also a Bosphorus site, isn't it?

It is, sir, but it really shouldn't be. The legend of Hero and Leander actually took place in the Hellespont, later known as the Dardanelles. But it's a legend, isn't it? So it probably didn't take place at all, but if it did—

It would have taken place in the Hellespont.

Yes, sir. That's another strait, and it connects the Aegean Sea with the Sea of Marmara. The stamp, Scott 256, is the 5 paras violet brown. And the 10 piastres red brown, Scott 266, shows the Sweet Waters of Europe, another site on the Bosphorus at the Golden Horn. I should probably mention the Garden Lighthouse, too.

Oh, by all means, you little show-off.

That's uncalled for, Arnold. What about the Garden Lighthouse, Edna?

Well, it's a lighthouse—

Duh.

Oh, shut up, Arnold. Fenerbahçe means "lighthouse garden" or "garden lighthouse," and it's a district in Istanbul on the Asian side of the Sea of Marmara. And it's attractive. You can see that on the stamp, the 10 paras green.

Scott 258. There's another stamp with a maritime setting, though it doesn't seem to be a specific one. It's the central subject that's the main attraction of the 2 piastres green and black, and it would recommend the stamp to collectors of a certain very popular philatelic topic. Rachel?

Ships on stamps, sir. That would be Scott 263, and the ship is a cruiser, the Hamidye. *She was ordered in 1900 by the Ottoman Navy, built in a British shipyard, and originally named the* Abdul Hamid *for the Sultan. After the Young Turk revolution of 1908, her name was changed to the* Hamidye, *and she was used that year to put down a Greek uprising on the island of Samos. She saw extensive service in the Balkan Wars of 1912–3, and sank a lot of Greek and Serbian shipping before battle scars forced her to sit out the rest of the war in the Red Sea.*

How does she know all this crap?

Shut up, Arnold. During the First World War—this would be after the stamp was issued, sir—the Hamidye *saw action in the Black Sea against the Russian Navy. When the war ended, the Treaty of Sevres called for her to be handed over to the British as part of war reparations, but after the Turkish War of Independence, Kemal Ataturk tore up the treaty of Sevres, and did you know you could do that, sir? Just tear up a treaty like that?*

Well, *I* can't, Rachel. And I don't suppose you could, either, but—

But it's different when you're Kemal Ataturk?

I think so.

Well, he did, and in 1925 the ship was returned to the Turkish Navy. There's a lot more I could tell you about the Hamidye, *right up to when it was sold for scrap in 1964, but maybe that's enough.*

More than enough. I know, I know. "Shut up, Arnold."

If only. Seth, I've a feeling you could point out other interesting aspects of the Turkish series of January 1914.

Plenty of them, sir. There's the ancient Egyptian obelisk of Tutmoses III, erected at the Hippodrome in Constantinople. It's called the Obelisk of Theodosius because he's the one who moved it there from Alexandria. And there's the column of Constantine, erected on that emperor's orders to mark the designation of Byzantium as capital of the Roman Empire. It was still Byzantium then, before it became Constantinople. And we don't want to forget the Castle of the Seven Towers, or the Fountains of Suleiman, or Sultan Ahmed's Fountain, or the War Ministry. It later became Istanbul University.

Who could possibly forget that?

Shut up, Arnold. Rats, sir, I'm forgetting one, aren't I?

The Monument to the Martyrs of Liberty.

Of course! The Young Turks had established a constitutional monarchy in 1908, and the following spring there was a counter-coup by reactionary forces who sought to restore full power to Sultan Abdul Hamid II. After a few days the army squashed the coup, exiled Abdul Hamid, and replaced him with Mehmed V. Kemal Ataturk was one of the army officers involved.

But not one of the martyrs, I trust.

No, they were the 74 soldiers killed in action, and the memorial was erected in their honor in 1911. Judging from the stamp, sir, it's a very attractive monument.

Very good, Seth. You've all done good work today. And it all stemmed from a single page in the Classic Catalog, and one that I chose not after great thought, but simply because it caught my eye while I was flipping pages, looking for a subject for today's class.

And now here comes the wrap-up, about the richness of philately, and how any stamp can teach us more than we'd learn in a classroom, and blah blah blah.

Not blah blah blah, because after all we're talking Turkey today. So that should be gobble gobble gobble. And, just for the record: Shut up, Arnold.

How Keller's Daughter Got Her Name
—From *Hit Me*

"Her legal name is Jenny," Keller said. "See, she was a breech birth."

"I beg your pardon?"

"A breech presentation. She was upside down in the birth canal, and—"

"I understand the term, Nicholas. What I don't begin to understand is why that would make her a Jenny instead of a Jennifer."

He reached for his cup, took a sip of coffee. "I'm not sure this will make any sense," he said, "but that's when we realized she wasn't going to be, you know, ordinary. And there were so many little girls named Jennifer, and we knew we weren't going to call her Jennifer anyway, so—well, that's why it says Jenny on her birth certificate."

"And it doesn't have to be short for Jennifer," Denia said. "Think of Pirate Jenny, in *The Threepenny Opera*. But your little pirate's name is Jenny Edwards. And does she have a middle name, Nicholas? Because I'm serious about putting that money in trust for her."

"It's Broussard," he said, and spelled it. "My wife's maiden name."

"Pirate Jenny," he said. "Maybe that's what you'll be next Halloween. We'll get you an eyepatch, and your mother can make you a cutlass out of cardboard."

"Daddy home," said the future pirate, bouncing happily on his lap. "Daddy home!"

"Daddy's home," he agreed. "And in fifteen years or so, he'll be the one stuck at home while you toddle off to college."

"And it's all paid for," Julia said. "You really think she'll go through with it? Set up our little bundle of joy with a six-figure trust fund?"

"Well, you never know," he said. "It was her idea, and I couldn't talk her out of it. She could change her mind, but I don't think she will."

"And where will the pirate go to college, do you suppose? She could follow in her mommy's footsteps and go to Sophie Newcomb, but they went and merged my old school into Tulane. I'm not sure it would be the same. With all that money she could go someplace fancy. All New England preppy. Where would you want her to go?"

"Nowhere, for the time being. Fifteen years from now? I don't know. Some school where there aren't any boys, how's that?"

"Aren't you the dreamer. How about Sweet Briar, in Virginia? I knew a girl who went there, and don't you know she got to keep her own horse there."

"Right in the dormitory?"

"In the stable, you idiot. Jenny, you'll be a pirate on horseback. How does that sound?"

"Daddy home," Jenny said.

"Well, you know what's important, don't you? Yes, Daddy's home. Aren't we lucky?"

After they'd put Jenny to bed and then gone to bed themselves, after the lovemaking and the easy shared silence that followed the lovemaking, she said she didn't think she'd ever known anyone named Gardenia.

"I gather no one ever calls her that," he said. "I believe she said she'd had it changed legally."

"Better than changing it illegally. Jeb, Jenny, Denia—all of y'all have got names that are short for something, except they're not."

"That's true, isn't it?"

"I guess. Is she pretty?"

"Denia Soderling? She's an attractive woman."

"Why didn't you sleep with her? Or did you? No, you didn't. What stopped you?"

"Huh?" He doubled up his pillow, propped himself up with it. "Where did this come from? Why would that even be a possibility?"

"Oh, come on," she said. "A beautiful lonely widow? A handsome mysterious stranger? You were her hero, you came to her aid to broker the sale of her husband's stamp collection. 'Stay in my guest room, it'll be so much more comfortable than that nasty old motel.' She didn't offer you the guest room in the hope that you'd stay in it."

"I guess she may have been interested."

"And you weren't?"

He considered the question. "The last night," he said, "when she wanted to set up a fund for Jenny's education, we talked about her name, and how it was just plain Jenny, and not short for anything."

"So they'd get it right on the paperwork."

"I suppose. I told her how Jenny was a breech presentation."

"And she got it right away? Or did you have to explain?"

What he could have told Denia Soderling:

"See, there's a very famous U.S. airmail stamp of 1916, Scott C3a. There were actually three stamps with the same design, a 6¢ orange, a 16¢ green, and a 24¢ carmine rose and blue. They all pictured a Curtiss biplane, called the Jenny because it was part of the company's JN series of aircraft.

"The high value, the 24¢ stamp, was a bicolor, and that meant each pane of stamps had to make two passes through the printing process, once for each color.

Only one sheet went through upside down, and as a result the stamps had what's called an inverted center.

"Now, this was an occasional consequence of bicolor printing. For some countries, where quality control wasn't a priority, or where enterprising employees had learned to make profitable mistakes, inverted centers turned up with some frequency. In 1901 the U.S. issued a stamp series to mark the Pan-American Exposition in Buffalo, the one where President McKinley was assassinated, and three of the six stamps could be found with their centers inverted. They all illustrated modes of transportation, so depending on the denomination, you'd have a steamship or a locomotive or an electric automobile, and it'd be upside down.

"Those three stamps were legitimate rarities, and nowadays bring substantial five-figure prices. But they didn't catch the imagination of the public the way that upside-down plane did. These were the first airmail stamps, and aviation was very new and very exciting, and here's this plane putting on an exhibition of philatelic stunt flying. You can buy a decent copy of the regular stamp, Scott C3, for around a hundred dollars. If you want the error, with the plane upside-down, you'll probably have to spend over a million.

"Our Jenny was turned around in the birth canal, and they were going to do a Caesarean because she was leading with her behind, and that makes for a difficult delivery. But the obstetrician managed to get her turned around some, so that she emerged feet first.

"We'd already decided that we both liked the name Jenny. It was high on our list. And then, when she flew into our lives upside down, well, that cinched it."

"She might have liked it," Julia said. "Don't you think? Her husband was a collector, and because of your efforts she now had a million new reasons to like the whole idea of stamps."

"I figured it would take a long time to explain. It was nothing she needed to know, and I didn't feel like going through it."

"So you didn't sleep with her, and you didn't tell her how your daughter got her name. You're some house guest, Keller. Glad to be home?"

My Newsletter: I get out an email newsletter at unpredictable intervals, but rarely more often than every other week. I'll be happy to add you to the distribution list. A blank email to lawbloc@gmail.com with "newsletter" in the subject line will get you on the list, and a click of the "Unsubscribe" link will get you off it, should you ultimately decide you're happier without it.

Lawrence Block has been writing award-winning mystery and suspense fiction for half a century. His newest book, a sequel to his greatly successful Hopper anthology *In Sunlight or in Shadow*, is *Alive in Shape and Color*, a 17-story anthology with each story illustrated by a great painting; authors include Lee Child, Joyce Carol Oates, Michael Connelly, Joe Lansdale, Jeffery Deaver and David Morrell. His most recent novel, pitched by his Hollywood agent as "James M. Cain on Viagra," is *The Girl with the Deep Blue Eyes*. Other recent works of fiction include *The Burglar Who Counted The Spoons*, featuring Bernie Rhodenbarr; *Keller's Fedora*, featuring philatelist and assassin Keller; and *A Drop Of The Hard Stuff*, featuring Matthew Scudder, brilliantly embodied by Liam Neeson in the 2014 film, *A Walk Among The Tombstones*. Several of his other books have also been filmed, although not terribly well. He's well known for his books for writers, including the classic *Telling Lies For Fun & Profit* and *Write For Your Life*, and has recently published a collection of his writings about the mystery genre and its practitioners, *The Crime Of Our Lives*. In addition to prose works, he has written episodic television (*Tilt!*) and the Wong Kar-wai film, *My Blueberry Nights*. He is a modest and humble fellow, although you would never guess as much from this biographical note.

Email: lawbloc@gmail.com
Twitter: @LawrenceBlock
Facebook: lawrence.block
Website: lawrenceblock.com

www.ingramcontent.com/pod-product-compliance
Lightning Source LLC
Chambersburg PA
CBHW051533260626
47170CB00003B/920